PEEPSHOW

PEEPSHOW

LEIGH REDHEAD

THE OUTFIT

PEEPSHOW

Copyright © 2004, 2009 by Leigh Redhead

The Outfit
www.outfitcrime.com

ISBN: 978-1-60701-150-7

First published in Australia by Allen & Unwin in 2004

To all strippers everywhere but especially
Dotti, Donna, Lara and Miranda

Monday 13 November

The tripper staggered out of the Palace nightclub into the bright hideousness of dawn.

"Fuuuck."

Ten years of raving and the new day still came as a shock to him. He was prepared, however, and fumbled in the pockets of his voluminous cargo pants until he found his sunnies. That was better. They were black framed with blue lenses and as well as looking incredibly cool they gave the morning light depth and softness. Mellowed everything out.

He chewed his sugar-free gum and considered what to do next. He couldn't go home to Craigieburn. The E he'd swallowed half an hour back was just starting to kick in.

"Be careful, mate," the dealer, clad only in PVC pants and a thin sheen of sweat, had said. "They're really strong, direct from Amsterdam. Better start with a half."

As if!

A half was for lightweights, which he most certainly was not. He'd even stuck a pill up his bum once 'cause he'd heard it made the rush more intense. But now, as he looked around the brisk St Kilda morning that seemed to shimmer a little, and crackle and pop, he thought maybe the dealer had been telling him the truth. Man, he was off his head. It was hitting him in waves, each one more powerful than the next. The only thing for it was to go to the beach and smoke a joint, chill out for a bit.

He stopped at a palm tree to hang a leak, rested his head against the rough bark and unzipped his pants. Damn drugs shrivelled things in the trouser department. He strained, but only a thin trickle of urine dribbled out. He gave it a shake.

Cars sped past along Marine Parade. It was Monday morning and people were off to work. Losers. Someone beeped and he waved at the traffic, then zipped himself up.

The beach had recently been graded and was flattened down neatly into corrugated ridges. Miniature waves lapped the shore, sounding like a new-age relaxation tape. The sky was pale blue and streaked with rosy wisps of cloud. Magic. He was patting his pockets, feeling for his dope tin, when he saw it, out in the bay.

Far out. It was a dolphin. The tripper loved dolphins. Always had. He was no hippy but liked to think he had a spiritual side, one he nurtured with copious quantities of chemicals. He was convinced dolphins were mystical creatures, possibly from another galaxy, sent to teach humans the meaning of life. He always bought dolphin-free tuna and had wanted to get a dolphin tatt until his friend George convinced him they were a bit girly, and he would be better off with a Celtic symbol.

He felt the dolphin calling him, using sonar pulses to communicate with his brain. Amazing. He loped to the water's edge, stripped down to his boxer shorts and started swimming. I'm coming, little dolphin. Wait for me. The dolphin kept disappearing and he thought he'd lost it when suddenly it bobbed up in the swell. He lunged and embraced the animal.

It wasn't a dolphin at all.

The tripper's arms were wrapped around a garbage bag that contained something squishy and buoyant. As he trod water the wet plastic slipped off the object and the sun, which had been hidden behind cloud, came out and reflected off the ocean with dazzling brilliance. He realised there was nothing under his feet and instinctively grabbed harder at the thing to stay afloat. It rolled towards him, the bag floated free and he found his arms around the neck of a corpse, his cheek pressed against a dead man's face. Rubbery lips kissed his skin and one cloudy eye stared directly at him. The other eye was not there. In its place was a hollow red socket with whitish tendrils of nerve, waving like sea anemone. The hole made a gurgling sound as it sucked in seawater.

Chapter One

I was lying on my back in the peepshow at the Shaft Cinema, legs in the air, wearing a peekaboo nightie and no knickers.

Two of the six booths were occupied, and every time one of the guys put a coin in I heard a buzz, the glass went from opaque to clear, and a small orange light came on above the window.

It cost them two dollars for forty-five seconds, and I got a dollar of that. The booths were dark and the men's faces shadowy, unless they pressed them right up against the glass. Not a good idea.

They kept putting coins in so I writhed around on the thin mattress, got on all fours, flipped my long dark hair around in faux orgasmic throes and pretended to play with myself. A portable stereo blasted out Madonna and the small room was lit with coloured disco lights. Mirrors on the walls and ceiling reflected each other and there were thousands of me, stretching out into eternity. You can see yourself from every angle in the peeps: right profile, left profile. I knew exactly what my pussy looked like. Forget those seventies women's encounter groups my mother used to go to, all sitting around in a circle inspecting their vaginas with hand mirrors. Work in a peepshow for an hour or two and really get to know your gash.

The peep's door opened and my best friend, Chloe, pulled across the tatty red curtain.

"Simone!" Her blonde hair was in rollers and she popped out of a small pink bikini top.

"You're keen." I glanced at the clock. It was three forty-five in the afternoon. "I've still got fifteen minutes."

"He's dead." She was clutching the pm edition of the *Herald Sun*. "That fat cunt's been murdered."

"What fat cunt?" I lay on one side and lifted my leg up, Jane Fonda style.

"Strip club slaying," Chloe read from the front page. "The body of a man discovered floating near St Kilda beach this morning has been identified as strip club boss Francesco (Frank) Parisi, thirty-eight. Police have confirmed Mr Parisi, Maltese-born proprietor of Flinders Street table dancing venue the Red Room, was brutally hacked to death before being dumped in the bay." Chloe worked at the Shaft during the day and moonlighted at the Red on Friday and Saturday nights.

I bent over in front of the windows and gave everyone a flash. "Did you knock him off?" I joked.

Chloe wasn't laughing. She hugged the paper tightly to her chest and chewed her bottom lip. "I think we'd better go for a drink," she said.

We crossed Swanston Street, dodging trams and Silvertop taxis, and headed to the Black Opal. It was a pokies place with cheap drinks and the men were too busy willing their machines to pay out to bother cracking onto a couple of off-duty strippers. Maxine was covering for us in the peeps. She should have retired back in the mid eighties but that was another story.

I bought bourbon and coke for Chloe and champagne for myself and we sat at a high table at the back of the bar, the newspaper between us.

I sipped my drink and waited for her to fill me in. She lit a Winfield Blue and looked around the bar with big scared eyes. Drama queen. I slid the paper over and read my horoscope. It worked.

"I never told you what happened on Saturday night," she blurted out. "I should've, but I was embarrassed."

When she paused for effect I flipped through to the employment section. She lasted five seconds.

"It was early in the shift and Frank called me into his office to do a line of coke. You know, kickstart the night."

I knew, even though I hadn't done any drugs for a year.

"I'd been alone with him before and nothing ever happened. But this time, after we've done a couple, he gets up and comes over to where I'm sitting and unzips his pants. Gets his cock out and tells me to suck it. Mate, I just fucking laughed at him, thought it was a joke, right? Then he tries to push my head down, like, hard, and somehow I manage to wriggle out of his hands and I bolt back into the club."

Shit like that made me really mad. If Frank wasn't already dead

I would have had to kill him myself. "Why didn't you tell me?" I asked.

Chloe took another slug of bourbon and rubbed her face with her hands. "I shouldn't have got myself into that situation. You wouldn't have."

It was true Chloe flirted and appeared promiscuous and up for anything. But that was no excuse.

"It wasn't your fault," I said.

She shrugged. "So there I am at the bar and I'm like, coking off my head but I'm also in shock and a couple of the girls are asking me what's the matter when Frank comes out of his office and tells me to clean out my locker, I'm fired.

"And I say, well that's OK 'cause I quit anyway and where's the two hundred you owe me from the night before? And he says he's not giving it to me. Fuck, mate, I just went ballistic. I earned that money. I worked fucking hard for every cent of it. I went off at him, called him every name under the sun and told him I was going to report him to the cops, charge him with sexual assault, drugs, you name it."

I raised my eyebrows. Chloe groaned. "I know, not the smartest thing to say to a prick like that. So he goes, you don't know who you're dealing with, bitch, you want to wind up dead? And I say, you don't fucking scare me, you better watch your back motherfucker 'cause I know people. And then Flame, she's kind of like his girlfriend, hands me the stuff from my locker and the bouncers drag me out."

"Do you really know people?" I asked.

"No, that bit was bullshit."

The card machines sang electronic songs and Chloe lit another Winnie off the butt of the first. I wanted one too but I'd given up a few months before.

"Tell me what I should do," she said.

I'd finished my investigative services certificate in October and gained an inquiry agent's licence soon after. Since then the girls at work considered me the last word on all matters of law and order. They asked me about custody disputes and apprehended violence orders, taxation and drug busts. No matter that I hadn't found a job and my training covered following people and pissing into a funnel.

"How many people heard you threaten Frank?" I asked.

"'Bout fifty."

"You should go to the cop shop now and tell them about Saturday night. Makes you look innocent."

"I am innocent!"

I drained my champagne. It had given me a nice buzz and I was tonguing for another.

"Come on, I'll take you."

We caught the number 16 tram and rattled down Swanston Street. The top end where it intersected Lonsdale was home to the Shaft and a bunch of sex shops. As we moved towards the river we passed takeaway stores, discount clothing outlets and shops with spruikers out front flogging perfume rip-offs and cheap sunglasses. The Flinders Street station end had all the druggies. Junkies in bad tracksuits hung around McDonald's and Hungry Jacks and the alcoholics congregated on benches outside St Paul's Anglican Cathedral. Swanston was the street they never showed you in the tourist brochures. I knew it well.

We passed the Queen Victoria Gardens and the Domain and got off at the St Kilda Road Police Centre. I led Chloe straight up to the reception desk.

"We're here about the Parisi murder," I told a young cop. "My friend worked for him and she'd like to speak to someone."

"I didn't kill him," Chloe exclaimed.

The uniform grinned. "That's what they all say."

Chloe smiled back. She was wearing a low-cut top with "Pornbabe" written across the chest.

I was good at flirting but Chloe was better. She could flirt for Australia. They stared at each other, smiling, while he picked up the phone and spoke to someone.

"Detective Talbot will be down in a moment," he said.

I sat in the corner and left them to it. Just as she asked to see his gun a door opened and a female detective with bobbed auburn hair stuck her head out a door. "Chloe?"

She followed the D and I settled back to wait. Crimestopper's posters adorned the walls and cops went in and out the automatic doors. I watched them and couldn't help wondering what they had that I didn't. I'd tried to join the police force a year before and hadn't got past the application stage. They'd rejected me when I told the truth about my work history. Either I didn't have the moral credentials to be a girl in blue or the Victoria Police had enough scandal without dropping a stripper into the mix.

It was a weird career to aspire to after growing up in a hippy community where the kids were taught to hate the "pigs" and our parents lived in fear of the choppers that buzzed the hills around harvest time. But aspire to it I did, partly from rebellion and partly because of something that happened when I was thirteen.

My mum had hooked up with a man named Russell, an ex-bikie, straggly but good looking in his own way. He'd come to our town to buy dope to sell in the city, but liked it so much he decided to stay. My younger brother Jasper and I weren't too happy when he first moved in, but he brought us round with jumbo packs of M&Ms and hand-held, battery-operated computer games. He even hooked up a small black and white TV to a car battery so we could watch Countdown.

The trouble was he had a problem with alcohol, and heroin, and when he was really drunk, or couldn't score, he'd lose the plot. Anything would set him off and his arguments with my mum escalated from yelling, to pushing, to slapping her in the face.

We wondered why she didn't just leave him. She'd been a women's libber in the seventies and had worked at a battered women's shelter, but Russell seemed to have her under some sort of spell. He could go from frightening to charming, and after one of his outbursts he'd be extra sorry and romantic, and promise never to do it again.

He'd been living with us for three months when Jasper and I were woken by shouting. We peered down from the attic loft where we slept. In the light of the kerosene lamps we saw Russell looming over our mum, hand raised, face twisted with rage. Jasper, who was only eight, started sniffling.

"I've called the police," she said, but this got him angrier.

"Are you fucked in the head, woman? I've got ten pounds drying in the shed. You have got to be the stupidest fucking unit I have ever met." He was pacing back and forth on the faded oriental rug, a bottle of bourbon in his hand. All of a sudden he dropped the bottle and punched her in the face. She staggered back, crashing into the unlit potbelly stove and knocking out the flue.

13

I half climbed, half slid down the ladder and ran at him as he raised his fist again, jumped up and hung off his arm. He swung it back and I flew off onto the floor.

My brother's cry was now a high-pitched wail. Mum was cowering in the corner, Russell advancing on her, when the front door crashed in.

"Police!"

Two uniformed officers stood there, one male and one female. Russell grabbed a poker from beside the stove and wielded it like a baseball bat. "Come on," he yelled. "I'll have ya!"

The woman had her hand on the butt of her gun. The male approached Russell with his hands out, talking in low tones, calling him mate. Russell swung at him and the cop leaned back and grabbed the poker, pulling him off balance, so he fell face first to the floor. It was the coolest move I'd ever seen. The female officer leapt into action, wrenching Russell's hands behind his back and digging her knee in as she cuffed him tight.

They made sure we were all right and took Russell away. It turned out there were a number of warrants out for his arrest, and we never saw him again. And since that day I'd wanted to be a cop. But the cops didn't want me. So I'd done the PI course, it had seemed like the next best thing.

When I'd graduated one of my lecturers said he might have a bit of surveillance work coming up. Tony Torcasio was an ex undercover officer who had his own agency, a good guy, but so far nothing had eventuated. There were ads in the paper for investigators from time to time but if you didn't have experience or weren't an ex-cop you didn't have a hope in hell.

I loved dancing but after three years it was time to quit. I'd turned twenty-eight two days earlier and although I could pass for twenty-three, I felt old. Maxine was a well-preserved forty-five but that didn't stop the younger guys yelling, "Get grandma off stage."

"All done." Chloe stood in front of me, wiggling her hips.

"They're not going to throw your arse in jail?"

"Nuh." She skipped off to the front counter, whispered something to the constable and handed him one of her cards. I could have sworn I heard "bring your handcuffs."

Ten days later, November thirteen, I was sitting on my balcony in Elwood among palms and potted herbs. My first floor unit is in a block of sixteen and although the building is ugly brown brick the one bedroom flats are renovated and the street, Broadway, is full of oak trees. Dean Martin was on the stereo and I had a glass of cask wine and half a pack of individually wrapped cheese singles in front of me. I love plastic cheese. It was Thursday evening, still light because of daylight saving, and I felt the itch to go out. It was a toss-up between seeing a band and getting so pissed I ended up pashing some grungy rocker, or going to the Godard version of *Breathless* at the Astor. Decisions, decisions. The wine flowed into my limbs, relaxing them, and a breeze that smelled of saltwater came in off the bay.

The phone rang. It was my mum.

"You're home, I don't believe it. How's work?"

"Great, fantastic," I lied.

"I worry about you, you know. Not so much the peepshows but the bucks' parties. What if the guys get out of hand? What if it turns violent?"

"It's really not dangerous. There's always heaps of security. And the bucks are more scared of us than we are of them. Just last weekend—"

"It irks me. It just does." She actually said irk. I wondered if I'd heard anyone say it in conversation before and decided I hadn't.

"I know." I started craving a cigarette.

"And apart from your physical safety I worry about your psyche."

"My psyche?" I would have killed for a cigarette. And something a bit stronger than wine. I leaned back in the canvas director's chair and put my bare feet up on the balcony railing.

"It's got to affect you, pandering to men, reinforcing ridiculous stereotypes about women, buying into the whole madonna/whore thing—"

"I don't buy into—"

"I know *you* don't but by working in that industry you perpetuate the myth. And to think I named you after Simone de Beauvoir."

My mum was an old school feminist who lectured in women's

studies and I couldn't win an argument with her. I turned into a petulant fifteen-year-old every time I tried.

"It's an art form, Mum, like . . . like Josephine Baker or Gypsy Rose Lee."

"Did Josephine Baker do 'floor work' and show the world what she had for breakfast? I think not."

I picked at an ingrown hair on my leg and didn't say anything until she changed the subject: "I heard from Jasper."

"What's he up to?"

"He's doing really well, said to say hi. He's in New York doing some stuff for GQ, then he's off to Canada for fashion week in Montreal."

My brother had scooped the family gene pool and worked as a model. I considered asking my mother if she didn't think modelling was similar to stripping but restrained myself.

"How's Steve?" I asked instead. Steve's my mother's "partner." They met a few years after the Russell episode and have been together ever since, eventually moving to Sydney where my mum became an academic. Steve ran courses in mud-brick housing and solar power at the College of Adult Education.

"He's great, really busy though, organising a rally against the government's stance on greenhouse gas emissions."

"I've got my inquiry agent's licence," I said. "There might be some work coming up."

"Why don't you finish your degree? You've only got one semester to go and you could finish it in Melbourne. I've looked into it."

"I'm a bit busy at the moment."

"You could study part time. A qualification would get you out of the sex industry."

"I dunno about that, heaps of strippers have arts degrees."

There was a beep on the line. Call waiting. Hallelujah.

"Mum? I've got another call, I have to go.

"Hello?"

"Simone," Chloe sounded out of breath, "you've got to come quick. Someone's trying to kill me."

Chapter Two

My 1967 Ford Futura shuddered to a halt next to the cop car. Chloe's ground floor unit was on the beach at Parkdale and pink and indigo clouds swept the evening sky. I knocked on the door and a female officer answered.

"I'm Chloe's friend," I said.

Chloe's place was tiny, one room full of stuffed animals and Marilyn Monroe posters with a kitchenette and small bathroom. Chloe sat cross-legged in the middle of her sofa bed, clutching a woolly lamb. This would have been the time to give her a hug but I'm not much of a huggy person. I looked around. Everything appeared normal except that her wizard shaped bong was absent from its usual place on the coffee table, probably hidden under the sink.

"What happened?" I asked

A fifty-something male cop came out of the bathroom with a page from a magazine in his hand. Chloe pointed to it.

"That was on my bathroom mirror."

He held it up for me to see. It was a nude shot of Chloe torn from *Picture* magazine and the glossy paper had been shredded across her neck, boobs and pussy. Red ink stained the gashes and a message read: Die Bitch.

Nice.

The cop slid the page into an envelope. "We'll send this off to the lab. If you get any more threats, call me." He tossed his card onto the bed and made to leave.

"Hang on," I said, "my friend's had her life threatened. What are you going to do to protect her?"

"I have a feeling she'll be fine." He glared at Chloe.

"What are you talking about?" I asked.

The female officer spoke: "She probably defaced the picture herself."

"I never!"

"Let me tell you about your friend." He consulted his notebook. "This is the fourth time in as many months a unit has attended these premises. She reported a prowler, a break-in there was no evidence of and an obscene phone call. On each occasion she appeared inebriated and on the last she attempted to seduce the responding officers. Tying up police resources is an offence." He looked at Chloe. "This is your first and final warning, young lady. Keep carrying on like this and I'll charge you with public mischief."

He slammed the screen door as they left.

"Attempting to seduce responding officers?" I said.

"The first two went for it. The last one must have dobbed me in."

Just when I think she can't be any more of a nut-job she goes and surprises me.

"Pack a bag," I said, "you're coming to my place."

An hour later we sat in my lounge room in our PJ's. Mine were a pair of old trackie daks and a singlet, and Chloe's were short and made out of pink satin. The radio played softly as she sat cross-legged on the floor packing dope into her travel bong and I reacquainted myself with the wine cask. We were waiting for pizza from Pavarotti's. Carbs are permissible the week before your period or immediately after death threats.

"I should hire you to find out who's trying to kill me." She clicked her Bic against the cone and the water bubbled.

"No one's trying to kill you." I opened the sliding balcony door to let out some smoke. "Someone's trying to scare you though. What about your ex?"

"He's a gutless wonder."

"Ripping up a picture's a gutless thing to do. Any obsessed customers?"

"I wish. Maxine told me that in the eighties this stockbroker was so hung up on her he bought her a BMW. Man, that shit doesn't happen these days."

A George Michael song came on the radio and Chloe leapt to her feet and turned it up.

"This is fucking awesome, this is my new stripping song." She began dancing around the room. The security buzzer squawked and I picked up the receiver. "Hello?"

"Pizza."

"Come on up." I pushed a button to open the security door.

Chloe lay on the back of the couch doing pelvic thrusts, rubbing her breasts and singing along. There was a knock on the door and I grabbed a fifty and opened it.

I thought, that's weird. There were two pizza guys, older than usual and wearing suits. One was holding the pizza. The other was holding a gun.

Chapter Three

Chloe shrieked, fell off the couch and hit the carpet with a thud. I backed up until my legs bumped the dining table. George Michael was singing about being a sexual freak.

The men came in and shut the door behind them. The one with the pizza sat in my armchair and put the box on the coffee table. He was dark and expensive looking, and his musk-scented aftershave hit me from two metres away. Gun guy turned down the stereo. He had spiky red hair and the wide, lumpy appearance of a rugby league player who'd seen better days. His suit appeared to have been purchased at Lowes. He pointed the gun at me and my limbs tingled and my mouth went dry.

"Get up." Pizza guy had a Mediterranean accent. I couldn't pick it. Chloe popped up from behind the couch like a meerkat at the zoo. She quivered like one too. "Do you know who I am?" he asked.

"You're Frank's brother, Salvatore? I danced for you at the Red once," she said.

"Do you know why I'm here?"

Chloe shook her head but I'm sure we both had a fair idea.

"She didn't kill him." It didn't even sound like my voice.

"Of course she didn't, look at her, five foot nothing in her stockinged feet. Blue—" He addressed the red-haired guy who went over to Chloe, grabbed her hair and put the gun to her head.

"Owww," she cried.

"Hey!" I wanted to run at him but my legs wouldn't move.

"Who'd you get to cut Francesco's throat?" Sal inquired, opening the pizza box and taking out a slice.

"No one!"

Blue cocked the gun. "Tell him, and I'll make it quick."

"It's true," I said. "She didn't have anything to do with it."

"And who are you exactly?" Sal took a bite.

"She's a stripper," said Blue. "Works with this one at the Shaft."

Sal chewed the pizza and wiped a piece of mozzarella off his chin with the back of his hand. "Sorry," he said, "you probably didn't have anything to do with the murder. Just in the wrong place at the wrong time, what you gonna do?"

God. That sounded so final.

"You don't have to do this," I said.

"My brother is dead." Sal threw the rest of the pizza back in the box and the corners of his mouth turned down. "I now have two responsibilities. To avenge his death and to send a message that anyone who hurts my family or my business interests will suffer."

This prick was serious. Chloe stood there paralysed and I knew I couldn't run, couldn't grab her and dive through a window. All I could do was talk.

"What if I could tell you who really killed Frank? What if I could prove it?"

Sal cocked his head to the side. "What do you know?"

"Well nothing yet, but I could. Easily. I'm a private investigator."

Blue sniggered.

"Check my purse." I nodded at my bag on the coffee table. Sal picked it up and opened my wallet. He found the inquiry agents licence, turned it over and laughed. "Simone Kirsch, private detective. How will you find the killer when the police cannot?"

"Because," my mind was racing, "I can go undercover at the club. People will tell me things they won't tell the police. I'll find out and I'll come straight to you with the information. You can waste the guy, send a message to the underworld, cops won't even connect the killing to you. No mess, no fuss."

God, that was lame. I was fucking dead. We both were. I hoped I lived long enough to be able to scrawl the bastard's name on the wall in blood.

No one spoke. The tick of the clock on the wall was deafening.

"OK," said Sal, "you've got a week."

"A week's not long enough. I need a month at least. I have to build up trust, it's essential to undercover work." All the stuff I'd learned in class was coming back to me.

"Two weeks. No longer than that. You better be a good private detective."

"I am," I lied, "I'm great at it."

"OK." Sal stood up and wiped his hands together to get rid of the last of the pizza crumbs. "We'll be in touch."

I couldn't believe it was that easy. Soon as they left we could call the cops. Maybe we'd have to go into witness protection.

Blue kept his hand on Chloe's neck and dragged her towards the door.

"Get your fucking hands off me," she spat.

"Whoa," I said, "I thought we had a deal."

Sal smiled. "She's the insurance. It will encourage you to find the killer and ensure you don't involve the police, some of whom are close personal friends of mine. We'll be watching, and listening."

"Simone!" Chloe struggled against his grip.

"Please—" I begged.

"Shut up," said Blue, and they were gone.

I raced out to the balcony and saw them get into a black sedan but it was too dark to see the make or numberplate. The car took off up Broadway towards St Kilda and I grabbed the phone, ready to dial triple zero. I hesitated, trying to predict what the police would do. Come over here for a start. What if Sal had someone watching the flat or had bugged it? I searched under the coffee table and around the stereo but couldn't see anything. What if he had someone outside with a directional microphone? We'd learned about those in class. Oh shit. I walked around in circles. Oh shit, oh shit, oh shit. If I called the police and Chloe ended up with a bullet in her head I'd never forgive myself.

Tears filled my eyes and I remembered when I first moved to Melbourne and found it really hard to make friends. Then I met Chloe when I started stripping at the Crazy Horse and she'd taken me around and shown me all the secret bars down alleyways and the best places to get a souvlaki at four am. Oh god.

I had to calm down and stop panicking. Chloe's Winfields were on the coffee table and I grabbed the packet and lit one. Cancer and heart disease were the least of my worries right now.

The act of sucking in smoke worked like a meditation—my heart rate slowed and my mind cleared. Chloe would stay alive while I was investigating, so that's what I had to do. It would at least buy me some time to think of a better plan. I took a deep breath, called the Red Room and asked if I could come in for a job interview. Now. The receptionist laughed and said it was great I was so keen and booked me in to meet the manager at one the next afternoon.

I threw the pizza in the bin and drank wine until it was no longer possible to think or stay awake.

Chapter Four

Friday 14 November

The Red Room was in a stately bluestone building on Flinders Street, around the corner from King and across the river from Crown Casino. The name was spelled out in neon above heavy wooden doors. I pressed a button on the intercom and looked around. It was the middle of the day and office workers hurried about like they were on important business. Lunch, probably. Slashes of deep blue sky were visible between buildings and the trees on the median strip had small green leaves.

It was different after hours. When it got dark this area turned into a nightclub precinct and was jammed with cabs and P-plated cars. Young girls with bare midriffs shared the footpaths with hyped-up guys from the suburbs and minibuses disgorged drunken hens and bucks. Drive-by shootings of club bouncers happened from time to time.

The intercom crackled to life: "Yeah?" a man answered.

I put my mouth up close: "My name's Simone, I'm here about a job."

"I'll be right down."

A minute later a key rattled in the lock and the door swung inward.

"Simone? I'm Jim." He was early thirties, blond, boyish and a little bit crumpled. He held a cigarette between his thumb and index finger.

"Nice to meet you." I stuck out my hand. He transferred the cigarette to his mouth and we shook. I noticed faded blue tattoos on his knuckles. Jim looked me up and down. I'd worn a black, knee-length skirt, slingbacks and a red halterneck top. Slutty yet sophisticated.

"This way." He locked the door and I followed him up a flight of stairs, past a cashier's booth and into the club. It was a cavernous, slightly shabby room and the predominant smell was stale smoke and beer. A bar took up the area to the right of the entrance and there was a stage on the left. Wooden podiums with brass poles dotted the room and red-upholstered couches and booths hugged the walls. I followed Jim across the crimson carpet, through an arch opening onto a hallway. The passage was home to the men's and women's toilets and a door marked "Staff only." Jim unlocked an unmarked door I hadn't noticed was there. Opposite us was another arch draped in gauzy curtains. He saw me checking it out.

"The private rooms are through there," he explained as he led me into the office. He sat down heavily in a leather swivel chair behind a large desk. I took a seat and glanced around the room. It was a bunker, small and grey with a concrete floor and no windows. A couple of filing cabinets were crammed into a corner and a bank of video monitors flashed onto different areas of the club. Jim rolled up his shirtsleeves and yawned.

"Sorry, we had a big one last night. Haven't been to bed yet." He lit another cigarette and held the pack out to me. I showed restraint and shook my head. "So, you worked tabletop before?"

"No, but I've stripped."

"Where?"

"Bucks' parties, Crazyhorse. Also the Shaft, the adult cinema."

He laughed, "Fuck, that place has been around since the seventies. I reckon some of the girls have been around since then too. Stan still run the place?"

I nodded.

"The Shaft," Jim chuckled. "No offence, Simone, but you're too good lookin' for a dive like that. Peepshows are like a retirement home for old strippers, four kids, tits down to here covered in tatts." He placed his hands at waist level and mimed pendulous breasts. "You don't have any tatts do you?"

"No."

"Good. The customers hate it. We get the girls to cover 'em with makeup." He grabbed a folder from a pile on the desk, pulled out a photocopied form and wrote on it. "Tattoos? No." He looked up at me: "Measurements?"

"God, I don't know exactly. I'm a size twelve. About five seven?"

"Bra cup?"

"B."

He made a note, put out his cigarette and leaned back in the chair with his hands behind his head, "You can make a lot of money in tabletop," he said. "A lot. But you've got to be motivated. You can't just sit on your arse and expect it to come to you. It won't."

I nodded, pretending to take him seriously.

"You've got to be able to talk to the guys, flirt with them. You've got to be bubbly and outgoing. There's an art to it."

"To hustling?" It just slipped out. Jim gave me a sharp look.

"We see it as customer service. Hustling's something prostitutes do. If you don't understand the difference then maybe you're in the wrong place."

Ouch. "I'm sorry, I didn't mean—"

He waved my apology away. "It's OK, don't mind me, I'm just tired." He offered me a conciliatory smile. "Diet Coke?" He pulled two cans from a bar fridge under the desk. "We have to be really careful here. The laws are outrageous. You get too close to a customer during a dance—the wowsers can say that's prostitution, close us down." He took my contact details and photocopied my driver's licence, which I wasn't real crazy about. "We need girls Friday and Saturday nights. Are you right for tonight?"

"Sure." I sipped my Diet Coke. It tasted like wet cardboard.

"Good, be here at eight so we can show you around. By the way, what's your working name?"

"Vivien."

Jim made a note, stood up and unlocked the door. I followed him out across the club. An Asian man with a vacuum cleaner harnessed to his back sucked cigarette butts off the carpet. As we descended the stairs Jim asked, "I'm curious, why did you come to the Red Room? Why not Goldfinger's or Men's Gallery?"

"A friend of mine used to work here. Chloe?"

He looked blank.

"Paris was her working name."

"Oh yeah, little blonde chick, great tits."

"Plus I heard it was really busy now after the, you know . . ."

"After Frank was murdered?" We were at the front doors and he stopped and looked at me.

"I'm sorry," I winced. "Did you know him?"

"Very well. But don't be sorry, you're right. The place is pumping. You know what they say about any publicity being good publicity . . ."

"See you tonight," I said. "It was nice to meet you."

"Ditto." Jim locked the heavy doors behind me.

I took the number 96 tram from Bourke Street to St Kilda. I never drove my car into the city, it was impossible to find a park. Plus I'd never got used to turning right from the left lane and there was a strong possibility the Futura would stall and a tram would ding its bell at me.

I wrote down everything I could remember about my encounter with Jim. Like they said at detective school: if it's worth a mental note it's worth a written note. Every time I thought of Chloe my guts clenched up. I was desperately worried. I was also paranoid. If someone glanced in my direction I imagined them working for Sal.

I got off the tram at the end of Fitzroy Street and walked toward Elwood along the path that followed the bay. It would conveniently take me past the stretch of water where Frank had bobbed up, the closest I'd got to a crime scene.

I passed the new St Kilda Sea Baths complex. I'd considered going to the gym there until I found out the annual membership fees cost four times what I'd paid for my car. It was for expensive people, the kind who never sweat because they don't have any pores. Rollerbladers and bike riders whizzed past and the fashionable crowd sat at outdoor tables in front of the Stokehouse, drinking champagne in the sun. It seemed wrong the day was so beautiful when Chloe was locked up somewhere. My slingbacks began to chafe so I kicked them off and walked barefoot in the sand. Sunbathers lazed on the beach and some folks were actually swimming in the flat, polluted water of the bay.

I sat on the sand in front of Donovan's restaurant where Frank's body had eventually been dragged to shore. I'd read all the newspaper reports. Pity the poor tripper who'd mistaken him for a dolphin. The Westgate Bridge gleamed in the distance and I tried to figure out how Frank's body had ended up in the bay.

He'd only been in the water for a few hours so he must have been dumped somewhere around St Kilda beach. If it was from a boat the police hadn't located it. I supposed someone could have just dragged him in, but the foreshore was so public, there were people around all hours of the day and night.

A small rocky headland jutted out to the left of the beach. It adjoined the marina and had a small lighthouse. You could dump a body off there in relative privacy. To my right the pier stretched five hundred metres into the bay. It was wide enough to drive a car down. I wrote the theories in my notebook, sketched the scene for good measure and felt like a proper detective.

I brushed the sand off my butt and continued home. On the way I bought a red icy-pole from a kiosk and ate it quickly before it melted. The path went right through the marina and I admired all the boats. The big ones were very Miami Vice drug dealer and I wondered what had become of Don Johnson. I passed the sailing school at the southern end of the marina. A middle-aged man was cleaning one of the school's yachts with a bucket of soapy water. It was twenty foot long and not very flash. No images of big-haired bikini-clad babes or guys called Pablo sprang to mind. I leaned on the high wire fence and watched him,

"Hi," I said.

"Hello." The man straightened up to talk to me. "Can I help you with anything?" He wore khaki shorts, deck shoes and a navy polo shirt.

"A couple of things actually. Do you teach the sailing school?"

"I certainly do."

"Good, because I jog past here a few times a week and I keep meaning to ask about sailing lessons."

"I can give you information about that."

"I also wanted some information about tides."

"Tides?"

"That's right." I smiled encouragingly. So far this inquiry agent business was a piece of piss.

"Hang on a sec." He put down his bucket and climbed off the boat onto the wooden decking, let himself out of a gate in the fence, and offered his hand. "Reg Bannister."

"Simone Kirsch."

"You have a pink tongue, Simone."

"Red icy-pole, Reg," I said. "Can't be helped."

He laughed and I followed him to the school headquarters, a prefab shed that shook when we walked inside. The walls were covered with posters of sailing boats and complicated looking marine charts.

"Do you have any sailing experience?" Reg asked.

"I worked on a prawn trawler when I was seventeen," I said. "Does that count?"

"'Fraid not. What you'd need is the beginners course."

"How much?"

"Private lessons or group?"

"Group. That would be cheaper, right?"

Reg picked up a brochure from a stack on his desk. "We run group lessons for beginners at ten am Saturday and Sunday right through the summer. It's thirty dollars for an hour and a half and you need to book. The information's all there." He handed me the leaflet. "Now what was it you wanted to know about tides?"

"Say something washed up on St Kilda beach," I said, "right in front of Donovan's, at about seven in the morning on the third of November this year. What direction would it have come from?"

"What are we talking about? A plastic cup? A life raft? A boat?"

"A dead body."

It dawned on him. "You're talking about that bloke, Mafia guy, with the strippers, some Italian name . . ."

"Parisi."

"That's the one. Cops were all over here a week ago, checking out boats, talking to people. Didn't ask about tides though. Guess they got their own people for that." He looked at me intently. "What's it to you? You know the bloke?"

"I'm a private detective, assigned to the case."

"Bullshit." Reg had a good old chuckle. "You're not a private detective."

"Yes I am." I took out my wallet and showed him my licence. Reg examined it, still chuckling, and handed it back. Wait till he told the boys at the sailing club. He tapped some keys on his laptop and connected to the Internet. "I'm just going to the VCA Victorian tide tables site," he said. "Let's see, tide had been coming in for about an hour . . ."

"He was in the water for about two hours," I said.

Reg rubbed his chin. "I'd say he'd have come from somewhere near the lighthouse."

"What about from the sand or the pier?"

"Doubt it. The way the currents move, it was most likely the lighthouse or a boat near there. If he'd been chucked off the pier he would have ended up at West St Kilda beach."

I wrote the information in my notebook, along with Reg's name and the date and time.

"Thanks, Reg, you've been very helpful. I'll give you a call about the sailing."

He showed me out the door. "How long have you been a private detective?" he asked.

"Eighteen hours," I said, and walked back to the headland to have another look.

I stood on the rocks and gazed down. More rocks and dirty water. I turned to Marine Parade and noticed a car park. I'd read the papers and watched the news and knew the cops hadn't found blood or other evidence, so maybe Frank was killed elsewhere and his body driven here. Then the killer had to get the body from the car, over the bike path and across one hundred metres of grass. Frank was a big guy so it had to be someone strong. Or maybe a couple of people. I looked around on the ground for some clues—perhaps the murderer had dropped his business card. I wasn't that lucky.

the key to the inside lining of my shorts. Aurora disappeared around the corner to the left and I trotted along behind her.

"This is backstage," she said. "The stage and podiums are up those steps and this door leads to the private rooms. If you do a private you can wear a fantasy outfit. They're in those boxes." She nodded to a shelf with boxes marked "schoolgirl," "cheerleader," "nurse" and the like. She led me up the steps and we stood in the wings. The main stage had catwalks leading to three of the podiums.

"Podiums one, two and three," she pointed. "Four and five are over there. A roster in the girls' room tells you which one you're on. It's twenty minutes every hour and a half." We walked the narrow catwalk to the middle podium. The first customer, a guy drinking alone, looked over. I tested the pole, it went all the way up to the ceiling and seemed sturdy.

"So how does it work when you're up here?" I asked.

"You haven't done tabletop before?"

"No."

"But you've stripped?"

"Yeah."

"I'll give you a crash course," Aurora said. "You come out and start dancing. Guys'll come and sit in the seats down there. Don't take anything off until they tip you. Ten bucks for your top, twenty for the bottoms. And dance for the guy who tipped you. Everyone else will try to get a look, cheap bastards, so go up real close. Watch how the other girls do it."

I nodded and she continued, "You dance for the guy who tipped you for a couple of minutes, then you put your bikini back on, thank them and give them a bit of a kiss on the cheek. Of course if they keep tipping you stay there as long as the money comes in."

"What if two guys tip you at the same time?"

"Go to one, then the other. Back and forth. It's easier to do than explain. It'll all come together when you're up there, after a couple of drinks. Speaking of which, you want one?"

"Sure."

Aurora sat down on the edge of the podium, then slid off to the floor. I followed suit and we headed for the bar.

"First drink of the night's free," she explained. "After that you have to pay." We both ordered champagne.

"What's the difference between a lap dance and a private dance?" I asked.

"A lap dance is twenty dollars and you take the guy to a couch and dance for two songs max. They have to sit on their hands. If they don't one of the bouncers'll come over and tell you off. You can get up real close, rub your boobs on their face, but you can't actually sit on their laps. No crotch to crotch contact, even if you're fully clothed."

"Sort of takes the lap out of lap dance, doesn't it?"

"You're not wrong. They changed the laws in ninety-nine and ever since it's been illegal to sit on someone's lap for money. Now it's prostitution."

"That's like the peeps," I said. "You can get busted for hooking if a cop comes into the booth and sees you playing with yourself. How can that be prostitution if the customer isn't even in the same room as you?"

"It's a fucking joke," said Aurora. "You want to see where we do the privates?"

The private area consisted of six rooms, two rows of three facing each other with gauzy red curtains instead of doors. Each had a fake animal print rug, a couple of chairs, a side table for drinks and a stereo on a small shelf. The walls were mirrored and the lighting was low. A black light made Aurora's dress luminous. I suddenly realised why everyone wore those fluorescent bikinis.

"It's fifty for ten minutes. You give the money to Emma at the bar and she gives you a tape. A bouncer will wander up and down the corridor. If you get the timing right you can do a bit of lap sitting, let the guy touch your boobs. Or not, it's up to you."

I nodded. I was dying to ask about Frank but it was too early. "Thanks for showing me around," I said.

"No problem. If you need help with anything just ask." Aurora returned to the girls' room and I knocked on Jim's door. It clanked as he unlocked it from the inside. High security. No one was getting in that room uninvited.

"Hey Vivien." Jim was bright eyed and chirpy. "How'd your tour go?"

"Great." I realised he'd been watching on the closed circuit television. "Aurora was really nice."

"She's a honey, isn't she? One of our top girls. Did you know she has an Honours degree from Sydney University?"

"No."

"Well she does. And top knockers. Not usually a fan of the fake ones myself but hers are real beauts."

"It's an excellent job." I agreed.

He picked up a Polaroid camera from the desk and aimed it at me. "Say cheese."

I held my hand up. "I don't—"

"We need it for your personnel file. Everyone's got one. Don't worry, you look hot." He snapped and the camera made a mechanical churning sound as the photo slid out. He waved it around in the air, waiting for it to develop.

"I've rostered your first podium dance at twenty past nine, gives you a bit of time to watch the other girls first." He showed me the picture. I looked like a cyber-vixen from the planet Zorg. "The security guys are Brad and Vince." He pointed to them on the video monitor. Brad was fair and Vince was dark and they both could've given Schwarzenegger a run for his money. "Now remember to be friendly and talk to the guys. I don't want to see any customer sitting on his own. That's why they come here, you know? Sure, they wanna see tits and pussy but they love havin' pretty girls pay them attention too."

The Red Room was filling up. I sat at the bar observing, working up some champagne courage. Suits sat in groups, pissed and loud, drinking since they knocked off work. Other guys looked freshly scrubbed and gelled. Their nights had just begun. Bouncy, top forty music thudded out of the speakers and the house DJ tried to get the blokes excited in his deep radio voice: "Hi, guys, and welcome to the Red Room. We've got some fine fillies on tonight so don't be shy. Ask 'em for a lap dance or go sit at the podiums. You gotta hand over the cash if you wanna see some gash, yeah."

Aurora, Betty and one of the other girls I'd been introduced to were slowly grinding on the podiums. More dancers had started and worked the floor. They were quick. Soon as the guys sat down girls would come and sit on the arms of their chairs or stand in front of them wiggling suggestively. I wondered what they could possibly be talking about. Current affairs? The state of the economy? The girls gave the punters five minutes and if they didn't bag a lap dance they moved on.

I drained my glass and asked for another, paying with money from my garter. It was now or never. I had to fit in and I'd end up leaving with less money than I came with if I sat at the bar all night. I slid off my barstool and approached a group of three men in business suits the other girls had given up on.

"Hi, guys," I sat in a chair opposite them. "Having a good night?"

"I hope you're not going to hassle us for a lap dance." The eldest of the three was fat, ruddy and smelled of scotch. "It's fucking mercenary. Every two minutes—do you want a lap dance? Twenty bucks? What do you get for twenty bucks? Can't even touch."

I shrugged. "You don't have to worry about me. I don't even know how to lap dance. It's my first night."

"Bullshit," he spat.

"It's true. You'll see when I get on the podium. I don't know what I'm doing. I don't know any pole tricks. I'll probably fall off the goddamn thing."

"You must have stripped before?" This one looked forty but was probably twenty-seven. He was balding and paunchy. Office jobs seemed to do that to a fellow.

"No," I lied.

"Are you nervous?" asked the youngest.

"I'm shitting bricks."

Fat guy leaned back and laughed, spilling scotch on his ample thigh. "So what made you decide to do this?"

"I'm studying to be a beauty therapist," I said, "and the fees are, like, so expensive. I was working part time in Coles but it just wasn't enough money."

"Not putting yourself through medical school then?" he sneered.

You impotent prick, I thought, smiling sweetly.

"Do you have a boyfriend?" The young one was awkward in his cheap suit. "What does he think about you working here?"

"No, no boyfriend." I tried to look wistful. "I don't think you can do this sort of work and have a relationship."

The young guy nodded. "I'm Tim."

"Vivien."

"Like that's your real name." Fat guy nudged bald guy. "Tim's in love." They laughed and Tim blushed. "Hey, Vivien, Tim's never been to a titty bar before. Why don't you give him a lap dance?"

"Yeah," laughed bald guy, "it'll be hilarious. Like two virgins trying to have sex."

Fat guy took out his wallet and angled it so I could see his big wad of cash. He plucked out a twenty and checked it carefully in the low light, making sure it wasn't a fifty. He held the note out then pulled it back when I reached for it: "Uh-uh." He pointed to my leg. His fat sweaty fingers fumbled around my garter.

"OK, Tim, let's go." I stood up.

"Can't you do it here?" bald guy whined. I shook my head and led Tim over to the couches. He sat down with his hands in his lap.

"I'm sorry," he said, "I've never done this before."

"It's pretty easy. You've just got to sit there and try not to touch me."

A schmaltzy song by some American boy band was playing. Not my preferred stripping music but it would have to do. I looked over at another girl lap dancing and copied her. I swayed in front of Tim, took off my top and shorts, and then my bikini. I put my knees on either side of his legs and pushed my breasts close to his face. When I put a palm to his chest for support I felt his heart beating like a frightened rabbit. At the end of the second song I bent over in front of him.

"There you go," I said, putting on my clothes.

"That was great." Tim stood up. "Do you want to come back over and have a drink with us?" His companions were laughing and waving. Aurora saved me.

"She's due up on the podium, sweetie." She took my arm and led me away. "I can't believe you got a dance out of those tight-arses."

"Hardest twenty bucks I ever made."

"It gets easier. You ever worked in sales?"

"No."

"I used to work at a cosmetics counter, commission work. It's quite similar." Aurora opened the door to the girls' room. "There was this one girl, Samantha, not that great looking, average body, but she came here with a telemarketing background. Direct sales? Made an absolute fortune. Bought a house."

"Wow." We were at the backstage area, peering through the curtains.

"You're on two," said Aurora, "the middle one."

A statuesque redhead was hanging upside down on the pole, spinning around.

"What the fuck," I said.

"That's Flame. She's a pole-dancing champion, won the state finals last year and came runner-up in the nationals."

"I can't do that."

"You don't have to. Just go and be sexy. You'll be fine."

Flame had spotted us in the wings and looked over.

"Go while she's there, that way the podiums are never empty."

I walked along the catwalk thinking, don't fall over. Three champagnes and no dinner had made me light-headed.

"Hi," I said as Flame prepared to walk backstage. "How's it been?"

"Fucking dead." She stalked off. Lovely. Still, I had to remember she'd just lost her "sort-of" boyfriend.

I gripped the pole with one hand and walked around it. You got a good view of things from up there. I checked out the other dancers. One of the girls sat on the edge of the podium with her ankles on a guy's shoulders so none of the other men could see between her legs. An old man wearing a cardigan sat down and I smiled at him and crawled up to the edge of the table like I'd seen the others do.

"Are you new here?" His false teeth clicked as he spoke.

"Sure am."

"You're very pretty."

"Thanks." I waited for him to give me money but he just sat there with his hand in his pocket. I got up and danced around the pole. This was getting embarrassing. I was glad I'd taken Anais's advice and stuck some money in my garter so I didn't look like a complete loser. Tim came up and I thought he should be good for a twenty. I got down on my knees in front of him, all sexy-like.

"Hi, Tim."

"Hi." He opened his wallet, took out a business card and handed it to me. "I really like you," he slurred. "I think you're a really nice person for a stripper. So, if you ever want to go out for coffee . . ."

Coffee? I thought. Coffee?

Tim looked back at his workmates. They were getting up to leave.

"I've got to go, beautiful. Call me." He walked off banging his leg into a chair. This was going from bad to worse. The old man sat there, moving his false teeth around with his tongue. Finally he withdrew a crumpled ten-dollar note from his pocket and held it up. I put it in my garter and noticed it was slightly damp. I unzipped my latex number and took off my bra. Everyone else in the place looked over, copping a free perve. Anais stalked down the catwalk trailing a whip. Thank god. I put my top back on and gave the old man a tight smile: "Gotta go."

Chapter Six

As I stood at the bar working on champagne number four I realised I'd made thirty dollars but spent twenty; hadn't learned a single thing about Frank and my feet were beginning to ache from the boots. Great result.

Two men walked in to the club and sat at a table not far from me. Five girls homed in on them but stopped when I got there first. The champagne was making me proactive.

"Mind if I sit down, gentlemen?" I plonked myself in a spare chair without waiting for a reply. "My name's Vivien."

"Alex," said the older and more suave of the two, "and this is my colleague Grant."

Grant had a buzz cut and a sunburned face. He was also extremely pissed and gaped at the dancers, eyes glazed and mouth hanging open.

"He's originally from Queensland," Alex explained.

"Ah," I said.

Emma came past and Alex ordered a double scotch for himself, beer for his friend and another champagne for me. Grant was mesmerised by Emma's tits and slowly reached out a hand like he was about to go the grope.

"Boobies," he said.

"Grant!" Alex smacked his hand down and Grant giggled. Alex and I exchanged a look. He had dark, sexy eyes.

"What have you boys been up to tonight?"

"Nothing much, been to the casino and now here. I like your boots."

"Puss in boots," slurred Grant. "Pussy in boots." He laughed at his play on words.

"Not only devilishly handsome but a rapier-like wit," I said.

Alex studied my face. "This your only job?" he asked.

"I'm studying to be a beautician." I tilted my head to the side and he looked dubious. Emma came back with the drinks. Alex paid and told her to keep the change while Grant stared at Emma's boobs like a starving infant.

"And what do you do, Alex?" I examined him over the rim of my glass. Dark hair, expensive haircut, maroon shirt, fabulous shoes.

"Guess."

"Dolphin trainer?"

"No," he laughed.

"Bikini waxer to the stars?"

"I wish."

"I give up," I said. "You may as well tell me."

He ran his hand through his hair and sighed. "I'm a cop."

My brain started buzzing. Cops have access to all sorts of information. And what was he doing here, so soon after the murder?

"You don't look like a cop," I said. He seemed pleased.

"My job doesn't freak you out?"

"No. Cops are tops. Just like the sticker says. What sort of cop are you?"

"I'm a detective with the CIB. Criminal Investigation Bureau."

A skinny stripper perched on the edge of Grant's chair and whispered to him. Her blonde hairpiece didn't quite match the colour of her hair. She took his hand and led him over to the couches.

Alex rolled his eyes. "I apologise for Grant."

"Don't worry about it." I plucked the strawberry from my glass and nibbled at it. "Hey, do CIB guys mix with cops from Homicide?"

"Sometimes." He was cagey.

"Do they have any suspects in the Parisi murder?"

He raised one eyebrow and almost smiled. "I'm not at liberty to comment."

"Have any theories of your own?" I asked.

"Why do you want to know?"

"He was a wonderful guy and a terrific boss. I just want to see the killer brought to justice."

"Come off it. He was a sleaze. You girls told the taskforce yourselves. If he hadn't been murdered it was only a matter of time before he was charged with sexual assault."

"My," I said, "don't we know a lot about a case we're not even working on? Why'd you come here? Why not some other club?"

"Professional interest. You ask too many questions. You're not an undercover cop but I don't think you're a stripper."

I smiled. "Why don't you get a lap dance and find out?"

"Nah." he shook his head

"Why not?"

"I always swore I'd never pay for a lap dance."

"Because you're too cheap? Can't afford it?"

"No."

I sat back and crossed my arms. "Would you feel like you were exploiting me?"

"Well . . ."

"Or that I'm exploiting you? Poor delicate flower."

"I'm just not that desperate," he smirked.

"Well, it was nice talking to you, Detective." I got up to leave. "But if you're not having a private dance I'm going to have to go and mingle." I tipped the last of the champagne down my throat and turned to saunter off.

Alex grabbed my wrist. "All right, how much?"

"Fifty dollars for a fantasy dance in one of the private rooms."

He took a leather wallet from his inside jacket pocket and slid out a green hundred.

"Keep the change."

"Follow me."

He grabbed his drink and I led him by the hand through the club. In the time we'd sat talking the place had really filled up. Blondes in fluorescent bikinis flirted convincingly with men in neat casual. There were suits, country guys, and the occasional tragic pisspot who'd been left behind by his friends. I even saw a minor soap star and the son of an ex-premier. Music pounded and the podiums were full. Frank's murder had given the club the sort of publicity money couldn't buy. It was notorious and when people came to the Red they felt like they were really taking a walk on the wild side, if only for a few hours. I gave the money to Emma, selected a tape, then took Alex to the private room at the end of the corridor. Two other rooms were busy and music melded together like an out-of-tune radio. He sat in the armchair and put his drink down. "I like the zebra rug, classy."

"Here at the Red Room the eighties never ended," I said. "I'll be back in a moment."

"Where are you going?"

"It's a fantasy dance. I have to get changed into my fantasy outfit."

"You mean that's not it?"

Backstage I found the box I was looking for, cop, and changed into navy hot pants, a light blue shirt and police hat. A utility belt with handcuffs and a toy gun fitted snugly around my waist. I swaggered into the room pointing the gun at Alex. "You're nicked, sunshine."

He groaned. "You have got to be joking."

I put the tape in, pressed play and the theme song from *Cops*, "Bad Boys," blasted out. Alex shook his head.

I swayed my hips and looked him straight in the eye. It's the most important part of striptease, the look, more important even than removal of the undies. The bold female sexual gaze, if you want to get academic about it. I swung my hair and ran my hands from my breasts to my hips. Alex swallowed. If he'd been wearing a tie he would have loosened it.

I remembered how much I loved stripping, not the hustle but the dancing, the rush of power and control. You could be sexual and shameless yet completely insular, intimate without giving any of yourself away. The tease, the ice princess. You want me but you can't have me. It was an affair with no sex, the endorphin rush when you fell in love.

I shook my arse in front of his face. His hand slid up my inner thigh and I spun around and grabbed it.

"No touching, officer. Contravenes amendments to the Prostitution Control Act 1999."

"The what?"

I unclipped the handcuffs. "Place your hands behind your back, sir."

"Come on . . ."

"Don't make me use this." I pointed the gun, cuffed him, and reholstered my weapon. I slowly took my shirt off and the press-studs went pop, pop, pop. Moving close I pushed my sparkly bra-clad breasts into his face and rubbed my nipples until they got hard. I bent over, sweeping my hand up my thigh and across the crotch of the hotpants. Alex squirmed in his restraints.

I faced him and inched the shorts down to reveal the G-string, then lay on the rug running my hands over my body. Kneeling and looking up at him I removed my bra. Let's just say he wasn't staring into my eyes at this point. I put my hands on the arms of the chair and slid myself up, breasts touching him all the way from the rough wool of his pants to the smooth silk of his shirt. His aftershave smelled expensive and woody.

I straddled his lap, arms over his shoulders, fingers gripping the back of the chair and his cheek scratched me as I rubbed my boob on it. When he tried to suck my nipple I slapped him lightly on the face, "Naughty boy," and felt his cock go hard beneath his trousers. So much for the ice princess—I was beginning to feel a little tingling of my own.

Looking around for a bouncer and seeing none I pushed myself against his erection a few times then decided to quit before it got messy. I stood before him, playing with my G-string, starting to take it off then stopping. Sitting in the opposite chair I parted my legs and unclipped my G. I slid it off, placing my hand over my pussy, then removed my hand and he couldn't help but stare. They all did, though to Alex's credit he didn't go slack jawed, just had an intent look, as if committing it to memory.

The tape finished and I put my G-string back on and kissed his cheek. "See," I said, "that wasn't so bad, was it?" I uncuffed him and gathered my clothes against my chest in a display of completely false modesty. "I'll get changed and take you back to the bar."

"Take your time." Alex looked downwards. "It'll be a while before I can re-enter polite society."

When I got back he was straightening his hair in the mirror.

"You look beautiful," I said. "Did you enjoy your first lap dance?"

"It's a sophisticated form of torture."

"Amnesty International have been after us for years." I turned to leave and he grabbed my wrist again. Feisty.

"Wait, Vivien." He handed me his card. "I know men must do this all the time but, fuck it. If you want to call then call. If you don't . . ."

"Thanks." I slipped it into my boot. "I'll put it with all the others."

Soon as we rounded the corner into the bar area I sensed something was wrong. Alex felt it too and stopped, like an animal sniffing the wind for danger. Then I heard it under the thumping disco beat. Yelling. Some shit was going down over by podium three.

Chapter Seven

"Fuck." Alex pushed through the crowd. I hurried after him and caught a flash of sandy hair. Grant. The whole club surged over, trying to see what was going on.

"You fucking bitch," Grant yelled. He held his hand to his forehead and I could see blood on his face. "You coulda fucking killed me, you slut!"

Alex was close but security, Vince and Brad, got there first.

"What's going on?" Vince grabbed Grant's arm but Grant shook him off.

"That cunt just kicked me in the head with them fucken high heels." Grant pointed at Aurora who stood topless, doing up the sides of her G-string. She put her hands on her hips.

"Throw this prick out, Vince. The dirty bastard tried to stick his finger up me so I kicked him."

Vince punched him in the guts and Grant folded but didn't go down.

"No fucking touching the girls." Brad was about to lay one in when Alex got there, put one arm around Grant's shoulders and stuck the other out to stop Brad.

"You want a go too, mate?" The tendons in Brad's neck stood out, steroids pumping through his veins.

"I'm a cop, mate." Alex kept his palm out. "We both are. We don't want any trouble. I'll get him out of here, OK?"

Vince moved in and Alex reached into his coat pocket for ID. He flipped it open and the bouncers backed off, their chests still puffed out and nostrils flaring. All that testosterone and nowhere for it to go.

"Get that cunt out of here." Vince wanted the last word. "No one touches our girls."

"Except management," Anais said quietly, standing behind me.

Alex helped Grant out and Vince and Brad followed. The crowd dispersed but a group of girls remained around Aurora as she repeated the story. "I was lying on my back on the table and he just tried to stick it in."

"Dirty prick." Dakota was petite with long wavy hair. "You did good, girl. Pity you missed his eye."

I looked around. Everything was getting back to normal. The soapie star and the ex-premier's son were talking animatedly. This was what it was all about: the underworld, sex and violence. It was too cool.

I picked up an abandoned glass of champagne and drank from the side that wasn't smeared with lipstick. Brad and Vince walked back into the club.

"Fucking cops," said Vince.

"Just as well I didn't deck him," Brad laughed.

Vince walked over to me, his walkie-talkie crackling. "You Vivien?"

"Yep."

"Jim wants to see you, in his office."

I got paranoid. Was I busted for going too close in the private? Did someone overhear me talking to Alex about the murder? I knocked and Jim unlocked the door and beckoned me in.

"Have a seat, Vivien. You all right after that little scene?"

"I'm fine. Does that kind of thing happen often?"

"Now and then. Most important thing is protecting our girls. You can't let pricks like that get away with it. I hope it didn't freak you out."

"No, I would have kicked him in the head myself."

Jim smiled. "Attagirl." He dragged on his cigarette then stubbed it out. "Time for a bit of wake-up juice, don't you reckon? Get us through the rest of the night." He swivelled around in his chair, opened a safe behind him and carefully extracted a mirror with four lines of white powder already laid out. Cocaine.

Jim snorted two lines faster than the speed of light and handed me a straw. I hesitated. I was investigating a murder, trying to save my best friend, and I didn't need my judgement clouded by drugs. On the other hand I'd fit right in if I did some. What would Tony Torcasio do in this undercover situation? He always said you had to become your character and I was Vivien, skanky stripper, confronted with two lines of free blow.

I held the straw up to my right nostril, blocked the left with my index finger and hoovered away. Amazing how your drug-taking skills never leave you, just like riding a bike.

A few seconds and I couldn't feel my nose, the back of my throat, or my front teeth. It was coke all right. I leaned back, tingling down to the roots of my hair, the soulless concrete room sparkling around me. The out-of-it detective. Jim grinned, eyes glassy. "Not bad, ay?"

"Mmm."

"Primo shit. You can't get this on the street." He lit another cigarette.

"Can I have one?" Any willpower I might have possessed was gone.

"I thought you didn't smoke, Viv."

"I don't."

He shook one out of a pack of fifty and lit it for me. In my drug-fucked state the cheap cigarette tasted sublime. Jim pulled out a Diet Coke and offered me one but I stuck with my second-hand champagne.

"Done many dances yet?" he asked.

"A couple. I did a fantasy dance, that was fun."

"For the copper?"

"Yeah. I thought he was bullshitting me. I even dressed up in the police uniform for a joke. I didn't think he was a real cop."

"Yeah? Why's that?"

"He didn't look like one, he wasn't fat enough."

Jim laughed. "You're funny, darl. Me, I can smell a cop a mile away."

"You can?"

"Uh-huh. Got a sixth sense about it." He tapped his forehead. "He ask you any questions?"

"Questions?"

"About this place, about Frank . . ."

"Actually," I whispered and leaned into the desk, "he did ask me who I thought murdered him."

Jim looked pissed off.

"Really? Fucking Farquhar. What's his game, sending one of his boys in here?"

"Farquhar?" I asked.

He shook his head. "Don't worry about it." He swivelled around to the safe and retrieved a small bag full of white powder. "Another line?"

"Sure, it's really good." That was the trouble, I never could stop at just one.

"When only the best will do . . ."

We snorted up the powder and Jim chain-smoked and swigged Diet Coke. He started pontificating about the stripping industry. "Strippers," he said, leaning back in his chair, "they're pretty fucked up, most of them. No offence Viv, but believe me, I have seen it and heard it all. Abused childhoods, a lot of them. And it's not just the money, though that's a big part of it. They want to take their clothes off. They like to flash their pussies. Most of them are very into sex, with bisexual tendencies, definitely, so if you don't swing that way . . ." He looked for a reaction to indicate I did. "Watch out, they'll try to lead you astray."

His walkie-talkie crackled and he put it up to his ear. "Tell him to come right up." He stood. "Well, Viv, better get you back to work."

I walked to the door but Jim didn't open it straight away. He moved closer, looking up at me, crystalline blue eyes sparkling with drugs.

"You're a good-looking girl, you know. In a classy way." He reached out and brushed a lock of hair off my face. "I think it's the dark hair. Elegant." I could smell cigarettes, Diet Coke and the washing powder he used to launder his shirts. His teeth were very white and I wondered if he'd had veneers put on.

There was a loud knock on the door and Jim opened it. I turned to see who it was and almost had a heart attack. Sal stood there, smiling down at us.

"Vivien," said Jim, "this is Salvatore, one of the owners. Sal, our new dancer Vivien."

"A pleasure." Sal shook my hand, palming me a note. Jim patted me on the arse. "Make some money, honey," he said.

Chapter Eight

I woke up the next afternoon, opened one eye and squinted at the bedside clock. It was three oh-eight. Jesus.

I lay very still for a few minutes and assessed the damage. Dry mouth, one blocked nostril, throbbing headache, sore feet, sore legs, thirsty as hell and needing to piss. I opened the bedside drawer and took out a packet of codeine and paracetamol that said PAIN TABLETS in big red letters. I popped out four and washed them down with water from an old Mount Franklin bottle.

After staggering to the bathroom and back I flopped into bed, waiting for the drugs to kick in and memories of the previous night to flood back.

There was the lap dance with Alex, the scene with Grant and, Jesus—Sal. The note had been from Chloe, big loopy letters and hearts instead of dots over the i's. "I'm all right," she'd written, "please find the killer."

I was due back at the Red at eight and knew I should be out researching Frank's background, or following someone, or devising a cunning plan to bring down Sal but I was paralysed with a hangover. Seriously, I felt like I was dying. No more drugs, I told myself, and only half as much champagne.

Backstage at the club all the girls looked like they'd just rolled out of bed. I'd spent a tragic afternoon on the couch eating tuna out of a can and watching crap Saturday TV, gardening shows and motor racing. My only effort to find Frank's killer involved reading an article about the murder in the paper. I'd found out Detective Inspector Gavin Duval was head of a task-force they'd dubbed "Velvet Curtains," that Frank and his brother ran a restaurant in Sydney before venturing into the table-dancing world, and that one of the strippers' boyfriends was "helping police with their inquiries."

I sipped champagne as I got ready and felt better for the first time all day. Aurora and Betty entered the girls' room.

"Back for more?" Aurora asked.

"Yeah, but I don't know how my knees are going to take it." My white minidress revealed bruises from kneeling on the wooden tables.

"Ouch," said Betty. "The podiums'll do that to you." She put her makeup bag onto the dresser next to me and I smelled dope smoke around her, like a cloud.

"Your knees will toughen up the more you do it," said Aurora.

I finished my makeup and laced up a pair of white boots. The shameful truth is I can't dance in those stripper heels. With my teased hair and liquid eyeliner I had a real sixties look going on.

"Love your outfit." Betty slipped into the leopard-skin number she'd worn the night before. High praise indeed.

"Thanks," I said. "Listen, could someone show me a few pole manoeuvres before we open? I felt like an idiot up there last night."

Aurora adjusted her fluorescent yellow bikini top. "Flame will. She's out at the bar." Oh great. Miss Congeniality.

Flame was smoking a cigarette and leaving lip-gloss marks on a tumbler of bourbon and coke. She wore an abbreviated sailor suit with gold epaulettes, brass buttons and a hat, and appeared seven foot tall but was probably five nine plus shoes. Hers had a spike heel and perspex platform with orange fish floating inside. Way cool.

"Great shoes." It was the universal compliment in stripper-land.

"I know."

"Aurora said you could show me some pole tricks."

Flame sighed and violently stubbed out her cigarette. She strode across the floor to the centre podium and I jogged behind on tippy-toes trying to keep up. She hoisted herself onto the table and I stayed on the ground. Now she was fifteen foot tall.

"What did you want to learn?" She crossed her arms.

"Oh, anything really, I dunno."

Flame wrapped her legs around the pole and shimmied up until she reached the ceiling. She frisbeed her hat onto a chair then hung upside down and slid back until her palms rested flat against the podium. The handstand turned into a backflip and ended in a sexy kneeling position. I clapped politely like they do at the golf. Flame did another handstand and teetered over until her platform shoes clanked against the pole. She scissored her legs, gripped the metal with her calves, raised her body and climbed to the top again. For the finale she spun down fast and came to rest doing the splits. Ouch.

"That's amazing," I said, "but I just wanted to learn how to spin around."

Flame snorted air out of her nose. "Take a run up, hook your ankle around the pole and extend your outside leg. The momentum will spin you around."

I did what she suggested but spun slowly and awkwardly, my skin squeaking against metal and the pole hurting my hand. So much for the seamless, elegant spin I had imagined.

"Or you can just hang on to the pole and dance," Flame smiled when she realised I wasn't going to set the table-dancing world on fire.

"I might just do that. Don't your hands get sore?"

She shrugged. "You get used to it."

"Flame," I said, "I just wanted to tell you how sorry I am about Frank. I heard you were going out and—"

"People die." She stared off into the middle distance. "That's life."

Jim had been watching from the bar and sauntered over, hands in pockets, walkie-talkie hanging off his belt.

"Flame showing you a few tricks, ay?"

I sat down on the edge of the podium, legs dangling. "It's not as easy as it looks."

"Nothing ever is." He sniffed and rubbed his nose. "If you need to see me at all tonight, don't hesitate, any time. Just get Vince or Brad to radio me first, OK?"

"Sure."

He headed back to his office.

"Jim seems really nice," I said, trying to be friendly.

Flame gave me a look. "That's why I'm going out with him."

I knew what that look meant.

I paced myself for the rest of the night, drinking just enough to keep me going and alternating water with champagne. I didn't touch any coke but saw most of the other girls duck into the office at regular intervals. Hopefully Jim was so high he didn't realise I hadn't visited.

It was hard hustling for lap dances without being off your brain. Every guy I talked to said the same old shit: you're too nice to be working in a place like this. Maybe they meant it as a compliment but I couldn't take it as one. It was like they were saying I'd made a poor career choice, possibly because of unfortunate personal circumstances, and they felt sorry for me. Give me a break. I made two hundred dollars but could see the other girls making more. And they were fast, talked to the guys for a couple of minutes then whisked them off to the lounges. Wham bam thank you sir and on to the next one. I wondered how they did it. I spent too much time talking to men who didn't want to hand over money, telling the beauty school story over and over, and shouting above the music until I was hoarse.

Finally the crowds ebbed for the last time and the house lights came up. Flame was draped over Jim by the bar, both smoking furiously, and she tapped her fish heels to muted top forty hits. They didn't look as good in the harsh lighting. Flame's skin had a greyish cast and dissipation showed all over Jim's face. He turned to me: "Hey, Vivien, good night?"

"Yeah, great," I lied.

"Wanna come back to my place for a drink with me and Flame? It's only just around the corner." His pupils were huge and he chewed the inside of his mouth. Flame looked off into space.

"I'm sooo tired," I begged off.

"We can fix that," he said.

"Maybe some other time."

"I'll hold you to that."

I walked to the staff room on aching legs. Aurora and Betty talked quietly while getting dressed. They seemed like good friends. Betty peeled off her leopard outfit and put on another fifties get-up: red pencil skirt, cap-sleeved blouse, bowling shoes and bobby socks. She dabbed makeup remover onto a cotton ball and rubbed her upper arm, revealing a dice tattoo. Red lipstick and a ponytail completed the look. Rock around the clock.

Aurora pulled on a pair of hipsters so low they would have shown pubes if she'd had any and a midriff-baring Che Guevara

T-shirt. Postmodern. Her twelve thousand dollar tits made Che's beret go lumpy. She examined her reflection in the mirror, caught me looking and smiled.

"How was your night, Vivien?"

"OK," I shrugged, "but I'm having a hard time getting any money out of them. I watched you girls. There's an art to it, isn't there?"

"Yeah, but it's hard to explain." She turned and sat on the dressing table. "When I first started I hardly made anything. After about a month, something seemed to click in and it became easy to make money. Is that how it happened to you?" she asked the others.

"Pretty much." Betty zipped up an old-fashioned crocodile skin case. All strippers need big bags. Chloe always trundled about with an air hostess suitcase, wheels and a pull-out handle.

"You've got to tell them what they want," said Anais, "don't wait for them to ask you."

Dakota said, "I just grab 'em by the hand and tell 'em it's time for your lap dance now."

"Isn't that a bit . . ."

"Rude?" said Betty. "Don't you think they're rude, the way one of them pays and the rest gather round for a free look? They act like you should be doing it for nothing and reckon twenty bucks ought to get them a head job. So fuck them."

"Hear hear," said Anais.

"Point taken." I changed into jeans, black boots and my Doug Mansfield and the Dust Devils T-shirt. It was a versatile look that could take me from the boardroom, to dinner, to out on the town.

The door to the girls' room burst open and Emma headed for her locker. "Thank Christ that's over. What a bunch of creeps. Where we going, girls? Expansion? They've got jugs of illusions."

"I want to go to the Gin Palace," said Betty.

"It's four in the morning, it'll be closed." Aurora hoisted her bag over her shoulder. "Coming for a drink, Vivien?"

"Why not," I said.

Expansion nightclub was half a block up King Street. Aurora smiled at the doorman and we bypassed the line out front. Who wouldn't let in a bunch of strippers, cashed up and wearing only marginally more than they did on stage? We dropped our bags at the coat-check and went upstairs to a room with lots of wood panelling and wall fans pushing smoky air around. People writhed to revamped disco hits under a paltry laser light show and drunk young men packed together at the edge of the dance floor.

I followed the others to a lounge area at the back of the room where it was quieter and leaned into Aurora: "Nice place, classy."

"I thought you'd like it," she smirked. "Drink?"

"Champagne?"

"Don't do it. The champers here is so cheap it's poison. You'll be sick as a dog for days. Can I get you anything else?"

"Would they have Irish whisky?"

"A girl after my own heart. I like her." She clapped me on the back.

"Well buy a fucking bottle, sweetheart." Anais opened a Hello Kitty wallet and brandished a crumpled fifty. Aurora waved her away.

"Not whisky." Betty screwed up her face. "I hate that shit."

"Me too. I'll get a shaker of illusions, eh?" Emma bounced off to the bar and I was left sitting with Anais, Betty, Dakota, and Carolina. Dakota and Carolina were talking, a coke-fuelled rave with too many words and too little time. They got up to dance. Jesus, who'd have the energy?

"So, Vivien." Anais leaned back in her chair. "What's your story?"

"My story?" I had a moment of panic. Were they on to me?

"How'd you end up at the Red?"

"Well, I've done bucks' parties, pub shows and I used to work at the Shaft . . ."

"Eeew, not the peepshows." Betty screwed up her face again.

"Yeah, so?"

"It's just so . . ."

"It's so what, Betty?" Aurora sat next to me on the couch. She had a bottle of Jameson and three glasses.

"You know . . ." she pouted.

Aurora twisted the cap off the bottle and poured. "I don't think someone who works in the sex industry has the right to moralise about anyone else in the business. Strippers, prostitutes, massage girls, porn actors, phone sex operators, we're all sex workers."

"Hear hear." Anais held up her glass and clinked it with mine and Aurora's. "I don't mind the peeps." She winked at me. "I like to pop a coin in myself from time to time. And not just for research purposes."

"Research?"

"Anais is working on her Honours thesis," Aurora explained. "The Vagina as a Social Space."

Betty had marched off to the ladies'.

"Don't worry about her," Aurora said. "She can get a little narky after too much nose candy."

"Or too little," said Anais. Emma came back with two jugs of illusions. I didn't know what was in them—something green. Betty returned from the toilets sniffing and in a much better mood.

"Do you like the Dust Devils?" She pointed at my T-shirt.

"Yeah, you know them?" I was surprised, they weren't exactly hit parade stuff.

"Saw them at the Greyhound once." She sniffed again, "If you like them you should come see my boyfriend's band at the Espy Tuesday night."

"What are they called?"

"Las Vegas Grind." She pulled a flyer out of her bowling bag. The name was spelled out in red and yellow flames and there was a picture of a hot rod, a pair of dice and a busty burlesque showgirl. "They're kind of like a mix of rockabilly, swamp-country and western swing. Aurora's coming."

"Yeah, you should come, Vivien," Aurora said. "Where do you live?"

"Elwood."

"No excuses then, it's just up the road."

Dakota came back from the dance floor and flopped herself onto Anais's lap. "Illusions!" She had a shot.

Anais bounced her up and down. "Still seeing that cop, babe?"

"Nah." Dakota shook her head from side to side, sending her wavy blonde hair flying. "His wife found out and cracked the shits."

"You were going out with a cop?" I asked.

"From the murder investigation." She seemed proud of the fact.

"We all got interviewed," Anais said.

"It wasn't Detective Duval, was it?" I took a big slug of whisky and it seared a path down my throat.

"How do you know Duval?" Aurora asked.

"Read about him in the paper."

"It wasn't Duval," said Dakota. "He's, like, a hundred years old."

"Come on," said Aurora. "He's no more than fifty. He's got really amazing eyes. I'd root him."

The girls screamed with laughter.

"I'd root Talbot," said Anais, "but she'd have to be wearing a motorbike cop outfit, full leathers with handcuffs and a . . . baton . . ." She wiggled her eyebrows. Emma stood up and did an impression of Harvey Keitel in *Bad Lieutenant*.

"Show me your ass." She pulled at an imaginary dick. "Is that what Detective Perlman used to say? Show me your ass . . ."

"No!" squealed Dakota.

I had tears in my eyes and even Betty was laughing. Guys looked over. They wanted to approach but seven cackling females were just too frightening.

"Fucking hell." I wiped my eyes. "Must have been full on, middle of a murder investigation."

"Tell me about it," Dakota said. "They closed the club for a couple of days and when we opened there was so much heat around you couldn't get a line to save your life."

Aurora said, "Had to keep shutting early. No one could stay awake."

"Those undercover cops were so obvious," said Betty. "Pathetic."

I had another sip of whisky. The more I drank the easier it went down. "You reckon it was a Maltese mafia thing, like they're saying in the papers?"

Anais snorted.

"Those newspapers don't know shit," Dakota slurred. She was getting messy.

"I've got me suspects," said Emma

"Who?" asked Aurora. "Come on, Miss Marple."

"Well . . ." Emma leaned forward and almost fell out of her top.

"You know that copper who used to get free drinks and dances, what's his name? Dick something."

"Dick Farquhar," Aurora said. "Dick by name, dick by nature."

"Well, the night Frank . . . was killed . . . I got a call to bring them scotch in the office. Before I knocked on the door I heard arguing. They stopped when I went in, and started up again when I left."

"Did you tell the cops?" I asked.

"No way," said Emma. "That D, he's fucking bent, right? And he's a nasty piece of work. I always got a real bad feeling about him. I'm here on a working holiday, you know, have a few laughs, don't want to be the next backpacker murder or nothing. I'm like one of them monkeys that don't see, hear or smell evil."

Betty lit a Lucky Strike. "I think Jim had the most to gain. He wanted Frank's job, which he got, and, I don't know, was secretly in love with Flame and had to kill Frank so they could be together."

"That's sooo romantic," said Anais.

"Did Frank and Flame used to be an item?" I asked innocently.

"Yeah," Aurora said, "but that didn't stop him from rooting around, only Flame couldn't fuck anyone else."

"Unless it was another chick and he watched," said Anais.

Dakota, who was passing out on Anais's lap, suddenly came to. "He had his dick cut off."

"What?" I said. Everybody stopped talking and looked at her.

"That wasn't in the news," said Aurora.

"Whoops, that's supposed to be a secret." Dakota covered her mouth with her hands like a little kid.

"Fucking hell," said Anais. "Maybe it was Shane then."

"Who's Shane?" I asked. This drinking session was a goldmine.

"Honey's boyfriend," Anais said.

"Who's Honey?"

"Honey's a bit of a ditz. Starts rooting Frank and Shane finds out. Get this, he works in an abattoir and one night comes for Frank with one of the knives they use to slaughter the animals."

"No way," I said. "What happened?"

"Brad, Vince and Frank beat the shit out of him. Left him in hospital."

"Do the cops know?"

"Oh yeah," said Emma. "Told 'em about that one."

"Maybe it was Ebony," said Dakota. "This black chick into voodoo."

"Now you're thinking of *Angel Heart*," Aurora said, "with Mickey Rourke and Lisa Bonet? There was voodoo and penis severing in that."

"Can we stop talking about Frank?" said Betty. "The guy was a prick, someone killed him, world's a better place, end of story."

I went to the toilet and grabbed a coaster on the way. I must have been drunk because walking a straight line was beyond me. After I'd pissed I took a lipliner out of my back pocket and wrote on the coaster. Shane, Honey, abattoir, Jim, Ebony and Dick Farquhar. I circled his name—where had I heard it before? As I washed my hands I saw myself in the mirror. Not good. Mascara had migrated downward creating a fetching panda effect, and my foundation had soaked so far into my skin I could feel it enter my bloodstream. Go home, girl.

Back at the couches Dakota had passed out on Anais's lap. I said goodbye and walked down the stairs, gripping the handrail all the way. Outside the air was cool and the sky was getting light. I slumped into the back seat of a cab and watched telegraph poles slide by. I saw the top of Crown Casino, a concrete overpass and even a tree. I thought of Chloe and felt useless and stupid. My eyes pricked with tears. Drunk and maudlin. I didn't remember getting into bed.

Chapter Nine

I woke up one o'clock Sunday afternoon feeling slightly hazy but not totally hungover. It was a miracle. I got up and drank a plunger full of strong coffee and headed to the gym before the buzz wore off.

The gym was up Glenhuntly Road, across the Nepean Highway where Elwood turned into Elsternwick. It was nothing fancy, a huge space with peeling lemon yellow paint and shabby grey carpet divided into two barn-like rooms, one with weights and cardio equipment and the other aerobics.

I went into the weights room and jumped on the treadmill. There's nothing like working naked with a bunch of skinny chicks for motivation, and I ran for twenty minutes, visualising the fat just melting off my stomach. The gym was empty except for a nuggety guy with back hair and an overweight woman in leggings and a floppy T-shirt. None of those no-pore rich bitches here.

My legs still ached from dancing so I worked my upper body and abs. I grabbed a bench in front of the mirror and did free-weights: shoulder press, side lifts, biceps, triceps, then lay down and did chest presses and flies. I got on the floor and managed fifteen push-ups, real ones not the girly ones, then found a fit ball to do crunches. I did four lots of fifty and my abs screamed in pain. Somewhere under this layer of fat there's a killer six-pack.

I was red faced, sweating and pumped up on exercise-induced endorphins. Doing weights always made me feel powerful and strong, ready to take on the world. I left the gym and popped into the solarium. It was Chloe who told me brown fat looks less fat than white fat.

As soon as I got home I cooked scrambled eggs and wrote down a plan. I was going about this thing all wrong. Torcasio had told us in class that the most important thing in a murder or missing person investigation is the victim. I had to find out about Frank. And maybe Sal while I was at it. Then I had to systematically go through the list of suspects. I took out my coaster from the night before. Jim, Shane and Honey, Ebony, Dick Farquhar.

Farquhar. Suddenly it hit me, Jim talking about Alex: "What's Farquhar doing sending one of his boys around here?" Did Alex work with Farquhar? Did I still have his card? I raced into the bedroom, grabbed my black boots, held them upside down and shook. Two cards fluttered out. One said Tim Purcell, Junior Accounts Manager, and the other had the name Alexander Christakos and a mobile phone number. Bingo. Before I called him I rang Tony Torcasio. He was at his daughter's under-eight netball game.

"Sorry to bother you," I said, "but I need information on a cop named Dick Farquhar."

There was silence on the line and I heard cheering in the background.

"Detective Senior Sergeant Richard Farquhar of the southwest CIB?"

"I guess so."

"Why do you need to know about him?"

"It's kind of a long story."

"I don't know what you're up to, Simone, but we need to have a little talk. Can you meet me at my office tomorrow?" Tony sounded serious. He gave me an address in North Melbourne and we arranged to meet at midday.

"Farquhar is not someone you mess around with. He's corrupt and he's dangerous. It's people like him made me leave the force."

"Got anything on a cop who works with Farquhar named Alexander Christakos?" I asked.

"Never heard of him, but I can find out. In the meantime don't do anything stupid, OK?"

"I won't," I said, and dialled Alex's number.

He answered after three rings. "Alex Christakos."

"Hi, it's Vivien. We met at the Red Friday night?" I was walking around in nervous little circles with the portable phone.

"Vivien," he sounded surprised and pleased. "I didn't think you'd call."

"Neither did I. How's Grant?"

He groaned. "I have to apologise for that whole scene. What a fuck-up. Anyway, what are you up to tonight?"

"Nothing much." I sat on the couch.

"How about dinner?"

I imagined sitting in a restaurant, all civilised. Hmmm. I flipped through the *Inpress* on the coffee table to check out band listings. Doug Mansfield was playing at the Greyhound at four o'clock.

"How about a band?"

"A country and western band?" The corners of Alex's mouth turned down in distaste. We sat a couple of tables back from the stage. Actually I was sitting, he perched on the edge of the chair like he might get something nasty on his trousers.

"Not western, just country," I said. "There is a difference, you know."

The public bar was half full. Old rock dinosaurs in flannelette shirts propped up the bar and over at a window table a group of rough-looking guys shared a jug of beer with a loud drag queen and a smacked-out hooker. A couple of diehard country fans sat up front near the band, a man and woman in their sixties, dressed in checked shirts and cowboy boots. The man wore a string tie. At the table behind them a group of backpackers drank beer, talked loudly and occasionally shouted yee-ha. Two large Islander guys had staked claim on the pool table and the barmaid looked tired. It was the Greyhound all right.

I had gotten to the pub early and was working on champagne number three. Alex nursed a scotch. He wore an olive green shirt that looked expensive for a cop who wasn't on the take and his hair was slicked back and slightly damp. I'd decided on a white sundress. I thought a virginal look might confuse him after red latex the other night.

There was an uncomfortable silence.

"Well," I ventured.

"So," said Alex. We laughed. I looked him in the eye and he returned the gaze. It was a stare-off.

"You have beautiful eyes," he said. "Are they real?"

I almost choked on my drink. "What do you mean, are they real?"

"They're not coloured contacts?"

"No."

"It's just that they're such a bright blue. You don't notice it so much at night but in the light they're amazing."

I squinted my eyes and leaned across the table. "You're a Libra, right?"

"How did—"

I shrugged. "You dress well, smell nice and you're not short on charm."

"I don't believe in star signs," he said. "Can I get you a drink?"

I said yes although I probably shouldn't have. I was knocking them back like water to quell the nerves and it was certainly working. With Alex gone I turned my attention to the band. They played that cool, honky-tonk kind of country. Songs about whisky and prison and heartbreak. And about Melbourne too.

Doug Mansfield sat on a stool at the front. He had a beard and cowboy hat, and walked with a cane. A guy in a checked shirt played pedal steel, the drummer and guitarist wore hats, and the bass player, handsome and dressed in black like Johnny Cash, looked over at me.

"That guy's checking you out." Alex was back with the drinks.

"I go to all their gigs," I explained. "He probably thinks I'm stalking him."

That statement led to another uncomfortable silence. Alex broke it.

"So, Vivien," he said, "tell me about yourself."

"Not much to tell really. I grew up in a trailer park, always wanted to go to beauty school and got into the entertainment industry to pay the tuition."

"Is that right?" he smirked.

"Yes indeedy. What about you? How long you been a cop?"

"Ten years."

"That's a long time. How old are you?"

"Thirty-five."

"You married?"

"Was."

"Kids?"

"No. Do you have a boyfriend?"

"Nuh-uh. It's difficult when you're in . . . show business . . ."

"Girlfriend?" He raised his eyebrows hopefully.

"You wish."

Alex laughed. "You're an unusual girl. I don't think I've met anyone quite like you before."

"I'm trouble with a capital T." I was getting a little tipsy.

"I don't doubt it."

I took another large sip of champagne. More of a gulp really. "Anyway," I said, "enough of this flirting. Let's get down to business."

"Business?" Alex looked amused.

"Come on," I said, "I know you're dying to ask me more about the Parisi murder. Although I'm not sure what your angle is."

"My angle?"

"I know you're one of Farquhar's boys . . ."

Alex's look of surprise only lasted a second.

"And I know Farquhar had some kind of deal going on with Frank. Word on the street is he and possibly his whole unit is corrupt." I had made that bit up. "Now I'm wondering if he sent you to the club to find out if anyone knows anything, or if you're operating on your own or maybe for someone else. What's your agenda, Detective Christakos?" While I talked I leaned forward and rested my bare knee against his leg. It would have seemed accidental except I kept increasing the pressure in small increments. After a couple of drinks I was a regular Mata Hari.

Alex sipped his scotch and smiled enigmatically. The band was between songs and I heard balls click on the pool table and the dull roar of drunken conversation. Outside the sky had gone molten orange. He leaned forward too and rested his hand where the hem of my dress met my thigh.

"And what's your agenda, Simone Kirsch?" My shocked expression lasted a fair bit longer than his had and seemed to please him. How the hell did he know my name?

"You can't have been working at the Red long as you weren't interviewed in the initial investigation. Let's see . . ." He took a small notebook from his pants pocket and began reading. "You're twenty-eight years old, live on Broadway in Elwood, drive a nineteen sixty-seven Ford Futura and your work history's a bit hit and miss. Jill of all trades, huh? You've moved around the country a lot, been in Melbourne three years, had a few parking tickets and done once for speeding. No criminal record though. Applied for the Victoria Police earlier this year but got knocked back—probably because you admitted you worked as a stripper—not that anyone will tell you that's the reason because the department doesn't want to get sued for discrimination. And here," he pointed to his pad, "here's the clincher.

You applied for and received your inquiry agent's licence two weeks ago." His palm was hot against my leg and his face unbearably smug. "So I'm wondering why you're so interested in the murder, who you're working for and what you want from me."

I pulled my leg away from his hand, sure I'd gone bright red, and excused myself to go to the toilet. I sat down heavily in the graffiti-ridden cubicle and groaned. It was because I'd called him from my home phone—what an idiot. On the wall opposite a poster warned that one in eight young Australians had genital herpes. Cheery stuff. Probably one in four if you picked up at the Greyhound. I stopped at the bar on the way back and downed two cocksucking cowboys before purchasing more champagne for me and scotch for Alex.

"You still haven't answered my question," I told him when I got back.

He shook his head. "You are something else." Then he leaned in close and whispered in my ear, "How'd you like to work as an informer for the police? You'd get paid."

"I already get paid, and very well," I said. "How about a simple exchange of information?"

"I can't do that," he said.

"Well, if you can't then neither can I." I shrugged.

The band asked for requests.

" 'Achy Breaky Heart,' " shouted one of the backpackers.

"How does 'fuck off' grab you?" Doug swigged from a can of Melbourne Bitter.

" 'She Dances on Tables!' " I yelled. As the title suggested it was a song about a Melbourne table dancer. Doug and the boys conferred briefly about the key and started playing.

"This one's my absolute favourite," I shouted in Alex's ear.

Doug sang: "Well she came into the city looking for a better life to live . . ."

"Come up and dance." I tugged at Alex's sleeve. "I want to dance."

"Now you're really pushing it."

I pouted and went over to the backpackers' table and asked if anyone wanted to join me. A young Swedish guy with white blond dreadlocks leapt up and followed me to the dance floor. We spun around to the chorus, his friends yelling encouragement.

". . . And she pays the rent, dancing around on tables, shaking it all about for the city boys . . ."

I was dancing in a style that could best be described as Daisy Duke meets Lola Montez and the Swede loped around like a demented hillbilly: knees up and hands down. The drag queen became inspired and began shimmying about and then the country couple got up, the man earnestly twirling the woman around the floor.

The crowd watched, whooping and hollering, and the band members grinned at each other. Alex shook his head as if he couldn't believe he'd gotten involved in something so incredibly uncool.

I danced over to him and made come-hither gestures with my hands. When he didn't budge I climbed up onto the table. It was a bit wobbly so I swayed without moving my feet, swinging my hips and lifting my skirt.

The blokes went wild, whistling, yelling and stamping their feet. Doug Mansfield chuckled as he tried to sing. I spun my skirt higher and was glad I'd worn my good undies when suddenly I felt a sharp pressure behind my knees. Alex had karate chopped me. My legs buckled. I started to fall and he caught me on the way down and dragged me out of the pub to a chorus of boos. It happened so fast we were halfway out the door before I had the presence of mind to start abusing him.

"Let go of me. What the fuck do you think you're doing?"

He hauled me into a laneway behind the pub and let me go near a wall. The sun had set and the twilight was purple. "You just can't help yourself, can you?" He looked really pissed off. I rubbed my arm where he'd held it.

"How dare you," I said.

"You're an idiot." His dark eyes flashed. "Don't you care about your own safety? Carrying on in a place like that. You could get yourself raped."

"What fucking century do you live in?"

"You're insane," he spat.

"And you're boring." I went to walk off but he pulled me back and held me by the shoulders.

"You're just a stupid little girl playing at being a detective. You're so out of your mind that the Victoria Police wouldn't even take you. You're living in some whacked-out fantasy world and you don't know shit about the murder. You don't know shit about anything."

I went to slap him but he grabbed my wrist and pushed me against the wall. I glared at him. "Dick Farquhar argued with Frank on the night of the murder," I said triumphantly. The expression on his face told me he hadn't known. "Now give me something."

"Stay away from Dick Farquhar," he said, and kissed me hard.

I kissed him back, bit his bottom lip and tasted scotch. He still held my arm up and he touched my breasts with his free hand and then slid it underneath my dress.

He rubbed my pussy through my knickers and I felt his erection pressing against my thigh. When he released my wrist and fumbled with his belt buckle I snapped out of it, put one hand on his chest and pushed him away as hard as I could. I'm not anti sex-against-a-wall but never on the first date, you know?

"Get away from me." My lips were bruised and wet and I wiped my mouth with the back of my hand. Alex's hair was dishevelled and his shirt untucked. Lipstick was smeared on his face. "Get the fuck away from me."

I backed down the laneway, not because I was scared but because I had lifted his notebook from his pants pocket and was holding it behind me. I turned right at the Greyhound and then right again down Mozart Street. I had just stuffed the notebook in my bag when I noticed a dark car following me. Alex. I whirled around to face him and the back door opened.

"Get in," said Sal.

Chapter Ten

"I don't think so." I stayed on the pavement, swaying slightly.

"Don't you want to talk to your friend?" Sal waggled a mobile phone at me, so tiny it made mine look like a house brick. Desire to find out about Chloe overtook my better judgement and I got in. The interior was roomy and leather upholstered but the new car smell was overpowered by the cloying musk scent of Sal's aftershave. The driver had black hair and he stuck to the fifty k limit, going slowly over speed bumps.

"You've been drinking," said Sal.

"Damn right I have."

"Women shouldn't drink," he said. "It's unladylike." I glared. I wasn't about to argue the finer points of feminist theory with him. "Who was that man you were with?"

"A cop. Don't worry, I didn't tell him about you. He's a source. Cops have access to the best information. I'm just doing my job."

"Have you found Francesco's killer?"

"Not yet, but I'm getting close. I've narrowed it down to a couple of suspects and I'll definitely have the proof you need by Thursday week. Gotta wait for the proof. Wouldn't want to wreak your terrible vengeance on the wrong person now, would you?" I laughed. He didn't.

"How do I know Chloe's all right?" I asked.

He flipped open the mobile and dialled, then pressed a button to convert it to speakerphone and rested it in his lap.

"Hello?" I said.

"Mate!" It was her.

"God, Chloe, are you OK?"

"Yeah, fine. I'm just bored shitless and tonguing for a bong. Blue here won't get off his arse and score me some weed. Will you, ya slack bastard?"

I heard Blue say something and laugh in the background.

"Has he hurt you?"

"No, but he bought me the ugliest trackies in the world. And all we eat is takeaway for breakfast, lunch and dinner, so my arse is getting huge. You've got to find the killer, mate. I don't have a hairdryer, or makeup, and all Blue wants to do is watch action videos. Steven Seagal and Jean-Claude Van Damme. Blue thinks he is Van Damme."

More muttering from Blue.

"Yes you do," Chloe replied.

Jesus Christ, it was like talking to an old married couple. Was it the Stockholm syndrome? Was Chloe turning into Patti Hearst?

Evidently Sal thought we'd talked long enough and pressed the end button.

"You see," he said, "I am an honourable man."

That was debatable.

"But I stand by my word. If you do not prove someone else killed my brother, she will die." The car stopped and he opened the door. We were outside my flat. "Naral iktar tard," he said, "See you later."

"Adios, amigo," I replied with more bravado than I felt.

The next day I drove to Tony Torcasio's office in North Melbourne, checking for tails the whole way. I changed lanes, turned suddenly, all the stuff Tony had taught us in class. I didn't see anyone but it didn't mean they weren't there. The day was stinking hot and overcast and I was sweating behind the knees and underneath my breasts. As I passed the deserted Vic Markets on Peel Street I popped another two pain tablets and washed them down with a bottle of water. Why did I have to drink so much? Because it was there? Maybe I should give it a rest for awhile. Go healthy and detox with wheatgrass juice and colonic irrigation. Eat raw foods and gobble antioxidants and get into yoga and turn into Gwyneth Paltrow. God, I felt like a drink.

I turned into Victoria Street then drove around some back lanes until I found Tony's agency. It was a small shopfront on the edge of a row of terrace houses that had been converted for commercial use. The front wall was opaque glass and covered in red and black lettering. A1 Investigations, it read, Corporate, Industrial, Domestic. A buzzer went off as I pushed open the door and I found myself in a small reception area. An Italian girl sat at a desk, typing on a computer.

"Can I help you?" She had a sleek black bob and big lips and nose.

"I've got an appointment with Tony for midday. Name's Simone Kirsch."

"Take a seat." She pointed to a black vinyl sofa. "He won't be long."

The lounge squeaked when I sat down and I looked around the waiting room. A fake palm squatted in the corner and framed certificates hung on the walls. The black melamine coffee table in front of me was strewn with magazines. *Elle* for wronged wives, *FHM* for suspicious husbands and *Investigator* for would-be private eyes. I flipped through it, skimming articles on crime scenes and ads for spy cameras and surveillance gear. I must subscribe, I thought, as the door buzzed open and Tony Torcasio walked in. He carried a can of orange mineral water and a white paper bag with a beetroot stain expanding on its surface. A salad sandwich, I surmised, using my superior powers of detection.

"Sorry I'm late," he said. "Just in here."

I followed him through a door beside the reception desk into a small office with a desk, two chairs, filing cabinets and a TV and VCR. I sat in a chair and Tony perched on the edge of his desk. He wore his usual shorts and Hawaiian shirt ensemble. It suited him. He was short and stocky with a barrel chest and muscly legs, the human equivalent of a Staffordshire terrier.

"You'll have to excuse me." He ripped open the bag and took out a white bread sandwich. "This is breakfast."

"Go right ahead. So, the nerve centre of A1?" I looked around.

"It's nothing fancy but it does the job," he said. Shredded lettuce fell onto his shorts and he brushed it to the floor. "Why the sudden interest in Richard Farquhar?"

"I'm helping out a friend and his name keeps coming up."

He watched me as he chewed his sandwich, waiting for me to elaborate.

"It's . . . confidential," I said. Tony rolled his eyes, balled up his paper bag and lobbed it into a small bin.

"You know, just because you've got a licence doesn't mean you're an inquiry agent."

"But the course—"

"Between you and me, the course is bullshit. I can't teach in a couple of months what it took twenty years to learn on the street. I was serious when I said I was going to give you some work. Out of all the students you seemed like a smart cookie, seemed to have your head screwed on right. But taking on a case that involves Farquhar—that's madness."

"She's in trouble," I said, "and he's involved."

"Let me tell you about Farquhar." Tony got up and paced around the room. "He's a bad bastard, old school. Grew up in Richmond before it got all trendified, with his violent mother who was an alcoholic and a whore. Worked vice in the eighties and was rumoured to stand over pros and have a stake in a brothel, before prostitution was legalised. One of the girls that worked there got picked up in a heroin bust and wanted to dob him in, in return for immunity from prosecution. When she got let out on bail she died of a hot shot."

"Farquhar?"

"Couldn't be proven."

"How does he keep getting away with stuff?"

"Friends in high places. Well, not exactly friends. He got a lot of young coppers into the graft twenty years ago and made sure he had proof of them doing it. There's rumours of videotapes, photos. Those cops have moved up the ranks now."

"Why hasn't internal affairs got him?"

"You're watching too many American cop shows. It's called Ethical Standards here."

"I thought they were cleaning up all the corruption."

"Farquhar's a smart bastard. He's been investigated. They couldn't find enough evidence and no one would talk. Besides, he's a bit of a hero, arrested the Bayside strangler in the early eighties."

"So they just let him carry on."

"Evidence, Simone. Makes the law enforcement world go round."

"And what about Alex Christakos? Did you find out about him?"

Tony shuffled through some papers on his desk and found the one he was looking for. "He works with Farquhar all right. Transferred from Richmond twelve months ago. What's this Christakos's story?"

"I don't know." It was true. Tony sat behind the desk flicking a pen between his fingers. In class he'd been a fun guy, always joking around. Now he was serious. More serious than I'd ever seen him.

"What I suggest is you drop the whole thing right now, and get your friend to talk to Ethical Standards. They'll protect her." He looked at me sternly.

"I'll call them," I said.

"You're out of your depth."

"I understand."

"So you'll drop it?"

"I will."

"Good." He seemed to relax. "You want to help me with some surveillance in three weeks time? It's only a few hours work. Fifteen bucks an hour. But it'll give you a start."

"Sure, that'd be great." A real detective job. I hoped I would still be alive to take it.

It was only twelve thirty so I drove to the State Library and parked on Latrobe Street. I don't know much about architecture but with its towering stone columns and marble floors the building could have belonged in ancient Greece. It was quiet and cool inside and I followed the signs to the newspaper reading room and sat down in front of a computer. I typed Farquhar's name into the search engine and got twenty-three hits. Most were from the early eighties and concerned the Bayside strangler case. A psycho was murdering St Kilda street workers and Farquhar had collared the guy single-handedly, right in the middle of the act. He'd been working vice back then and the arrest had gotten him a promotion, bravery medal and lots of good publicity. As I kept reading I realised he had a knack for great press. If he wasn't in the news for coaching a footy team of underprivileged kids he was raising money for charity, or visiting schools warning children of "stranger danger."

Frank Parisi's name appeared forty times. I'd read most of the articles but there were some from a few years back. I opened a file from nineteen ninety-nine.

RESTAURATEUR BEATS RAPE CHARGE
By Curtis Malone

The owner of upmarket Bondi restaurant Deluxe, Francesco "Frank" Parisi, was found not guilty yesterday of raping an eighteen-year-old woman last year.

A jury took just over two hours to find Mr Parisi, thirty-five, not guilty of assault and rape.

The woman, a waitress at Parisi's restaurant, claimed he raped her after the eatery's star-studded opening night.

Paris maintained the sex was consensual.

He was jubilant and punched the air with his fist when the jury handed down the verdict.

"I always said I was innocent and this proves it. I want to put this whole mess behind me and go back to what I do best—running Deluxe."

Apparently Frank didn't run Deluxe all that well because an article a couple of months later explained how the restaurant had gone belly-up and the Parisi brothers were moving to Melbourne to get into the lucrative table-dancing industry.

I printed a selection of articles then went to the microfiche area to copy some photos. I found a picture of Farquhar from the early nineties, posing with his young footy team. *Our Hero*, read the caption. Puh-lease. He was chunky, with sandy, blow-waved hair, a handlebar moustache and small, flinty eyes. I printed it and a picture of Frank taken not long before he was killed. He was a younger, gaudier version of Sal and favoured thick gold chains and blond tips in his hair. He wore a suit jacket over a black T-shirt, his arms were crossed and his chin tilted arrogantly towards the camera.

I left the library and sat down in a little Japanese place on Swanston to eat some sashimi, took Alex's notebook out of my backpack and looked at it again. It was small and bound in brown leather and unfortunately for me seemed relatively new. There was the information about me and after that a page had been ripped out. Well that was easy. I borrowed a pencil from the waitress and rubbed over the blank page. Something came up but it was hard to see in the dim light. I paid my bill, gave back the pencil and went outside. I could just make out *52 Newcowell Rd 6 pm Monday*. It was Monday today.

Chapter Eleven

The only Newcowell Road was in Springvale, right opposite the railway line. Number 52 was a rundown brick veneer in a street full of rentals. The yard was overgrown grass and one straggly native tree and the blinds were shut tight. I was driving a brown Corolla I'd picked up from Rent-a-bomb, an '83 model with cigarette burns all over the upholstery, and I'd dressed in a long skirt, floppy T-shirt and baseball cap over a blonde wig.

The wig was a bit ratty, a hangover from my early stripping days when I'd had the idea of going blonde and changing my name to Marilyn. I'd lasted a week. The wig was itchy and hot as hell and it was a nightmare trying to fit my own hair into the skullcap underneath. Not to mention the ever-present danger of flicking the thing off and looking like a drag queen halfway through a show.

I'd parked down the street from the house, facing away so I could check it out in my rearview mirror. As I watched a man came out, adjusted his tie, trotted across the road to his car and drove away. A couple of minutes later a battered ute pulled up and a labourer in paint-spattered overalls went into the house. Then a guy in a suit emerged from a shiny new four-wheel drive and did the same. After half an hour the labourer left and drove away. It was quarter to six and although Alex might have turned up at any second I had to confirm my suspicions about what was going on in there.

I'd converted my green backpack into a private detective bag of tricks and I pulled out a tin, clipboard and pad of raffle tickets and approached number 52, heart beating double time. What if Alex arrived early? Seedpods from the tree crunched between my feet and the concrete path. I knocked on the opaque glass door and plastered a smile on my face when I saw a shape approach. The Asian woman in the black evening dress who opened the door also had a smile that disappeared as soon as she saw me. I launched into my spiel.

"Hi," I enthused, "I'm selling raffle tickets for the local primary school, they're two dollars a ticket and they're to raise money for, um, computers and it would really, really help if you could buy a ticket or two." I checked out the house behind her while I talked. All I could see was a hallway with old floral wallpaper and threadbare carpet. The air smelled of cigarette smoke and cheap, rose-scented air freshener.

"What you want?" the woman said sharply.

I rattled my tin. "Money? For the children?"

A door opened further up the hallway and the suit who'd gone in earlier popped out with a white towel around his waist. He walked up the hallway and out of sight. A couple of seconds later a woman came out the same door. She was late thirties and had short blonde hair, thin eyebrows and an impressive bust. She was tucking her white blouse into a navy skirt when she saw me and marched over.

"Hi," I started my spiel again, "I'm—"

"We don't want any." She slammed the door in my face.

Fair enough. I walked away and pretended to knock on neighbours' doors for awhile, in case anyone was watching. I grabbed a local paper from a letterbox and took it back to the car with me. It was full of real estate ads and paid endorsements for local restaurants disguised as reviews. What I wanted was at the back in the classifieds.

The relaxation therapy column came right after the adult section. A notice at the top read: "Advertisers in this category have signed a legal disclaimer stating that no sexual services are on offer." Well, they would say that. I ran my finger down the listings until I got to a line ad that read, "Springvale Aus-Asian Relaxation. New Open! New Staff! New Feeling!" I rang the number on my mobile and a recorded message told me the address. 52 Newcowell. I ripped out the ad and wedged it in my notebook. Interesting.

At a couple of minutes to six the man I'd seen in the towel came out and drove away and two Commodores, one maroon and one white, pulled up in front of the house. Alex got out of the maroon car and Dick Farquhar the other. Holy shit. I sunk lower into my seat and watched them in the mirror. Alex looked up and down the street but Farquhar strode straight to the front door. He knocked and they went inside. Forty long, boring minutes later they reappeared, talking and laughing. They shook hands and climbed into their respective vehicles while I started up the bomb. When they'd driven past I followed at a safe distance. Farquhar turned left at the end of the street and Alex indicated right.

I went after Farquhar. I tailed him for ten minutes, hanging a couple of cars back in the traffic until he turned off into a residential street and there were no more cars between us. He parked in front of a small block of blonde brick units and went inside. I pulled over further up the street.

By this time I was desperate to pee. I took a funnel and an old drink bottle with a screw top out of my bag. Right. I wished I'd had a practice run at home. I stuck the neck of the funnel into the bottle and manoeuvred the apparatus underneath my skirt. Wrong angle—the wee would go everywhere.

I felt underneath my seat and pulled a lever to slide it back, then perched right on the edge of the seat, using one hand to raise my arse up, and put the contraption back again. The angle seemed fine. A few cars drove past and I tried to release my bladder but felt like I was pissing in public. Nothing happened. I forced myself to think of streams, rivers and finally great gushing waterfalls swollen in flood.

That did it. Sweet relief. I hoped I wouldn't overflow the bottle. It took five hundred millilitres but how much was the average urination? I didn't have a clue. Finally I was done and I wiped myself and the funnel down with a handy travel pack of wet ones and screwed the lid back on to the bottle.

Just in time. Farquhar came out of the building, shoving something in his pocket, and when he looked in my direction I almost had a heart attack. I was too low down in my seat for him to see me though, and he hopped in his car and drove away. There was no way I could push my luck and keep following him so I decided to call it a night.

I went home and ordered Thai takeaway, tom kha gai and beef salad. I had two glasses of wine, which counts as detox for me, and went to work moving the corkboard from the kitchen to my bedroom desk. I removed all the photos of Chloe and me in various stages of drunkenness and undress, and the "overdue—pay now" notices, and devoted the left-hand side entirely to Dick Farquhar. First I stuck his picture up, then the ad for Aus-Asian Relaxation, and finally Post-it notes with information supplied by Torcasio and the girls.

Frank's photo and the article about him went on the right and I pinned my smudged coaster from Expansion in the middle. When they do this in the movies it enables them to make subconscious connections and solve the case.

Let me tell you right now, it doesn't work.

Chapter Twelve

Tuesday 18 November

I had a jug strip at the Royal Hotel. I'd cancelled all my shifts at the Shaft but this one had been booked a couple of weeks earlier and I really needed the money.

The Royal's on Punt Road in Richmond, opposite the Richmond cricket ground and not far from the MCG. A sign outside advertises TOPLESS BARMAIDS & STRIPPERS 12-2 & 5-8. I parked at the side of the pub, hoisted my big bag off the bench seat beside me and went in.

"Hi, Dave." I waved at the manager. He sat at the bar doing the *Herald Sun* crossword.

"Hi." He probably didn't remember my name.

I let myself into the girls' room. It was small, windowless and furnished with a full-length mirror, wonky barstool and three hooks in the wall. In its previous life it had been a broom closet. A skinny goth chick was wriggling into a leather outfit and I said hello. She nodded and looked me up and down. I dumped my stuff and went to the bar.

"Able," said Dave, "Six letters."

"Adept?" Elise the barmaid poured beers for a bunch of tradesmen. She had long red hair and pendulous freckled breasts.

"No. That's only five."

"Adroit?" I said.

Dave scribbled it in. "Thanks."

I grabbed a glass beer jug from the end of the bar and prepared to do the rounds. Most pub shows were jug strips where you went around and collected money from the punters before the show. It meant the venue didn't have to pay you, just like table dancing. I hated it, it felt like panhandling, but I gritted my teeth and did it anyway. I wore a knee length black skirt and a low cut top. You had to save something for the show.

The pub was full of tradesmen who'd knocked off when the mercury hit thirty-five degrees, all dressed in blue singlets and anything by King-Gee. Most of them knew the drill and put in at least a two-dollar coin. Some gave me shit and asked why they should put in any money. I had my answers ready: "The more you put in the hotter the show. Guys who put in the most money get all the attention."

A couple of men put in ten-dollar notes and I made a point of remembering their faces.

After five minutes I'd milked them all I could and Dave was on the mike announcing Destiny was about to perform and to give her a big hand. The guys started yelling and the girl from the change room stalked out, all studded leather and eyeliner. Her music was loud industrial metal and with her matchstick legs she moved like a praying mantis. I could hardly watch. It was the wrong sort of show for the Royal. Pub strips called for eighties hits and girls with a bit of meat on their bones. I sat next to Dave on the far side of the bar, bought a glass of cask wine and added up my money. One hundred and twenty, not bad. Elise changed it into notes and held it for me while I went and got changed.

I pulled a nurse's outfit from my bag. It was a nylon number with a zip down the front, hat and plastic stethoscope. I'd bought it from Club X in the city one night when Chloe and me had been rampaging around, off our tits. Thinking about her made my stomach tighten. I wasn't doing enough to help her.

Destiny came through the door, naked and sweating.

"Fuck it's hot out there."

"How's the crowd?" I asked.

"Rooted." She wiped herself with a towel and began changing into a black velvet skirt.

Dave poked his head in and handed Destiny her stage outfit and tape.

"Sharon's just going round with the jug," he told me, "So you'll be on in five. Bankrupt, nine letters, last letter T?"

"Insolvent," said Destiny.

"Right, cheers." He closed the door.

I put on white stay-up stockings, white bra and knickers and teased my hair.

"You don't know a dancer called Ebony?" I asked.

"Black American chick?"

"Yeah."

"Everyone knows Ebony." Destiny pulled on big black boots. "She's grouse."

I zipped up the nurse outfit. "Do you know where I could contact her? I know someone who wants a black girl for a show."

"Then he's out of luck. Ebony doesn't strip anymore."

"Retired?"

"Nah, she's into B&D now, working at the Marquis and making a shitload. Wouldn't mind getting into that line of work myself."

Dave opened the door. "Got your tape?" he asked. I handed him a cassette, white fluffy rug and bottle of Nivea moisturiser. Destiny stuffed her leather number into an army duffel bag and said goodbye. I stood with the door slightly ajar waiting for Dave's intro, feeling nervous. After three years I still got butterflies performing before a crowd.

Dave introduced me and I heard the opening guitar riff of Bon Jovi's "Bad Medicine," the ultimate nurse show song, beloved of strippers from every nation. I strode through the bar in time to the music, swinging my stethoscope around and thinking how someone was probably doing this exact same show, right now, in a yurt on the Mongolian steppes. The tradies sang along, headbanging and playing air guitar while I walked around the crowd, smiling, checking pulses with my finger and heartbeats with the stethoscope. I climbed onto the small stage and danced, unzipping my uniform part of the way, then got down on my knees for a bit, making it up as I went along.

The guys were loud, really getting into it, and I was feeding off their energy and giving a really good show. Like any live performance stripping depends on the audience, and working-class ones were always the best. They'd usually seen heaps of shows and knew where the line was and not to cross it.

White-collar blokes were a different story. They didn't have the experience and saw you not as a performer but as some amorphous, sexually available creature they had a good chance of fucking. They were more likely to make snide, degrading comments and grab for your pussy.

At the end of "Bad Medicine" I unzipped the outfit all the way and it fell to the floor. There were cheers and whistles and I felt like a rock star. The next song started without a break: "Doctor Doctor," by Huey Lewis.

I got up on the bar and crawled along like a cat, everyone grabbing their beers out of the way. My hands and knees got all sticky from spilled drinks but I didn't care. One of the guys who'd put in a tenner was at the bar so I stopped and sat in front of him, opened my legs and nuzzled my breasts in his face. His mates cheered him on. I hopped off the bar and spun his chair around so he faced the crowd, then put the stethoscope to his crotch and pretended to listen. A highly unoriginal move but it went down a treat.

I found the other ten-dollar guy, sat on his knee and let him undo my bra. After I'd bounced up and down on his lap a few times I strutted to the stage where I prepared to slide down my G-string.

Dave got on the mike: "Do you want her to take it off?"

"Yeah!"

"Well let's make some noise!"

I cupped my hand to my ear like I couldn't hear them, and when they cheered loud enough I slid my knickers down to my ankles then stood up with my hand over my pussy. What a tease. I stepped out of the G and removed my hand. Ta da!

The last song was Warrant's "Cherry Pie," not exactly of or pertaining to nurses but a classic pub strip song nonetheless. Dave threw me my rug and I got down with much writhing around and flipping of hair. I dripped moisturiser on my tits to simulate that just-been-cum-on look then I went over to the ten-dollar guys and let them rub the lotion in. That'd teach the cheapskates. Right before the last song ended I was back on the rug for a bit of open leg work culminating in a final squirt of Nivea down there.

I stood up and took a bow and got a standing ovation that lasted until I was well into the girls' room, sweating like crazy, the hair at the back of my neck damp and matted. It had been a good show.

Chapter Thirteen

When I got home I had a cold shower, made myself an iced water, took the phone out to the balcony and called the Marquis Centre for Bondage and Discipline.

"Yes?" the receptionist was stern right from the get-go.

"Hi," I said, "I was wondering if I could talk to Ebony?"

"I'm afraid we don't allow personal calls."

I thought fast. "It's just that, I'm a stripper and I want to get into the B&D industry and a girlfriend of mine knows Ebony from when they used to strip together and suggested I talk to her . . ."

"Oh all right." Her voice instantly changed to bubbly and chirpy. "Ebony's not actually in today. Were you looking for work as a top or a bottom?"

"What?"

"A dominant or a submissive?"

"I hadn't really decided yet."

"Well, I'll tell you right now that there's not much work around for mistresses," she said.

"Really?"

"There's a bit of a glut in the market. You need a lot of experience and training or else have something special, different. Ebony does very well because she's the only African-American mistress in Melbourne."

"I see . . ."

"But we're always looking for submissives," she said brightly, "and the money's very good."

"What does a submissive have to do?"

"Be available for paddling, whipping. We have this new A-frame rack that's really popular."

"Is sex involved?"

"The mistresses don't generally have intercourse but the subs are required to provide it, yes."

"That's interesting, but I'd still like to talk to Ebony about it.

Can you give me her number or tell me when she's going to be in?"

"I'm not allowed to give out the workers' numbers," said the receptionist, "but she is going to be at Sexpo this week, from tomorrow. We've got our own stand this year. Ebony and our other workers will be able to give you a bit more information."

"Thanks." I hung up and punched in Kelvin's number. He ran a small agency called Extreme Promotions and got me bucks' parties and pub shows. I could have got more work through the larger agencies but Kelvin looked after the girls, provided security and paid a better percentage. He was a big, cuddly Sri Lankan guy with a penchant for soul music, Sam Cooke and Al Green. Girls constantly screwed him around because he was so nice.

"Don't tell me you didn't make the show today," he said by way of a greeting.

"Come on, Kel, I've never cancelled a show yet," I said. "I was wondering if you had a stand at Sexpo this year."

"Sure do, we've got a prime position this time, right next to the main stage."

"Do you need promo girls?"

"Yeah. You offering?"

"Can I do a few hours tomorrow?"

"I can give you ten till four but it's only twenty dollars an hour. Didn't think you'd be interested or I would have offered you the work. You hard up for cash?"

"I'm fine," I said. "Just wanted to get in for free."

"OK then, see you there." He sounded puzzled.

Soon as I hung up the phone rang. I steeled myself for Sal but it was Aurora.

"I got your number from Jim," she said. "I hope you don't mind."

"No. What's up?"

"I'm just calling to remind you about the band tonight, Las Vegas Grind? Betty and I really want you to come. We think you're one of the coolest people we've met in ages."

Me, cool? I'd always thought I was a bit of a dag. I'd totally forgotten about the invite but figured it'd be a good opportunity to find out some more information. Plus there would be music and alcohol and dancing, a few of my favourite things.

"Sure, I'll be there," I said. "They're on at the Espy, right?"
"Front bar. I'm so glad you're coming. See you about nine?"

At eight fifty-five I climbed the Espy steps in my faded jeans and pink checked shirt, ready to rock and roll. It was the perfect summer night and when I got to the top I turned and looked out. The bay was black beyond the Royal Yacht Squadron, coloured lights reflected off the water and oil tankers balanced on the horizon, lit up like party boats. It was so beautiful that something like infatuation welled up in my chest, and my eyes pricked with tears. Did I usually notice this stuff or was it that life and death situations made everything more intense?

Jesus. Get a grip, I told myself as I nodded to the Maori bouncer and entered the pub.

The band hadn't started yet but their instruments were on stage. It was pretty packed for a Tuesday and the audience was mostly rockabilly. The girls looked like Betty with their liquid eyeliner and Victory-rolled hair and the boys wore bowling shirts and gravity defying quiffs.

Aurora waved from the bar and I sidled through the crowd. She stood up and hugged me and gave me a stool she'd been saving.

"Which do you prefer," she asked, "Vivien or Simone?"

"Simone, I guess, if I'm not at work. What about you?"

"Aurora. I loathe my real name. It's awful." She waggled her champagne glass at the bar boy and held up two fingers.

"What is it," I asked, "Hildegard?"

"Don't laugh, you're not far off." She handed me a drink.

"Why'd you pick Aurora?"

"I love Greek mythology, it was my favourite subject at uni. Aurora's the goddess of dawn. I actually wanted Persephone but didn't think anyone would be able to pronounce it. How come you chose Vivien?"

"Vivien Leigh. I like her. She's a Scorpio and according to Hollywood legend a nymphomaniac."

Aurora tipped her head back and laughed. With her perfect blonde looks you'd expect a sound like a pealing bell but hers was gutsy and throaty, like an old blues singer. She was dressed in a backless black singlet top and wore pants and high heels and long dangly earrings.

She looked like a Penthouse Pet come to life and all the rocker boys snuck peeks at her while their girlfriends pursed their lips.

"You look a bit like Vivien Leigh," she said.

"Most people say Xena."

"Hi, guys." It was Betty. "They're on in a couple of minutes. Come to the loo for a line?"

I shook my head. "I would but I'm working at Sexpo tomorrow, can't get too fucked up."

Betty looked at Aurora, who thought about it for a second.

"I'll pass this time, Bett," she said.

Betty looked offended. "Fine." She marched off to the ladies'.

"I didn't want to take it if you weren't." Aurora leaned in and touched my arm, "There's nothing worse than hanging with someone on coke and you're not."

"How long have you been working at the Red?" I asked.

"Five months."

"And before that?"

"I was in Sydney."

"Me too," I replied, then changed the subject.

"Do you know Frank's brother Salvatore very well?" I had to get something out of this night besides a new friend and some free champagne. "It's just that I met him the other night in Jim's office and he kind of creeped me out."

"Sal creeped you out? Just as well you didn't meet Frank. Sal's the older brother. Married, three kids. He runs the business end of things while Frank controlled the day to day running of the club. Don't get me wrong, Sal's no angel, there's rumours he's knocked off business associates, people who owed him money, and when he visited the club he always used to get a dance, but he never tried to fuck the dancers, not like Frank. God, Frank used to have this boat and he'd invite all the girls out to it for parties. I never went. A boat. Can you imagine? There's no escape, it's—"

A loud drumbeat and smattering of applause cut her off and I swivelled on my barstool to look at the stage. A single red spotlight illuminated the singer. His leather pants were tight and his red velvet smoking jacket appeared to have been pinched from Hugh Hefner's wardrobe. He twined himself around the mike stand like a snake and crooned a few bars of "Blue Moon," dyed black hair flopping over hollow cheeks. Aurora leaned in close and I smelled strawberries and roses. "That's Betty's boyfriend."

He stopped singing and sipped from what looked like a quadruple scotch. "Good evening and welcome to the Esplanade lounge bar," he drawled, mouth close to the mike. "I'm your host, Johnny Del Rey, and this is LAS VEGAS GRIND!"

The lights came up and revealed the rest of the band but I only saw the lead guitarist. Holy mother of god he was a stone cold spunkrat. I felt my pupils dilate and knickers go moist and I had an overwhelming urge to throw my panties at the stage.

"And who's that?" I had to shout in Aurora's ear as they launched into a twisted hillbilly rendition of "Viva Las Vegas."

"Mick Halliday."

"He your boyfriend?" Please say no.

"I'm not really doing the whole boyfriend thing at the moment," she said. "He is something though, especially if you go for the bad-boy type."

Mick had Elvis sideburns and dark messy hair, charcoal eyebrows and intense eyes. His black cowboy shirt was jazzed up with red piping and a rose appliquéd over his heart. The rolled-up sleeves revealed strong arms covered in multicoloured tattoos, right down to his wrists. Lordy mamma, it was suddenly hot in there.

The band performed for an hour and I liked the music almost as much as I liked watching Mick play it. The songs ranged from toe-tapping numbers about hot rods, girls and Saturday nights to darker, dirge-like pieces on sex, madness and death. I liked Aurora too, she was smart, easy to get along with, and after a few drinks I considered spilling my guts to her about Chloe and Sal but it was too soon, and I was too paranoid.

At ten thirty Las Vegas Grind gave up the stage to the headlining band, The Swamp Daddies.

"I should go home," I told Aurora, tracking Mick's movements out of the corner of my eye.

"You're not getting away that easily," Aurora said. "Everyone's going back to Betty's for a drink. If we leave now we won't get roped into carrying any gear."

We grabbed an obscene amount of champagne and took a taxi to a back street in Prahran. Betty lived in an unrenovated weatherboard house with a wire fence and sagging porch. Aurora took a key from the dead potplant on the verandah, shook off the dirt and opened the door.

I was in retro heaven. Elvis and Betty Page posters covered the walls, a zebra-print rug hid the tatty carpet and lamps with fringed shades produced an orange glow. A lava lamp perched on an old TV set and a large fishtank housed a dozen goldfish swimming in and out of a sunken galleon. I was particularly taken by the glowing Jesus picture over the record player.

"Cool," I said.

Aurora led me through a beaded curtain to a kitchen with a round-cornered pink fridge and black and white lino squares. I sat at the chrome and laminex table while she leaned against the sink and opened the champagne.

"Just one more drink," I said, "and then I have to go."

"Whatever you say." She popped the cork and poured us both a glass. "So why'd you move to Melbourne?"

"A lot of reasons, I guess."

"Man trouble?"

"I broke up with my long-term boyfriend. We were going to get married. Shit happened. I thought it would be best just to move interstate." I could see Aurora wanted to press for more details but I was saved by a wave of people from the pub staggering through the front door.

Half an hour later the house was full. Aurora had melted away somewhere and I was stuck by the fridge talking with the fat drummer about how hard it was to get a break in the music industry these days. Mick was leaning against the opposite wall talking to a blonde with a ponytail and an upswept fringe. They seemed to know each other. She had a tattoo of roses and thorns around her wrist and tapped him lightly on the forearm as she talked. I tried to catch his eye but he didn't look over.

God, this was pointless. I was drunk and pathetic and it was time to go home. I asked the drummer where the toilet was and excused myself and went off down a hall. I had a pee, flushed, and when I came out saw an open door to my right. Another kitsch extravaganza? I poked my head in but was disappointed. Just a mattress on the floor with a crumpled doona and a couple of squashed looking pillows. A guitar case was propped up in the corner next to a milk crate full of CDs and books. I tiptoed over to have a look. On top was *The Lost Get-Back Boogie* by James Lee Burke and a Lucinda Williams CD, *Car Wheels on a Gravel Road.* I had just picked up the CD and flipped it over to read the playlist when I heard, "You right?"

It was Mick.

Chapter Fourteen

I started and turned around. He leaned against the doorframe, a long-neck of Coopers in one hand and a joint in the other, staring at me with big green eyes.

"I'm sorry," I blushed. "I didn't know this was your room. I didn't know you lived here."

"I'm just staying for a while," he said, gaze steady. He nodded at the CD in my hand. "You like Lucinda Williams?"

"Yeah."

"Most girls don't even know who she is."

"I'm not most girls."

"I noticed." He looked me up and down.

"Bullshit, you've been ignoring me all night."

Mick laughed. "Poor baby." He toked on the burned-down joint and offered it to me. I shook my head and he pinched it out and flicked it into a large glass ashtray on the floor. "You work with Aurora, right? Must get plenty of attention at the Red. Don't need any from me."

"That's true," I said. "If you'll excuse me I have to go home now."

He turned side on to let me through the door and I handed him the CD on my way out. When I was halfway up the hall he called, "Simone."

He'd found out my name. I turned as I reached the kitchen door. He was in the doorway holding the CD.

"I'm putting it on if you want to have a listen."

I grabbed a fresh bottle from the fridge and fiddled with the foil, deciding what to do. I desperately wanted to accept his invitation but I didn't want to give the cocky bastard the satisfaction.

"Vivien-Simone!" Aurora was pissed and in high spirits. "I wondered where you'd got to. Come and dance." She pulled me toward the lounge room where the music was booming.

"Actually—"

"Where are you going with that bottle of champagne?"

I looked toward Mick's room and Aurora giggled. "You and Mick, I knew it."

The blonde with the roses shot me a filthy look.

"We're just listening to Lucinda Williams," I said.

"Who? Well, sweetie, I won't wait up for you."

"It's not—" but Aurora had skipped off to the lounge. The blonde gave me the death stare and I stared back until she looked away. I had to go to his room now, just to piss her off.

Mick lay on the mattress with one arm behind his head, smoking a rollie and looking at the ceiling. He'd turned off the bare light bulb and lit a candle in a beer bottle. He was hopeful. Lucinda Williams sang "Drunken Angel."

"What do you think?" he asked.

"I like it. All my favourite country songs involve drinking hard liquor and being on the run from the law."

He laughed, a slow, stoned chuckle. "Mine too." He propped himself up on one elbow and I sat cross-legged on the floor and drank out of the champagne bottle. We looked at each other and didn't say anything. Lucinda finished the first song and started another.

"You don't say much," I said.

"Most people talk just for the sake of talking." He flicked the cigarette into the ashtray and swigged his beer. "Come here," he said.

"Nuh-uh." I shook my head.

"Are you scared?"

"No, I'm not scared."

"I think you are," he smirked.

"Fuck you." I took a huge gulp of champagne and crawled onto the mattress and straddled him. Big mistake. Wherever my body touched his I felt heat and tingling, zapping me right through two layers of denim. I tried to slide off but he grabbed my hips and pushed me down onto him. Oh my god. He was hard and I felt my pussy start to throb. Mick placed his hands on my face and pulled me down to kiss him. His mouth was soft and he used just the right amount of tongue and gently bit my bottom lip. Despite the beer and tobacco he tasted sweet and up close smelled like sweat and clean washing. He put his hand inside my shirt and when he brushed my nipples I pushed harder against him. His cock strained at his jeans. He rolled on top of me and unzipped my hipsters while we kissed, and when he slid his hand into my knickers I almost came on the spot.

It was like there was some kind of energy between us, electric, otherworldly. Or maybe I'd inadvertently inhaled some of that dope smoke.

I could have kissed him forever but there was something else I wanted in my mouth. I whispered in his ear, "I have to suck your cock."

Not surprisingly there was no protest from Mick and I went down, undid his brass belt buckle and unzipped his fly. He wasn't wearing any underwear and his hard-on sprang free. I licked the head and the shaft then took the whole thing in my mouth and heard him moan. After a few minutes he pulled me up and kissed me again and began to tug off my jeans.

"Wait," I said.

"Don't you want to do it?" He drew feathery circles on my clitoris with his fingertip and made me really *really* want to do it.

"Yes." I pulled away from him, breathing hard, all messed up. His shirt was off and the tattoos on his arms and chest writhed in the candlelight. "That's why I've got to go."

I escaped via the back gate, stopped in a cobbled laneway and leaned against a wall, breathing deeply to slow my heart rate. Jasmine curled over the fence opposite, filling the warm, thick air with its scent. There weren't many stars but the moon was almost full and traffic hummed on nearby Chapel Street. I could still feel him, still taste him, and I stayed by the wall, hugging myself until I was composed enough to go look for a cab.

I had it bad.

Chapter Fifteen

"You're late."

"I'm sooo sorry." I looked around Sexpo. The exhibition centre was huge and blow-up dolls dangled from the ceiling.

"That's all right, mate, don't stress." Kelvin chucked me on the shoulder. "I'm just surprised."

"News flash," I said, "world's most reliable stripper late for Sexpo."

"Big night?"

"You could say that." I willed the pain tablets to kick in. I was getting too old for this shit.

"We'll have to go out some time for a kick-arse curry. It's been ages." He swigged from a water bottle. "It's just hard with the new baby."

"How is she?" I asked. "And the wife?"

"They're fine." Kelvin's dark round face beamed. "Amara's beautiful, sleeps a lot. What about you? When are you going to pop out a couple?"

I laughed so hard I thought I might throw up. Kelvin handed me a T-shirt and I went to the toilets to get changed. Exhibitors were still setting up their stands full of videos, sex toys and lingerie and the ladies' was packed with women squeezing into wigs and latex gear. I changed into hotpants, boots and a padded bra and put on the tight black T-shirt Kelvin had given me with extreme promotions emblazoned in white lightning letters. The padded bra was great. Cost me five bucks at a seconds shop in Richmond and was an instant tit-job, no mess, no fuss, no scarring. I painted on slutty red lipstick to match my bloodshot eyes, slid my inquiry agent ID into my back pocket, and headed to the cafeteria to get a coffee.

I tried not to think about Mick. Each time I did I got shivers and went into a dreamy swoon followed by angry recrimination. I should be ashamed of myself. Almost fucking a musician two seconds after meeting him. We'd hardly said a word to each other. And I knew the type of guy he was, the kind that as soon as he's had you he doesn't want you anymore. I'd learned about that shit the hard way.

I paid for the long black and dumped my bag under Kelvin's stand. Promotional posters of the girls hung on the booth walls and a large television screen showed a video of one of the tamer shows. Sexpo was strictly R rated. The strippers on the main stage weren't even allowed to take off their G-strings.

Sipping my coffee I looked around. The booth next to us was Swingers Scene, manned by a couple from the suburbs. The husband wore neat casual and the wife looked like a soccer-mum. They smiled and I gave them a little wave. In the distance a beige dinosaur thing ambled along, spurting water out of its head.

"What the fuck is that?" I asked.

"Penisaurus." Kelvin straightened the cards and flyers on the table. "He's the official Sexpo mascot."

"Good god." I shuddered, "This place is turning me off sex already. So what do I have to do?"

He handed me a bunch of flyers. "Just walk around and give these out. We're also promoting topless shots with the girls. Ten bucks a pop."

"Can I pass on that?" I yawned.

"Sure."

I walked around giving people flyers and cards, checking out the exhibitors. One of the top brothels had a bed and spa on their stand and a raffle to win a Harley Davidson. Next to them a small booth promoted "Uberglide," a revolutionary German designed lubricant. I passed the velvet-draped Marquis stand but couldn't see anyone fitting Ebony's description and when I got to the far end of the room I found the "lifestyle" booths, beauty, chiropractic, natural therapies. You could tell your friends you just went to Sexpo to get your spine realigned. Yeah right. I signed an anti-censorship petition at the Eros stand and went into the draw at another to win fifty porn videos. That would be sure to impress any potential suitors.

All the exhibitors were really friendly. In fact the whole place had a family atmosphere that made whatever kink you were into seem acceptable, wholesome and healthy. I was appalled. Sex was supposed to be dirty and bad. What if my erotic life never recovered? That got me thinking of Mick again and I just wanted to lie down on the cheap grey carpet and roll about. Sexpo was probably the place to do it. Everyone would just stand around watching politely then ask for a brochure. I blushed when I remembered sucking his dick. I'd really jumped the guy. Chloe would be so impressed. Shit, Chloe. The thought of her snapped me out of my dreamy reverie. I had to find Ebony.

Back at Kelvin's stand a girl with curly blonde hair extensions and an Extreme Promotions T-shirt handed out leaflets.

"Hi, I'm Vivien," I said.

"Sabrina," she yawned. "Gawd, early enough for ya?" It was two o'clock.

"You girls should do a double show." Kelvin sat on a folding chair at the back of the booth reading an adult contact journal he'd picked up from the swingers next door.

"Fair go, Kel," said Sabrina. "I'm not growling out some chick I've never even met—no offence."

"None taken," I smiled politely. "Can I go on a break, Kelvin?"

"Yeah, sure, whatever." He was engrossed in his magazine.

I bought a bottle of water to combat the dry horrors and went to the Marquis' booth to see if Ebony was there yet. On the way through the maze of stalls I saw the Red Room stand. Little blonde Dakota was gyrating sullenly on a makeshift table. I didn't blame her—god-awful lighting, tinny music from a faraway PA, everyone staring but nobody putting money in your garter. I went over.

"Hi," I said, and when it looked like she couldn't quite place me, "Vivien, from the club."

"Oh, hi Vivien." She kneeled down to talk to me. She had a breathy, girly voice.

"Tough gig."

"Fucken tell me about it. Jim owes me big time. This is the pits. You working tonight?"

"No, just Fridays and Saturdays. You know, they sell alcohol at the cafeteria."

"Really?" Dakota's face brightened.

"Yeah. Say hi to Aurora and Betty for me."

"Sure."

A man in black latex underpants and a gimp mask was tied to an A-frame rack at the Marquis' stand. Probably a Supreme Court judge. A bored-looking dominatrix, way too white to be Ebony, whipped him from time to time and a barrel-chested man in his forties stood beside the rack, handing out cards. He was balding and had done that thing where they shave off all the remaining hair. Studded armbands ringed his biceps and his leather pants had the arse cut out, exposing hairy white buttocks. He should have looked ridiculous but carried himself with the natural authority of a man who beat the shit out of people for a living.

"I'm the Brigadier." His phony English accent reminded me of Vincent Price.

I shook his hand. "Nice to meet you. How's the legs?" The floor was concrete under the thin carpet.

"Killing me." He rolled his eyes then slapped a cat-o'-nine-tails against his palm. "Complimentary whipping?"

"No thanks, just had one. Couldn't take another lash. I was wondering if Ebony was around."

"Oh yes," he said. "Here she comes now." He nodded at the Hustler stand and I saw a statuesque black woman stride towards us. A red rubber corset pushed her breasts skyward and impossibly high black boots were laced to the tops of her thighs. She wore a white, Louis XVI wig with a mini top hat and veil, rouged cheeks, a heart-shaped beauty spot and a stern expression. The leashes in her hand led to dog collars around the throats of two flabby middle-aged men dressed like the guy on the rack. A Liberal Party MP, I guessed, and possibly a Catholic priest.

"Ebony." The Brigadier clapped his hands together. "This delightful young lady would like to speak with you."

Ebony looked me up and down and I felt very short, very white and very skanky in my hotpants and cheap T-shirt.

"How can I help you?" She had an American accent.

"I'd like to talk to you about getting into some bondage work," I said.

She looked down at me and arched an eyebrow. "Talk to Felicia." She looked at the other mistress. "Or the Brig. I'm busy." She snapped the leads like an arctic explorer "mushing" the huskies and began to walk off.

"Wait," I said sharply. I was over all this bullshit, hungover and running out of time. "I'm not after a job. I want to talk to you about Frank Parisi's murder."

Ebony's eyes opened wide and she put her hands on her hips. "And who the fuck are you exactly?"

"I'm a private detective." I took my licence out and handed it over. The Brigadier, who was pretending not to listen, did a double take and nudged Felicia. Ebony studied my ID and laughed.

"A private dick." She chuckled. "Always wondered what you guys wore under those trenchcoats."

"I strip as well. It's the new millennium—multi-skilling and all that."

"Tell me about it, sister, but I don't know if I can help you." She handed back my licence. "I already talked to the police."

"Anything you can tell me about Frank would help."

"I'm going out for a cigarette," she said. "You can join me if you want." She handed the leashes to the Brigadier and the men sat on their heels like begging dogs and whined. One crawled over and licked Ebony's boot.

"Fuck off." She kicked him away.

We left Sexpo and walked through the glass-walled foyer that overlooked the Yarra, then out a side door to some concrete steps. About twenty exhibitors in various states of undress hung around, eagerly sucking in smoke. We sat down and Ebony stretched her legs out, took a packet of Cartier cigarettes from a small velvet bag and offered me one. I shook my head and she lit it for herself with a small gold lighter. Her fingernails were long and gleamed with dark red varnish.

"How'd you get my name?"

"I've been talking to the girls at the Red and they mentioned you used to work there."

"Why you so interested in who killed Frank?"

"It's a long story. I have to find out to help a girlfriend of mine. She's a stripper too. I can't really tell you any more."

Ebony nodded sagely and blew out some smoke.

"What was going on at the club before Frank was killed?" I asked.

She shrugged. "Shit, same old same old. Frank coked up and

arrogant, king of the castle, Jim handing out drugs like candy, Sal coming in to collect the cash now and again with some heavy-looking dudes. There was the night Honey's boyfriend Shane got beat up by Frank and the bouncers."

"What about a cop called Dick Farquhar?"

"He'd come in once a week. I used to stay away from that guy."

"Did Frank ever try to crack onto you?"

"Hell no," she laughed. "He was scared of me. I used to do this voodoo themed show and he stayed well away. They're superstitious, those South Americans."

"You really know voodoo?" I asked.

"Shit no, I'm from Connecticut. I only know what I see in the movies. Thing is, anyone I meet in this industry, I let 'em know straight away I ain't taking no shit from no one. One time in Soho this asshole tried to touch my jewel. I broke his fucking arm, you know what I'm saying?"

I nodded. Yes I did. Ma'am.

"I worked all over," Ebony continued. "New York, Vegas, London even. Some of these girls though, they're eighteen. A young eighteen. Don't know how to play the game and get taken advantage of."

"Like Honey?"

"There are a million Honeys out there, all trying to please daddy." Ebony took a final drag and crushed out the cigarette butt with her spike heel.

"I heard she was having an affair with Frank."

"An affair implies consent."

"Did she tell you he forced himself on her?"

"She didn't have to say anything, I could tell by the look in her eyes. She acted like she didn't mind but that was to save face. When something like that happens you feel stupid, like in a way it's your own fault."

I wondered if Ebony was talking from experience, from some long ago time, before she'd started snapping ulnas like twigs.

"So if Shane knew, that's a pretty good reason for offing Frank."

"I'm not speculating, sugar. You should talk to him about it."

"Know where I could find him?"

"I don't have a phone number or anything but Honey's in

the Miss Striptease finals at Crystal T's tomorrow night. Shane'd probably be there. Won't want to talk to you though."

"I'll think of something," I said. "You in the comp this year?"

"Nah." Ebony lit another thin white cigarette. "I've had it with stripping and I'm really enjoying the B&D game. Beating the hell out of guys and getting paid a shitload. I think I've finally found my niche."

I got up and brushed specks of grit off my hotpants. "Just one more question," I looked around, paranoid. "What do you know about Frank's brother Sal?"

"Not much, bit of a mystery man. Rumour has it he imports the coke that's around the club and has some pretty heavy connections. Maltese Mafia. Not someone I'd ever fuck with."

Indeed.

I went back inside and handed out more leaflets, then watched a couple of strip shows on the main stage. Two unattractive women in the audience were making bitchy comments about a gorgeous stripper, picking at the tiniest things.

"She's got cellulite on her arse."

"Her tits are a bit saggy."

I came up behind them and said loudly, "Jealousy's a curse, ladies."

They turned and opened and closed their mouths like guppies before hurrying away.

The guys and girls were good, award winners some of them, but the audience hardly made a sound. I finished up at four when a couple of girls came in to replace Sabrina and me. Kelvin paid me a hundred and twenty bucks, cash. Every little bit helps.

I drove through Macca's in South Melbourne and bought two McOz burgers. When I got home I threw away the buns and ate them on a plate with a knife and fork. The burgers, the day and the hangover had made me tired and I fell asleep on the couch.

I woke in darkness to the phone ringing, not sure what time it was. I picked it up off the coffee table: "Hello?"

" 'Folson Prison Blues.' "

"Johnny Cash," I croaked, still half asleep.

" 'Too Many Nights in a Roadhouse.' "

"Junior Brown. Who is this?" I asked, struggling to sit up. But I already knew. It was Mick.

Chapter Sixteen

I arranged to meet Mick at the Doulton Bar where Acland Street smacked into Barkly. It was one of the few watering holes in St Kilda that looked like a pub rather than a space lounge or an eighteenth century brothel. It even had pub carpet. I'd dressed up for the occasion, jeans and my "damn right I'm a cowgirl" T-shirt and had spent an hour putting on makeup so it looked like I was wearing none.

I walked inside and couldn't see a thing. Everywhere in Melbourne has dim lighting—anything over forty watts seems to be illegal—and Sydney is fluorescent by comparison, dazzling and over-lit. Rather than peer around like an idiot looking for him I walked straight up to the bar and ordered a chardonnay. I felt wine would leave me with a modicum of composure that just wasn't possible with champagne. My heart hammered as the pouty bar girl poured the wine. It was ridiculous. I was more nervous now than when Blue had pointed his gun at me.

A voice behind me, low and sexy. "Hello, Miss Vivien Leigh."

I took my wine and turned around. It hadn't just been the champagne-goggles. He was gorgeous.

"Mr Halliday." Deciding to play it Jane Austen style.

"I've got us a seat."

I followed him to a couple of brown vinyl armchairs, sat down and kept my knees together. Mick sprawled in his chair with his legs wide apart. He wore an electric blue shirt with the neck open and sleeves rolled up and the same jeans as the night before. Probably still without underwear. I resisted the urge to unzip him and check and pressed my knees tight. How long since I'd had sex? A couple of months at least.

"Why'd you call me?" I broke the silence. "Was I the root who got away?" So much for Jane Austen.

Mick held up a palm. "You've got me all wrong."

Had I? I smoothed down my jeans, even though they didn't need smoothing. "I was pretty drunk last night," I said.

"I was pretty stoned."

"I have to apologise. I don't usually do . . . that, on the first date."

"Do what?" He was pretending to be serious but the corners of his mouth tugged up.

"You know." I glanced at his crotch. "That. I don't do that to someone I don't even know. It was out of character."

"No need to say sorry," Mick said. "I really enjoyed that. I think you're very good at it."

"Will you excuse me?" I got up and ran to the ladies' and leaned against the wall by the mirror softly banging my head against the tiles. Then I scrunched up my face and did a little scream. Aaaarrgh. A woman came out of a cubicle. "Are you all right?" she said.

"Now I am," I smiled.

When I got back Mick was rolling a cigarette and I asked him to make one for me.

"How long have you been with the band?" I felt better after my little episode in the bathroom.

"Not long." He handed me a rollie as tight as a tailor-made. "I've only been in Melbourne three months. Met the guys at the Byron blues festival earlier this year. They needed a guitarist and I came down. Tom, the drummer, got me some building work. Can't live on guitar playing alone."

Building. That explained the arms.

He leaned over and lit my cigarette with a match. "What about you? Do anything besides stripping?"

"No," I said quickly. "Byron Bay? You from up that way?"

"I'm from all over. My folks have a farm near Kyogle. You know it?"

"Yeah, my mum has a place in the hills fifteen minutes from Byron. I used to live there when I was a teenager."

"Hippies?"

"Uh-huh. What about your folks?"

He shook his head. "Rednecks." A pause. "Do you think we know each other yet?"

"Not hardly." I drew back, ashed. The skill of smoking never left you.

"What else do you want to know?"

"Where do I start? Star sign?"

"Pisces."

"Age?"

"Twenty-seven,"

"Married? Kids?"

"When I was nineteen. Not anymore. My nine-year-old son lives with his mother."

"Ever been in jail?" I was just joking.

"Once."

I raised my eyebrows. "Really?"

"Yeah." He drained his beer. "I'm hungry. You want a laksa?"

We walked down Acland Street to Chinta Ria, sat at an outside table and ordered king prawn laksas and beers. St Kilda went crazy on warm nights and around us music and people spilled from fashionable bars and trams number 16 and 96 disgorged their cargo. Mick was a lot more talkative than he'd been the night before, telling me about the places he'd lived in Queensland and New South Wales and all the jobs he'd done—jackeroo, miner, building boats and finally houses. I in turn gave him selected highlights from my ridiculous life: my parents splitting when I was five and my dad moving to America, leaving home at sixteen, running away to sea, countless crap jobs, constantly moving.

"How'd you get into stripping?" he asked.

"Bit of a long story."

"I've got time." He settled back to roll a cigarette.

"When I first moved down from Sydney I worked at Coles on Elizabeth Street," I told him. "The Crazyhorse adult cinema's on the same block and every time I walked past I was fascinated by the place. You know, flashing neon lights, blaring music and the stairs going down below street level, like they led to some mysterious subterranean underworld. It drew me in."

Mick nodded like he understood.

"There was always a hand-written notice stuck in the window: 'Dancers wanted, no experience necessary, apply within.' I always wanted to know what went on in there but never had the guts to get down the stairs.

"Anyhow, one time at the supermarket I was having a shit of a day, a common occurrence in retail, when this Toorak rich bitch comes in. I handed her the wrong pack of cigarettes and she called me a stupid girl. You know when you get so angry, you literally see red?"

Mick smiled wryly, ashed his cigarette. He knew.

"I ripped off my name badge, chucked it at her and came out from behind the register. I walked towards her, real slow, and she backed away. Her mouth was opening and closing, like a guppy, no sound coming out. And when I got to her, I reached out, hugged her, looked her in the eye and said, 'I forgive you.'"

Mick laughed. "No way. I would have smacked the silly bitch. What happened then?"

"She started screeching for security and I walked out the doors, up the street, and down the stairs to the Crazyhorse. The woman at the counter looked like a truck-stop waitress and I asked her for a job. She gave me a two-dollar coin to put in the peeps and I had a look. When I came out of the booth she said, "Reckon you could do that, love?" And I said yep and the rest is history. I went from there to the Club X Bar, to the Shaft, and picked up a bit of agency work along the way. Now I'm doing a couple of shifts at the Red."

"You must make a lot of money."

I shrugged. "Some days you do, some you don't. And quick as it comes it goes out again. Waxing, solarium, hair, nails, shoes, costumes. I never seem to have any left over. Some strippers are paying off houses, investing in shares, but they're few and far between."

"Do you like the job? I think Aurora does but Betty seems to hate it."

"Hmmm. Love–hate. When you're on stage dancing to the music you like and everyone's cheering it's the best job in the world. After an hour in the peeps for a lousy twenty bucks, or a show for a bunch of unappreciative arseholes, then it sucks.

"I love the people you get to work with, though. Everyone's a little left of centre. To tell you the truth I've never been totally comfortable in normal society, and hanging out with freaks and misfits I feel right at home."

"Tell me about it," Mick said.

"And the really great thing about stripping, as opposed to hospitality or retail, is that the customer is always wrong."

He laughed at my joke and I was glad. The waitress removed our empty bowls and we order another beer each.

"So what about you?" I asked. "What were you in jail for?"

"Shot a man in Reno."

"Ha ha, no really."

"Assault."

"A woman?" My stomach clenched. Our beers arrived. Bottles glistening with condensation.

"No. A man. A very bad man, who deserved everything he got."

"Who was it? What did he do?"

"Sorry." Mick picked up his drink. "You don't fuck on the first date and I don't spill my guts."

"So we're on a date, are we?"

"What do you reckon?"

We had a couple of whiskies back at the Doulton Bar and Mick drove me home in his battered ute. I didn't know if I'd invite him up or not. Sitting next to him, in amongst empty Tally-ho packets, beer bottles and crumpled building plans, the urge to touch him was immense and if it led to that I wasn't sure I'd be able to say no.

"This is it," I told him, and we screeched to a halt in front of my place. He switched off the engine.

"I'll let you walk me to my flat," I said, "but that's it." Trying to pretend I wasn't a slut.

I led him up the interior stairs and when we got to my place I turned and leaned against the door. We stared at each other for a long time. He had an intense way of looking at me that made my inner thighs turn to liquid. His mouth was only a foot away but the distance seemed impossible to traverse. I bit the bullet and moved hesitantly towards him and in a rush he scooped me up and put his mouth on mine. He pushed me back against the door and put his leg between my thighs, held my face and kissed me hard. I felt his broad back beneath the soft material of his shirt, his hips pressing against me and lost all resolve. I had to get him inside the house and inside of me as soon as was humanly possible. So what if I was the slut from hell? So what if he was a fuck-'em and leave-'em guitar player? I flashed to the incriminating noticeboard in my room but that was OK, we probably wouldn't make it further than the floor inside the front door.

I was fumbling for my keys with one hand and his belt buckle with the other when he suddenly pulled away and cupped my chin in his hands. He stared at me, almost as if he was puzzled, and said, "Where did you come from?" Then kissed me on the forehead, turned on his Cuban heels and walked down the stairs.

I waited by the door like a stunned mullet. What had just happened? Hopefully he was nicking to the car for some condoms and—

The ute started up. Shit. I unlocked the door, raced through my flat to the balcony, and got there just in time to see him speed off down Broadway.

Motherfucker. That was my trick.

Chapter Seventeen

The taxi crawled along Sydney Road, Brunswick, past two-dollar shops, Lebanese restaurants and pool halls. It was eight at night and I was on my way to the Miss Striptease competition. I had two hours to try and talk to Honey and Shane as Kelvin's driver was picking me up at ten. A last minute booking for a show at Noble Park— apparently they had asked for me by name.

Mick had called at midday from a building site, the staccato tap of hammering in the background and the whine of a circular saw.

"Okie from Muskogee."

"That's so easy I'm not even going to answer," I'd replied.

"What are you doing tonight?" he asked. "Wanna go see a band?"

"I'm working from eight till midnight."

"What about after work?"

"I don't know. What if you run out on me again?"

He laughed. "Now you know what it feels like."

"Evil bastard," I said. "Was that revenge?"

"An eye for an eye, lady."

I had told him I'd call when I'd finished my show.

The neon Crystal T's sign stuck out from the building at a crazy angle, surrounded by flashing lights. I paid the cab driver and zigzagged through traffic to the other side of the street. I nodded to the bouncer out front, paid ten bucks to get in and left my backpack with the girl behind the front counter.

Crystal T's had been around for years, catering for bucks' parties and hens' nights. The interior was eighties "nite spot" and the furnishings RSL bistro. The stage to my left had glittery curtains and tables full of guys crammed in front and on my right the floor tiered upward and there were more tables and a sound and lighting booth. The bar was at the back and I headed there first for cheap champagne before settling at a table in the raised section with a good view of the club.

I was right on time. The Miss Striptease theme blasted out and a mirror ball sparked points of light across the walls and ceiling. A smoke machine cranked up and a cloud drifted across the stage. Exciting stuff.

The DJ's voice boomed over the PA: "Good Evening and welcome to the Victorian finals of the tenth annual Miss Striptease competition!"

The music and lighting became more frantic and the contestants began to appear. Men down the front clapped and yelled. The dancers all wore variations on the same bondage theme and got ten seconds to do a little dance before moving to the rear and striking a pose.

A young-looking blonde shimmied down to a squat at the front of the stage and the DJ introduced her as "Honey, sponsored by Dominique's Elite." A guy stood up, punched a fist in the air and yelled, "Yeah!" I guessed that was Shane.

When all eight contestants had created a tableau an explosion sounded and glitter rained down from the ceiling. It was just like Miss Teen USA, but with open leg work.

The girls exited and the DJ introduced: "Your hostess this evening, Dominique Dubois!"

A forty-something woman with waist length black hair walked to the centre of the stage and welcomed the audience. She wore a leopard-print sheath with huge fake boobs popping out. Dominique was famous. She'd been an award-winning stripper in the eighties and now ran Melbourne's most successful agency, due to her knack for publicity. Her latest trick had been running for parliament on a law and order platform, campaigning with four busty strippers in skimpy cop outfits. It guaranteed her a spot on the news every night: "And now the lighter side of the election race."

"Are you ready to see the crème de la crème of Melbourne's striptease artistes get down and dirrrty for you?" Dominique said.

"Yeah," yelled the crowd.

"Tonight the girls are competing for over a thousand dollars in cash and prizes, the cover of *Picture* magazine, and the chance to represent Victoria in the national finals. Now you gentlemen have an important role to play. The judges will take into account appearance, personality and the quality of the show but also audience reaction. So when you see your favourite dancer we want you to make plenty of noise, all right?"

"Yeah."

Dominique cupped a hand around her ear. "I can't hear you."

"Yeaaahhh!"

"Show us your tits," someone shouted. Dominique didn't miss a beat.

"What, these old things?" She jiggled her boobs with her hands. "When you're about to see the best breasts and butts in the business? Gentlemen, the first part of our competition: Body Bitz!"

Dominique left the stage and the dancers began parading past a screen with the mid section cut out. You couldn't see their heads or legs, just tits and bums. I was glad my mum wasn't there. I'd never win the argument about stripping objectifying women and reducing them to parts. Not tonight.

There was an interval after Body Bitz and I bought another drink and took it back to my seat. I couldn't see the guy I thought was Shane. A man at the table next to me was smoking Peter Jacksons and I was considering bludging one when he noticed me looking and scooted over. He was mid thirties, dishevelled, and smelled very strongly of beer.

"How you doing? Curtis Malone, *Picture* magazine." He held out a hand and I introduced myself. His palm was slightly sweaty.

"Is that the judges' table?" I nodded to where he'd been sitting.

"Yeah, I'm one of them. That dude in the middle? He won a reader's comp to be guest judge."

I glanced over. The guy was deep in thought, looking down at his scoresheet and scratching his head with a stunted pencil. His light beer was hardly touched. I raised my eyebrows.

"Yeah," Curtis conceded, "he's taking it a bit seriously." He offered me a cigarette, lit it and I drew back gratefully.

"So he doesn't know the competition's rigged then?" I blew out smoke.

Curtis opened his mouth in mock shock. "Blasphemy!" Then he leaned in: "Ever done any glamour modelling?"

"Nope."

"How'd you like to be in *Picture*?"

"I don't know."

"Come on, every girl wants to be in *Picture* magazine."

"I am a fan of your publication."

"Really?"

"I love the words you guys come up with. Tockley, Smoo. And Cuntox, that's my favourite."

"No shit, Cuntox was one of mine."

"It's a heck of a word, congratulations."

"Thanks," he said. "I worked on the *Sydney Tribune* a couple of years ago, court reporting, sports pages. But I never got to make up a word, you know."

"It's a beautiful thing," I agreed. The lights dimmed and Dominique announced the individual dance event.

"Anyway," Curtis got off his chair, "here's my card, we're always looking for new girls and it's worth a couple of grand if you make the cover."

The performances began with a cheerleader, followed by a devil with glittering red horns and a girl who started in a fat suit and emerged thin and naked. I tried to note good moves for my own shows. Then Honey skipped onto the stage in a St Trinian's style school uniform: blazer, straw hat, ripped stockings. She was tiny even in stripper heels, with no hips and small perky breasts. The guys at Shane's table went wild as she jumped around like Mighty Mouse on speed, concluding the show by covering herself with whipped cream and a sprinkle of hundreds and thousands.

The next girl was a high-kicking blonde with big tits and then it was interval time again. The clock on my mobile said twenty-one thirty so I marched down to the table by the stage. A few guys sat around.

"Is Shane here?" I asked.

"He's at the bar," said a chunky blond guy. "After Honey I thought your show was the best."

"I'm not in the competition," I said.

"You should be," piped up a skinny young guy with bad skin. "You're hot enough."

"You're sweet." I resisted the urge to ruffle his hair. "She did a great show."

"Yeah," said Blondie, "Honey's grouse for a stripper, not stuck up or nothing."

A guy approached the table with a cluster of VB stubbies in his arms.

"Hey, Shane," the skinny one said, "this chick's here to see you."

Shane looked me over warily. At first glance he was quite good looking with straight blond hair that flopped over his face and a body like a kick-boxer, wiry and muscular. When I studied him a bit longer I noticed details like his chin was too pointy, his lips dry and thin and his eyes too close together.

He put the beers down. "What can I do for you?"

"I'd like to talk to you about something, in private."

A few of the guys sniggered.

"Why can't we talk here?" He picked up a beer and had a swig.

"It's about Frank Parisi's murder."

Shane rolled his eyes and ran his fingers through his hair. "You another fucking cop?"

"I'm an inquiry agent."

"Fuck off," he laughed.

"I am." I hoped I didn't sound too whiny and got my licence out again. Maybe I would be more convincing in a hat and trenchcoat. Shane took it and passed it around for his mates to see before handing it back.

"What do you want from me?" Shane jutted his chin out defiantly. "I didn't fucking do it. I've been over this a million times with the cops. I'm sick of this shit and I know I don't have to talk to you." He swigged his beer again and ripped the label off the bottle.

"Do the cops believe you?"

"Nuh, it's harassment. What happened to innocent before proven guilty?"

"Hear hear." His mates clinked their stubbies in support.

"I've got a fucking alibi," he said, "and there's no murder weapon, no DNA evidence."

"But you've got a motive."

"Who didn't?"

"What is your alibi?"

"Why should I tell you?"

Shane's mates were looking back and forth from him to me like spectators at the tennis. "Are you happy with the way the police are conducting the investigation?"

"What do you think?" He took a pack of Horizon 50s out of his shirt pocket and lit one with a Crystal T's lighter. "They're fucking useless."

"I don't think you did it," I said. "I've got information on a few suspects and if you talk to me I might get a line on the real murderer and get those dumb cops off your back."

He shrugged.

"I'm trying to help you, Shane," I said.

He ripped some more label off his beer bottle and pushed hair off his forehead again. "OK," he said finally. "Let's go out to me car."

I heard the competition start up as I followed him to the car park. Shane made a beeline for a late model ute in midnight blue, leaned against the curved bonnet and crossed his arms. "What do you want to know?"

"Your alibi, to start."

"I was home all night with Mel. That's Honey's real name."

Not the most convincing alibi in the world.

"Tell me about the fight with Frank," I said.

Shane sighed. "When I found out about him and Mel I was ropeable, mate, mad as a cut snake. I knew he musta forced her into it 'cause she wouldn't cheat on me, specially not with that sleazy cunt. I had a few bourbons, more like half a bottle, and drove into town. We live at Werribee."

Half an hour out, semi-rural.

"What date was this?" I asked.

"The second of November, Sunday. I remember 'cause I had to do a statement for the cops."

"Was Honey working?"

"Nuh, at her mum's. She only did Friday and Saturdays."

"What time did you get to the club?"

"'Bout ten. Don't know exactly."

"And what happened?"

He flicked his cigarette butt away in a glowing arc and did the thing with his hair. If I'd had a pair of scissors I would have cut that forelock off.

"I went up to the bar and told the girl to get Frank for me. When he came out the office I shoved him against the wall. Had a knife on his throat, boning knife from work. I said something like, what do you think you're doing fucking with Mel, cunt? And he said, who? And I said Honey, and pressed the knife so a little bit of blood came out and then someone king-hit me on the side of the head."

"Were you knocked out?"

"Nah, I hit the ground but wasn't out cold. Frank's two security goons were there, as well as a short blond bloke. Frank told 'em to take me out the back and they dragged me out this doorway and down these concrete steps so my head was banging on each one. I got a few punches in but each time I did they laid in worse. Down the bottom of the stairs the others stood back and let Frank lay into me. He was kickin' me in the guts, the kidneys, the head."

Shane took out another Horizon and lit it.

"Woke up the next afternoon in hospital, pissing blood. I was there for three days, lost a couple of teeth." He put his hand to his mouth and pulled out a bridge with false teeth attached, then put it back in. "It's only temporary, I'm gonna get those fake teeth they put in your jaw with titanium screws. They match them exactly to your real teeth. I'm saving up."

"You must've wanted to kill him," I said. "I would have."

"I did," he laughed bitterly, "and we were going to get him, me and the boys. We were working on a plan but someone beat us to it and now I'm the prime fucking suspect 'cause I was telling anyone who'd listen."

"Honey didn't keep working at the club?"

"Fuck no. She wouldn't have anyway but the cunt rings her mobile while I'm bleedin' out in the back lane and fires her. Wouldn't let her get her stuff from her locker and owed her two hundred bucks." He flicked his second cigarette butt in the same trajectory as the first. "Ha. But he's dead now, isn't he? Instant karma, ay?"

"What happened to the knife?" I asked.

"No idea. Must have lost it when I first got hit."

I heard the tap-tap of high heels behind me and turned around. Honey stood there in stage makeup and a feathered robe. Cars beeped at her from Sydney Road.

"What's going on?" She'd taken her hair out of pigtails and

boofed it into an elaborate, Dynasty-style do that was too big for her small head.

"She's a private detective," said Shane, "trying to find out who offed Frank."

"Can I talk to you about him?" I asked her.

"I don't wanna talk about that prick, it's over and done with. Come on," she told Shane, "the final parade's about to start, then they announce the winners."

He pushed off the bonnet and walked towards Honey.

"I hope you find the killer," he said. "When you do I'll buy him a beer." He put his arm around his girlfriend and they headed for the club.

"Shane!" I called out, and he stopped and turned. "How'd you find out about Frank and Honey?"

She was staring daggers at me. I didn't blame her.

"I got a call. Some guy I didn't know told me over the phone."

Chapter Eighteen

"Vivien." Wesley had pulled up beside the car park. He was Kelvin's driver and one of his three thousand cousins.

"Hi." I waved. "I'll just grab my bag."

He put it in the boot of the Celica and opened the door for me. Wesley was dark and thin and very polite around all the girls. Apparently he knew karate but no one had ever seen him use it.

"Have you had dinner?" he asked. "We could stop at McDonald's on the way."

"Maybe after. I don't want to be bloated for the show. But we need a bottle shop."

We stopped at a pub on Nicholson Street and I had a pee and bought two half bottles of Omni. It was a vibrator show tonight so I had to be a little drunk.

It was mostly vibe shows these days. I had a theory that because everyone was nuding up, pop stars, actors, lifestyle show presenters, a naked female wasn't the slightest bit risqué anymore. Bucks' parties had to up the ante, and strippers worked "hot"—vibe shows and lesbian doubles.

We drove down Hoddle Street past the housing commission flats, then onto Citylink and the Monash Freeway. I drank champagne through a straw and fiddled with the radio, feeling pretty positive, considering. There was a week left to find the murderer and I was leaning very strongly towards pinning it on Dick Farquhar even though I wasn't sure he'd done it. It seemed strange that a cop would use a knife instead of a gun, but it wasn't my problem. I just had to find enough proof to convince Sal.

And I was meeting Mick after the show. I squeezed my thighs together in anticipation. Everything was going to work out OK.

We pulled up outside an unremarkable brick veneer on a quarter acre block. Wesley got my bag and a portable tape player out of the boot and we walked up the path to the house and knocked on the door. A middle-aged man in jeans and a T-shirt answered.

"Entertainment's here," said Wesley.

"Come on in." The man shook his hand.

"Is there somewhere Vivien can get changed?" he asked.

"Yeah, sure, down here."

He led us along the hallway and opened the door to a small bathroom. It was an unrenovated seventies job, cream and brown tiles and orange moulded fittings. The mirror above the sink was speckled and old. Oh well, I'd had worse.

Wesley went off to collect the money and set up the boom box and my fluffy rug and I got changed. I was going for a NYC hooker look this evening with suspenders and fishnets, black lace G-string and bra, satin micro-mini and a long sleeved black mesh top. I slipped a black dildo, moulded, "realistic" looking, into a satin purse with a small bottle of baby oil, put on extra makeup and teased my hair at the roots. Wesley knocked on the door and stuck his head in.

"Got the money?" I asked.

"Yep, show's in the lounge room." He looked back down the hall. "You're not going to like it though."

"Why not?"

"There's only about eight guys there."

"You're kidding." You couldn't feed off such a tiny audience.

"I'll try and get them going, get 'em to make some noise."

Jesus, this was going to be painful.

"OK," I drained my second half bottle. "Let's get this over with."

I waited at the doorway until I heard the thudding intro of Madonna's "Erotica" and slinked up the hall. I sidled up to the doorframe and ran my hands over my body while I checked out the room. There were actually seven guys, not counting Wesley, a couple sitting on an old couch, three on chairs and two standing. All were dressed casually and aged between thirty and fifty. They were drinking Tooheys out of cans and the atmosphere was sombre. Some party. I dropped to my knees and crawled into the room like a cat.

I rolled around on the rug and Wesley clapped and shouted "Yeah," but no one else got into it. I crawled over to the couch, put my hands on one of the guys' knees and hoisted myself up, then bent over in front of them. No reaction. I smiled lasciviously at the two standing by the mantelpiece and they didn't meet my eyes. Time dragged, a minute seemed like an hour. This was worse than the time I'd danced for a bucks' party off their brains on Es, everyone peaking so badly their eyes were rolling back.

I had everything off bar the stockings by my second last song and I gave Wesley a look which said fade this one out early, and he nodded. Prince was singing "Nikki" and I took the baby oil out of my purse and drizzled it over myself, then removed the dildo.

Wesley whooped and said, "Come on, fellas, let's make some noise," but to no avail. I sucked on the vibe, rubbed it on my breasts and then spread my legs and slid it in and out a few times. Men think you're totally getting off when you do this but while concentrating on a show it's about as arousing as inserting a tampon. You can enjoy a vibe show if you have a good crowd, but it's not physical, more of a naughty thrill from doing something really sleazy.

Alas, there was no thrill for me tonight. Wesley, god bless him, faded out my music and I stood up and took a bow. He started up a round of lacklustre applause that was over before it began and I gathered my rug around me and made for the bathroom. Thank god that was over.

I washed baby oil from my hands and wiped the excess off my body with a towel. I was just about to unclip the suspenders when the door burst open.

"Wes—" I started but it wasn't him, it was the two men who'd been standing up.

"Excuse me." I held the towel against myself. Wesley was hovering behind them and I wondered why he hadn't beat the shit out of them, Jackie Chan style.

"I tried to stop them but they're . . ."

It was then I noticed they held identification in their hands. Police identification. What the fuck?

"I'm Detective Sorenson." He wore a white T-shirt and his thinning blond strands were slicked back. "And this is Detective MacIntyre." MacIntyre had thick dark hair and looked around nervously.

"What's all this about?" I asked as Wesley threw my clothes through a gap in between the burly detectives. He was hovering around, looking panicked.

"You've just violated the Victorian Prostitution Control Act," said Sorenson. "You're under arrest."

Chapter Nineteen

"What?" I tried to wiggle into lace knickers while holding the towel but it wasn't working so I dropped the towel and pulled my undies on in front of them. "You can't be serious. This is some kind of set-up." I clasped the bra and hoisted up my satin mini.

Sorenson gave his partner a look and MacIntyre pulled my hands behind my back and cuffed me before I realised what was going on.

"I don't believe this," I protested.

Wesley flitted about in the hallway looking more like a distressed hummingbird than a crouching tiger, his mobile phone pressed to his ear. "I can't get on to Kelvin, it's just going through to voicemail . . ."

"You'll have to come with us, miss." Sorenson steered me into the hall by my elbow.

"What about my stuff?"

"Detective MacIntyre will take care of that." Sorenson marched me outside to a blue, unmarked Commodore. I noticed everyone else from the "party" had already left. Wesley ran behind us and draped his black jacket over my shoulders.

"Don't worry, Vivien," he said, "I'll get in touch with Kelvin, he'll know what to do." And then to Sorenson: "Where are you taking her?"

Sorenson didn't reply, just opened the back door and put his hand on top of my head as he guided me into the back seat. The door shut with a dull thud. MacIntyre came out with my bag and handed Wesley the cassette player. He locked the front door of the house and put my things in the car boot. Wesley watched us drive away.

A few minutes later we pulled up in front of a small suburban cop shop.

"Where are we?" I asked.

"Dingley," said Sorenson.

The southwest was Farquhar's stomping ground. A cold dread washed over me. But how? I was sure he hadn't seen me follow him. Had Alex dobbed me in?

"What have you got?" The female desk sergeant raised an

eyebrow when she saw how I was dressed.

"Prostitution," Sorenson replied.

She sniggered, "No, really?"

They took me out the back, took off the cuffs and photographed and fingerprinted me. No one else was around.

"Are you sure this is the correct procedure?" I asked, dubious. "Aren't you supposed to interview me first? And what about my phone call?"

Neither replied. MacIntyre went through my stuff and bagged the vibrator for evidence.

"Can I get changed?" I pointed at my street clothes.

"No." Sorenson took me to a small interview room with a melamine-topped table and three chairs, trimmed in blue cloth. A camera was mounted on the wall above a sealed video recording unit and two flat-bed microphones were attached to the table.

He cuffed my hands behind my back again, making Wesley's jacket gape open.

"Is that completely necessary?" I asked but he didn't reply, just left and locked the door.

I sat down and tried not to cry. Tony Torcasio wouldn't. What would he do? Not get busted for illegal prostitution, for a start. Try to see the funny side of it, I told myself. It'll make a great dinner party conversation in years to come.

Christ, who was I kidding? I felt humiliated and ashamed. And scared shitless. Tears pricked my eyes and I blinked rapidly to get rid of them.

After what seemed like an hour I lay my head down on the table in front of me. My wrists, arms and shoulders sparked with pain and the panic had been replaced with exhaustion. I'd tried kicking the door and yelling but no one had answered. None of the recording devices were switched on and I was sure this was illegal. Then the door opened and I sat up ready to protest my treatment but the words caught in my throat.

Farquhar. The panic came flooding back.

He was older and fatter than the photo I had, dressed all in grey, slacks, shoes and a shirt with sweat-stained armpits. Above his navy tie with football club motif he had no neck, just a face that seemed to be melting. Even his light brown moustache drooped toward the floor.

Dick Farquhar smiled. There wasn't much that scared me, apart from evil clowns and singing karaoke, but now I felt the sort of elemental fear Neanderthals must have experienced in the face of a slavering sabre-tooth. My heart raced and sweat dripped down my back.

I forced myself to sit up straight and look him in the eye. Don't show fear. Or was that just for dogs?

He sat opposite, plonked down a plastic bag of Kentucky Fried and removed a box of chicken, large fries and container of gravy, filling the room with the damp salty scent of KFC. He peeled the lid off the gravy and dunked three fries at once, gelatinous globs dripping onto the table as he lifted them to his mouth. Wiping his fingers on his pants he reached into his back pocket for my charge sheet and smoothed it out.

"Simone 'Vivien' McCullers," he said, "haven't we been a naughty girl?"

I just stared at him. He picked up a stringy leg of chicken, poked it in the gravy, and popped it in his mouth, sucking off the liquid before chewing the meat. I had been very hungry but not anymore.

Farquhar read the charge sheet and made a clicking sound with his tongue.

"An unlicensed prostitution service provider can cop five years." He threw the chicken bone back in the box. "Got anything to say for yourself?"

"I'm not a prostitute."

"According to the amendments to the Prostitution Control Act you are. Prostitution means the provision by one person to or for another person of sexual services in return for payment or reward. The definition of sexual services under section three includes permitting one or more persons to view a person introducing, to any extent, an object or part of their body into their own vagina or anus."

The bastard had memorised the Act.

"It was a strip show and this is a stitch-up."

Farquhar chuckled slowly, dunked some more fries and hadn't quite finished chewing when he said, "Now why would anyone want to stitch you up? You're a fairly unremarkable suburban stripper and the law's the law." He plucked out more chicken. It wasn't a leg. It wasn't a wing. I couldn't tell what part of the bird it had come from. He crunched slowly, savouring every bite.

"I hope you realise you're in a lot of trouble here. It's a serious offence. Not just in this country but all over the world. A conviction for prostitution can follow you around for a long time. The amount of jobs that require police checks these days . . . could ruin a girl's career."

"You'll never get a conviction." My voice came out gravelly and I cleared my throat.

"Won't I? Seven witnesses, all of them police officers."

"It'll get thrown out of court."

"I don't think so," he said. "These amendments are relatively new and the government wants to show they're not all talk when it comes to the tough new laws. There'll be lots of publicity, the media loves this stuff."

"Look," I said, trying to reason with him, "what's this all about?"

Farquhar's eyes narrowed and his avuncular bad guy act vanished. He leapt out of his chair so suddenly it tipped over and was at my side with a speed that belied his size. Face pink with fury he hauled me out of my chair and slammed me into the wall so my head went thwack and things became brown around the edges. He raised his fist and I squeezed my eyes shut in anticipation of the blow. Instead he punched the wall so hard it shook. He was close and I smelled fried chicken and underneath that a rotten smell like tooth decay. Sweat beaded on his forehead and the open pores of his nose. His breathing was rattly and deep.

"What's all this about?" he bellowed. "What's all this about, you stupid cunt?"

I turned my face away from his fury and the specks of spittle flying in my direction but he grabbed my jaw, turned it back and spoke through clenched teeth. "It's about you trying to fuck with me, following me around with your brand new inquiry agent's licence, taking me for a mug. You're playing a very dangerous game, Simone. Who are you fucking working for?"

"No one," I said. "I don't know what you're talking about."

He slapped my face with a meaty palm and brought tears to my eyes. "Don't bullshit me." His hand was clamped on my upper arm, fingernails digging in.

"I'm investigating Frank Parisi's murder," the words came out in a rush. "It's for a girlfriend of mine, she's in trouble because people think she had something to do with it and I'm trying to prove she didn't."

"And you reckon you're going to pin that fucking wog's murder on me?" He shook his head. "Nothing worse than a stripper thinks she's got a brain. You've got no idea who you're messing with, do you? People have disappeared for less." He cocked his hand like a gun, stuck it between my eyes and laughed. "But then I thought, shame to waste such a nice piece of arse. If you were more of a dog, who can say?"

Farquhar let go of me and stalked back to his chair, sat down and dunked some more fries.

"Siddown," he ordered, and I did. "This conviction can ruin your life, I'll make sure of it. I'll be pushing for jail time and you can kiss your licence goodbye as well as any other job worth having. However, if you want to make it up to me," at this he smiled, "I can make it go away. In fact I've got something coming up you can help me with. You want to be a good girl? Help me out? Make it go away?"

I wanted to kill him but I nodded instead. "What do you want me to do?"

"Nothing yet, I'll tell you when the time comes. Wouldn't want to ruin the surprise. So don't go leaving town or crying to any other coppers 'cause I guarantee it'll get back to me. I wasn't even here tonight, darling, I was investigating a case in Geelong, so . . ." He gathered up the KFC detritus, placed it in the bag and swept crumbs off the table. "I've got your number and address. I'll be in touch."

He let himself out the door and I began to breathe. Five minutes later Sorenson uncuffed me, handed me my stuff and told me I was free to go.

I knew something was wrong as soon as I let myself into the flat. It was dark although I'd left a lamp on when I went out. I switched on the overhead light and looked around, couldn't see anything out of place. The newspaper was still on the dining table where I'd left it, next to a bowl containing the remains of a tuna salad, but something didn't feel right.

I crept into my bedroom and switched on the light.

The noticeboard was gone.

Chapter Twenty

I felt violated and angry. Someone had been in my space. My first instinct was to call Alex's mobile and it went to voicemail.

"Thanks for sicking Farquhar onto me, you lying scumbag piece of shit. Was it you or him who broke into my flat?"

Kelvin was beside himself with worry and apologised profusely when I called to let him know I was all right. I assured him it wasn't his fault, I was fine and no charges were going to be laid.

When I got on to Mick he was home at Betty's and it sounded like another party was going on. I wondered if the blonde tart with the tattoos was there. Meow.

"You took your time," he said.

"I got arrested." Now I started blubbering. What a baby.

"I'll be straight over."

"You don't have to—" He'd already hung up.

I jumped in the shower, washing my hair and scrubbing myself to get the stench of Farquhar and fried chicken out of my pores. I slathered on mango body butter and slipped into grey tracksuit pants and a pale blue singlet. My hair was wet and I didn't bother with makeup. If Mick didn't like it, tough.

He arrived a few minutes later with a six-pack of beer and a bottle of wine.

"How you doing?" He touched my shoulder.

I sniffed. "OK, considering."

He went to the kitchen and opened the wine and ripped a beer off the sixer for himself.

"What's going on?" He looked concerned, not like an arrogant guitar player at all.

I had no idea if my flat was bugged so I suggested we go for a walk. I took him down Broadway towards Glenhuntly Road and turned left at the Elwood canal. We found a bench and sat down beside the oily black water, crickets chirruping and bats flying overhead. Mick drank a beer and I swigged wine straight from the bottle. He rolled a cigarette, gave it to me, then started one up for himself.

"I lied when I said I didn't do anything apart from strip," I said, and told him everything. Sal kidnapping Chloe, going undercover at the Red, following Farquhar and Alex to an illegal brothel, and my arrest.

Mick didn't say anything, just sat there and smoked. I had expected more of a reaction.

"You're not surprised I'm a private investigator?" I asked.

"I knew there was something different about you, and not much surprises me anymore." He put out his cigarette. "What's the favour this Farquhar character wants you to do?"

"I don't know yet. He's going to contact me. He has a history of setting up his colleagues and filming them with hookers and drugs."

"Nice. Do you think Farquhar killed Frank?"

"I don't know. I'm pretty sure he was demanding protection money so the club never got raided." I shrugged. "I'm just guessing."

"Are you going to go to the cops?"

I shook my head. "Sal reckons he'll kill Chloe if I contact the police and the last time a girl tried to dob in Farquhar she ended up dead of a suspicious heroin overdose."

We walked back to my place and in the interior stairwell Mick said, "Want me to sort them out?"

"For god's sake," I whispered, "thanks for the offer but one's a cocaine kingpin and the other one's the police. They have guns. It's my problem. I never should have laid this shit on you."

Inside my flat I put on a Cowboy Junkies CD and Mick turned to me: "It's my problem now too."

"What are you talking about?"

"There's something going on between us," he said. "Don't tell me you don't feel it." His took my hand and put his lips on my wrist and sparks shot up and down my veins.

"Do you use that line with all the girls?" The words almost stuck in my throat. He shook his head and traced my lips with his fingertips and the fluttering in my belly became unbearable. He pushed two fingers into my mouth and I sucked on them, my blood on fire. We were standing in the middle of the lounge room and his hands were twined in my hair pulling my mouth onto his. He tilted my head back and sucked and bit my neck. My knickers were soaked and I felt him hard beneath his jeans.

Mick picked me up and carried me to the dining table, sitting me down and sweeping the newspapers and other crap onto the floor.

"Mick," I whispered, "Someone might be watching the flat."

"Then they're going to get a good show," he said, laying me back and taking off his shirt. I stared at his tattoos and his muscles, finely honed from years of physical work. My eyes trailed down his flat stomach to the line of hair that disappeared into his jeans, to the bulge in those jeans. He slid my top over my head and dragged my trackie daks and sodden underwear off. When he leaned over to kiss me his brass belt buckle was cold against my stomach.

He whispered in my ear, "You are so fucking beautiful," then kneeled down in front of me, opened my legs and put his mouth on my pussy. He knew exactly what he was doing and he slid two fingers inside as he licked me. I tried to pull him up to fuck me but he didn't stop until I came. I lay there, legs shaking, breath ragged, and watched him unbuckle his jeans and then he leaned over me, holding my wrists above my head and looking into my eyes. When he finally pushed his cock inside me it felt enormous, hard as steel, and my mind and body were white light, white heat.

Chapter Twenty-One

The next day we drove to Portsea and got a room at the pub. I'd called the Red and told them I was violently ill. Jim wasn't happy but what could he do? I had to get away, get my head together, and I didn't think the Mornington Peninsula counted as leaving town. Besides, there was sex to be had.

We holed up in the room and fucked on the bed, the floor, the dresser, the shower, in front of the mirror. I couldn't get enough of him and the more I got the more I wanted. Mick seemed to feel the same way. In between we drank and smoked cigarettes and talked, the intimate, heads together, endlessly fascinated talk of new lovers. Mick was gradually explaining the meaning of his tattoos. A clock without hands represented his time in prison, a jaguar was for a friend who'd died in a mining accident and a guitar for the first time he'd played on a stage. A flaming crown of thorns stood for his Catholic upbringing and a Medusa-like figure on his right shoulder blade symbolised strength.

We emerged at dusk, sore and hungry, and wolfed down steaks from the bistro at an outdoor table overlooking the darkening waters of the bay. A cover band started up and we watched it, drinking whisky and kissing until the bar manager told us we'd better leave.

We stayed Friday and Saturday night. Mick had to be in Melbourne for a show at the St Kilda Inn Sunday and I had to get back too. Guilt about Chloe was seeping in. I knew I'd been escaping the whole situation, drowning it out in sex and booze and infatuation. I had to get my shit together, put my plan back into action.

Mick dropped me off at my flat and asked if I wanted him to stay with me but I said no. I needed Sal to contact me and I didn't think that would happen with Mick around. We arranged to meet at the pub at seven, before the show.

I slept for a couple of hours then got up and had a strong coffee and put on a black dress with small red roses and a push up bra. I was waiting at the bus stop for the 600 when a familiar black sedan pulled up. I stuck my thumb out and Sal opened the back door.

"Boy am I glad to see you," I said. "Couldn't give me a lift to the corner of Barkly and Grey, could you?"

Sal smiled. "Certainly. Did you enjoy Portsea?"

"Didn't see much outside my hotel room," I said.

"I'm aware of that. Do you have any information for me?"

"I know who the killer is," I said.

"Who?" Sal leaned forward.

"Let me talk to Chloe first."

Sal got out his phone.

"Chloe?"

"Maaate!"

"How are you?"

"Not bad. Blue's massaging my feet. He's quite good at it. When are you going to get me out of here?"

"Soon, I've found the killer."

"Who?"

"Tell you later."

"I can't wait to see you. I can't wait to sleep in my own bed. And I'm so bored. We watched every fucking action movie ever made so I decided it was time to educate Blue about classic movies so I got him to get *Beaches*, you know?"

Chloe's taste in flicks was terrible.

"And he really loved it. He was crying at the end."

I heard Blue say, "No I didn't," and "No I wasn't."

"And we've also hired out *Titanic*, *Speed 2*, *Dead Calm*—"

"Great," I said. "Can you hang on a minute?"

"Sure."

Chloe was silent and I strained for some clue as to her whereabouts. Sal realised I was up to no good and hung up the phone.

"Who's the killer?"

"Detective Senior Sergeant Richard Farquhar," I said. "They argued before Frank was killed."

Sal nodded slowly. "Proof?"

"Not yet but I'll have it by Thursday. More proof than you'll ever need." It was an outrageous bluff but I said it with such confidence Sal seemed to believe me.

"Good," he said, a little surprised, and let me out at the pub. I went straight in to the bar in the middle and watched Mick set up on stage. He wore the black cowboy shirt and his hair fell over his face as he bent to tune his guitar. The drummer said something and Mick tipped back his head and laughed. Golden stage light illuminated his face and I squeezed my thighs together and felt short of breath. Control yourself, girl. What's the female version of pussy-whipped—cock-thrashed?

"You and Mick, hey?" Betty propped herself up at the bar next to me. Her eyes were glazed and she swayed slightly.

"Yeah, me and Mick."

She took a Lucky Strike out of her bowling bag and tried to light it with a box of matches. She couldn't get the matches lit and they kept falling to the floor. I took the box and struck one up for her. She blew smoke in my face.

"So how are you doing?" I asked carefully.

"Fucking great," she said. "I haven't been to sleep for three days and I'm not even tired."

"Is Aurora coming tonight?"

"How the fuck should I know? I'm not her mother." Betty laughed crazily, sat on a barstool, and put her handbag on her lap. She rummaged through until she found a tiny plastic bag of white powder, scooped some out with her fingernail and snorted. I looked around, paranoid. Betty sniffed and wiped her nose with the back of her hand, then spotted a friend across the bar. She slid off the stool and tottered over. I was relieved.

Mick finished setting up, came over and gave me a long, passionate, get-a-room kiss.

Betty was staring at us from the other side of the bar.

"I missed you," he said. It had been three hours.

"Betty's off her head," I told him.

"She usually is."

"You haven't told anyone about my day job, have you?"

"A few, but I killed them straight after."

"Ha ha," I said.

Mick leaned against the bar. "That scumbag copper contacted you yet?"

"No, but the scumbag drug-lord did. I spoke to Chloe, she's OK. She's a clever girl. I think she's made the hired muscle fall in love with her."

"Smart."

"It's just Sal I'm worried about. I've heard things about him. Bad things. He'd be prepared to kill her even if Blue wouldn't. I have to find a way to convince him Farquhar's the killer."

"We'll come up with something. You should tell Aurora, she's smart, she'll help you out."

"I probably will."

The band headed up to the stage and Mick reluctantly joined them.

"Come dance up front," he said, "where I can see you."

"Viva Las Vegas" blared out to the usual rockabilly suspects and backpackers who'd wandered down from the dorms upstairs.

I danced after a couple more champagnes. It was hot and crowded at the front of the stage and Mick winked at me. Sweat slid down my back and between my breasts and bass notes thudded inside my chest cavity.

Someone grabbed my arm from behind. Betty?

I turned and my stomach contracted and blood rushed to my head. It was Alex. Had he come to collect me for Farquhar's favour?

"I need to talk to you." His face was stony as he shouted in my ear.

"Come to do Dick's dirty work?" I shouted back.

"No." He gave me a disparaging look as he pulled me out of the crowd. I shook him off.

"Then what the fuck do you want?"

"To talk. It's urgent."

"Why should I talk to you? You sold me out to Farquhar."

"It wasn't me, I tried to warn you off him."

Alex walked toward the door and I followed him, venting my frustration, whispering loudly into his ear: "He's charged me with unlicensed prostitution if I don't do what he wants, when he wants. He broke into my flat and got my files. You're his little right-hand man, aren't you? Visiting illegal brothels, getting your cocks sucked together."

Alex had led me out of the pub and down a small side street. He whirled around and grabbed me by the shoulders.

"Will you shut up for a second and listen to me?" He hissed between his teeth, looking around: "I want to bring Farquhar down just as much as you do. I'm undercover for Ethical Standards and I'm putting my whole operation on the line here by telling you, but I need your help. Together we can bring down Farquhar and half the department. I'm trusting you—"

"Well I don't fucking trust you. Why should I?"

"Are you drunk again?"

"No I'm not drunk. I'm happy. I've only had three—"

"What the fuck's going on here?" It was Mick.

"Piss off, mate." Alex's hands were still on my shoulders. "This doesn't concern you."

Mick's eyes gleamed, he was all keyed up. "Get your hands off her. You're that fucking cop, aren't ya?"

"It's not Farquhar," I told him, "it's Alex."

Alex took his hands off my shoulders and looked Mick up and down. "Is this hillbilly your boyfriend?" he sneered. "Spare me."

Mick was on him in a second. He pushed Alex's chest then swung a punch. Alex dodged and Mick's fist bounced off the side of his head. He staggered back a couple of steps and then came at Mick.

Mick was taller than Alex, and more muscular, but Alex had some pretty nifty moves he must have picked up at the police academy.

Alex squared up to punch Mick in the face and when Mick put his fists up and leaned back to avoid it, Alex kicked his feet out from under him and Mick hit the ground. Alex jumped on top of him and Mick sucker punched him in the mouth before Alex grabbed his hands and then they were rolling around in the gutter, silently wrestling.

There was something kind of sexy about two hot guys grappling around like that.

"Hey," I said, "do you even know what you're fighting about?"

They wrestled for a bit longer, grunting with exertion, slowed down gradually and eventually stopped. They stood up and Mick spat on the ground. Alex wiped blood off his lip with the back of his hand and both kept eye contact like a couple of alley cats. If they'd had tails they would have swished them slowly from side to side.

Mick pulled a crumpled rollie from his shirt pocket and lit it. A vein in his temple throbbed and his hair was damp with sweat.

Alex tucked his expensive olive shirt back in and coughed. "Anyway, Simone, give me a call." He walked toward Barkly Street and for a second it looked like Mick was going to go after him. Instead he dragged so hard on his cigarette it imploded at the butt.

"Fucken jacks, what did he want?"

"He says it wasn't him who dobbed me in to Farquhar. He wants to help me."

"He wants to fuck you." Mick laughed mirthlessly.

"What?"

"It was obvious, the way he looked at you. He was all over you." I shook my head in disbelief.

"Are you going to call him?" he asked.

"Fuck Mick, I don't know. Probably. I need to get Farquhar off my back."

"Fine." He turned and stalked up the lane to the pub and I was left standing there thinking, what the hell was that all about?

I got back to the pub as the band started up again and sat at the bar drinking champagne until the gig was over. Mick didn't look at me once. The band began to pack up their gear and one of the backpackers put Oasis on the jukebox and cleared out most of the rockers.

Betty disappeared into the toilets for a really long time. I had to pee myself so I went in. One of the cubicles was locked and I bent down to look under the door and saw her two-tone saddle shoes. I used the next cubicle.

"You all right in there?" I asked.

"Yeah." Betty sounded funny.

I flushed and went out to wash my hands. The lock on her cubicle clicked open and Betty came out with her head back, holding a wad of toilet paper to her nose.

"Fucking nosebleed." She threw the bloodied paper in the bin and looked at herself up close in the mirror. After ten seconds a fat trickle of blood seeped from her left nostril.

"Aww fuck." She returned to the cubicle for more toilet paper, sat on the lid and tipped her head back again.

"Do you want me to get Johnny?" I asked.

"I said I'm fine, just fucking leave me alone."

Back in the bar the band had packed up and Mick was talking to the blonde with the tattooed wrist over by the stage. She was touching his forearm again, tapping it to make a point, and they were both laughing.

Blood rushed to my head and I marched to the bar and ordered a double Jameson, straight up. I knocked it back in no time flat and ordered another. Mick and the girl were leaning against a wall now, still talking. Cosy.

Betty came out of the bathroom and her and Johnny sat off in a dark corner. It looked like she was crying. They got up and Johnny put his arm around her and she leaned on him as he walked her out of the pub.

I couldn't stand it anymore and went up to Mick, stood there. They ignored me.

"Hi," I said. Both glanced over and kept talking.

"Are you pissed off at me?" I addressed the question to Mick but blondie looked at me and smirked.

"I'm not pissed off at you." Mick's voice was flat. "You can do what you like."

"Well fine, I will then." I looked in Mick's eyes and didn't know what I saw there. Fathomless pools? A murky swamp? He looked away and I walked out of the pub. I wanted to go straight backed and dignified but was so pissed I bumped my hip into the pool table on the way out.

I crossed Barkly Street and tried to hail a taxi. All occupied. Johnny and Betty were down the lane beside the pub. Betty vomited in the gutter and Johnny held her hair back. I started walking, stunned, numb. How had everything shifted so suddenly between Mick and me?

I became aware of a car slowing down behind me, following. Not again. I turned and saw four hoons in a hotted-up Commodore with P-plates and a thudding stereo.

"Hey, babe." The guy in the front passenger seat leaned out the window. "How much?"

I ignored them and kept walking.

"Don't be like that, we got money." He held out a ten-dollar note, "How much for a suck, baby?"

The other guys laughed and I felt rage, red hot, behind my eyes. I approached the car and kicked the passenger door, over and over, until the metal buckled. The car sped up and the hoon yelled back at me: "You're fucking ugly anyway, cunt."

I cried drunken tears as I wobbled home on my high heels. When I got there I drank some more and listened to every depressing song in my CD collection. Mick didn't call.

Chapter Twenty-Two

Monday 24 November

The next day I called Alex from a public phone and arranged to meet him on the hill at Point Ormond, near Elwood beach. I jogged there, ducking down cobbled lanes and sprinting across sports fields to shake off any surveillance. It was a bad day for a run, clouds hung low and heavy and the air was thick, oppressive. As I laboured up the hill toward the white wooden beacon my neck itched with sweat and my puffy eyes stung from crying the night before.

I leaned against the wood and stretched out my quads. You could see everything from the Elwood hill, the city skyline, the Westgate Bridge, the Bellarine Peninsula on a clear day. Alex walked up from the other side, past a grove of scrubby bushes where guys cruised for other guys.

"You look like shit," he said.

"Who's talking?"

His lip was cut and swollen and his cheekbone grazed.

"Nice guy, that boyfriend of yours. You've done well for yourself."

"Forget him," I said. "Let's talk about Farquhar."

"What happened when he arrested you?"

I told Alex about the arrest, Farquhar threatening me, and my flat being broken into. "Has he contacted you yet?"

"No. Maybe he's forgotten about it. Maybe he just wanted to scare me off."

Alex shook his head. "He'll contact you soon. I know him, he's got something in the works. He'll want you to have sex with someone while he films it."

"What?"

"That's the way he operates. What did you think he'd want you to do? Run a couple of suits to the cleaners?

"We think he'll contact you at work. It's pretty hard to hide a wire when you're naked, so we want you to wear these." He pulled a small brown envelope out of his shirt pocket and tipped a pair of earrings onto his palm, big and gold, with a cluster of fake pearls.

"I can't wear those," I said.

"Why not, you've got pierced ears?"

"They're off, totally eighties. I wore something similar to my Year Ten formal."

"They need to be big to hide the transmitter. Besides, I hear the eighties are back. Put them on."

I slipped them in my ear lobes.

"It's the only way," said Alex. "Farquhar's not going to approach you anywhere that might be bugged so I want you to work the Red tonight, every night until he shows up. Go along with everything he says. Someone from my team will be following you until this thing goes down. Wear the earrings everywhere until then, OK?" His mobile rang and he answered, listened briefly, then hung up. "The transmitter works fine."

"Go along with everything he says?" I repeated. "When exactly does the cavalry come and rescue me?"

"We want you in the room with the mark because we need all the evidence we can get. You don't actually have to go through with it though, unless you want to."

"Prick." I punched him on the arm and he smiled for the first time, then winced as blood oozed from his lip.

"You never told me who you're working for," he said. "I'm guessing the family?"

"Yeah," I said, and left it at that.

"Don't get too involved with them, they're into some pretty heavy stuff. You don't want to be tied up in it when it comes crashing down around them. And it will."

"I won't," I said. I wanted to tell him then about Chloe but I couldn't. I still didn't completely trust him. I didn't trust anybody and I wasn't going to shoot my mouth off with radio transmitters for earrings. "There's just one thing I want for helping you out."

"What's that?"

"A copy of Frank's autopsy report."

Alex groaned. "I can't—"

"Yes you can, if you set your mind to it."

"I'll see what I can do. Thanks for helping us out, Simone. I had the wrong idea about you. You're a smart girl."

"Woman, Alex. Are all you cops so un-PC?"

"'Fraid so," he grinned.

At home I lay in bed with tea bags on my eyes to bring the swelling down and fell asleep for a couple of hours. I woke at five and got ready for work, washing my hair, putting on makeup and painting my nails. I was about to leave when I heard a knock.

So much for the security door downstairs.

I took a deep breath and reached for the knob. Farquhar? Sal?

I opened it.

Mick leaned against the hallway wall, looking the worse for wear. He was smoking a cigarette and held an almost empty bottle of bourbon under his arm.

"Can I come in?"

I nodded and he walked past me and sat down heavily on the couch.

"Did you call him?" He swigged from the bottle.

"Who?"

"Who do you reckon? That fucking jack."

I sat next to him and whispered in his ear: "That fucking jack is going to help me with the you-know-who situation." I shook my head. "Jesus, what's your fucking problem, Mick? Everything was going fine and then out of the blue you attack him then act like you don't even know me for the rest of the night. That really hurt."

"You've got to understand—"

"No, you've got to understand. I'm not going to put up with this shit. I went through it years ago. It's so unnecessary."

"It was my first instinct," he said, head in his hands. "It's like, I dunno, you want to push someone away before they do it to you."

"Well, you did a great job of pushing me away. You and that blonde bitch. Did you fuck her?" The words just burst out.

"Yes."

Tears pricked my eyes. I thought he would at least lie. I flung open the front door.

"Get out."

He came up and kissed me, breath sweet with bourbon. I tried to move my mouth away but he held my face and pushed his crotch into mine.

My brain went into meltdown and all my resolve was lost. Suddenly I was hungry for him, hungry for his cock. I bit his lip, hard, and he pulled my black skirt up and shoved my knickers to the side. He leaned me against the wall. I wrapped my legs around him and he pushed his cock into me, fucking me standing up. The door was still open and any one of my neighbours could have walked by. I clawed his back with my nails, wanting to draw blood, hurt him, mark him.

"I hate you," I gasped, "I fucking hate you."

I did. I hated the hold he had on me.

It spurred him on and he fucked me harder, deeper, like a man possessed. My head banged against the wall and the wall shook. It was so intense I thought I'd pass out.

When he came he said he loved me. Must have been drunker than I thought.

I told him I had to work and kicked him out, had another shower, fixed my makeup and called a cab.

It wasn't until I got in the taxi that I realised I'd had the earrings on the whole time.

Twenty minutes later I walked up the stairs of the Red, smelling cheap perfume and stale cigarettes. It was seven o'clock and three girls danced on podiums. A few guys milled around but I couldn't see any corrupt policemen. I went to the girls' room and had just changed into my red latex outfit when Aurora walked in wearing a fuchsia dress slashed to the groin. She already had a couple of hundred dollars in her garter.

"Simone." She hugged me then held my shoulders, concerned. "What's been happening? I heard there was a scene at the St Kilda Inn."

"It's a long story."

She let go and I crammed my bag into my locker.

"Tell me over a drink," she said, "and don't take this the wrong way, but I'd lose the earrings."

We sat at the bar drinking champagne.

"Fill me in," said Aurora. "Mick leaves a party last Thursday, goes to your place, and the two of you disappear for two days."

"Portsea."

"So I hear. Nice and romantic, then a punch-up at the pub and you leave separately. What gives?"

"Mick got jealous, attacked a guy, then we had a fight. I saw him half an hour ago but I don't know what's going on between us."

"Who was the guy Mick was fighting with? Someone told me it was a cop."

"I can't tell you what's going on right now. Maybe in a few days." I touched the earrings selfconsciously.

"If you're in some kind of trouble, if you need any help, I'm here for you." She touched my arm. "All the girls are."

Jim came up then, walkie-talkie crackling. "What's going on, ladies? There's a table full of guys, no one talking to them. Have your little gossip session in your own time, that's not what I pay you for."

"We're independent contractors," said Aurora, "you don't pay us at all."

We wandered over to the table of suits and Aurora perched on a chair in the middle and went to work. I was watching, trying to figure out how she did it, when I felt a hand on my arse. Occupational hazard. I turned around to tell the guy to quit and came face to face with Dick Farquhar.

Chapter Twenty-Three

"How much?" Farquhar asked. He wore his corrupt detective on a night out look, a short-sleeved shirt patterned with swirls of red, blue and green. Abstract parrots? Wiry grey hair sprouted from the open neck.

"How much for what?" I tried to remember to breathe. In, out.

"A dance."

"Twenty for two songs, fifty for ten minutes in the private room."

He set his scotch on a nearby table and reached into the back pocket of his tan pants for his wallet. It was bowl shaped, moulded to his arse. He took out a fifty and shoved it roughly into my top, the plastic scratching my skin.

"Follow me." I led him toward the private rooms, feeling dizzy, still not breathing right.

I took him into the first one we came to but Farquhar wanted to choose his own. Paranoid. He sat down and smiled and his teeth didn't glow.

"What do you want me to do?" I asked.

"Take your clothes off. I did pay for it." He sipped the scotch and his mouth made a wet smacking sound. I stood up, unzipped my top and chucked it in the corner. I was about to do the same with my shorts when Farquhar laughed and held up his hand.

"Whoa," he said, "not much of a dancer, are you? Put on some music, shake that ass."

I glared at him and pressed play. Some sleazy R & B number came on, the singer crooning about rubbing his baby up and down. Great. I moved awkwardly to the music, taking off my hotpants and bra. Farquhar stroked himself through his trousers. Apparently there was a cock somewhere under that stomach.

"You're not allowed to do that," I told him.

He laughed. "I can do whatever the fuck I want."

I shed my bikini bottoms with minimal grace and swayed in front of him. He leaned over and grabbed my arm, pulling me onto his lap. A small hard bulge pressed into my left butt cheek and one of his hands cupped my boob and wobbled it. Very erotic.

I looked around the room for a deadly weapon. Ashtray to the head? Stiletto heel through the eye socket?

"We're going to the Uptown Hotel on Queens Road." His breath was hot and sticky in my ear. "A conference is winding up soon and there's a man I want you to seduce. I've got a couple of grams of coke. If you can get him to imbibe, so much the better. Meet him in the bar, take him to your room and confine most of the action to the bed. That's all you gotta do. One night, and I wipe the slate clean."

"Where's the camera?"

"You don't need to know."

"What if he doesn't go for it?"

"You'd better make sure he does. Just don't tell him you're a stripper, I don't want him to get suss. I'll have someone watching you every step of the way so don't do anything stupid. Be a good girl and I destroy all the paperwork and forget I ever caught you following me. Think I can't tell when someone's got me under surveillance?" He shook his head. "Twenty-five years I've been in this game. Fucking amateur."

My face flushed red and Farquhar let me off his lap. The synthetic material of his pants had made the backs of my legs sweat. Disgusting. He took a folded photograph out of his pocket.

"This is Bob Lange. Take a good look."

I held the photo up to the light and studied it. The man was middle aged, balding, average weight. Farquhar took the photo back and I got dressed. The tape stopped with a clunk.

"Get changed into your civvies and meet me out in the bar. You've got two minutes."

"I'm in the middle of my shift," I protested.

"Me and Jim go way back, he won't mind."

I raced to the dressing room in a panic. I had no way of knowing if Alex and his crew had picked everything up from my Maxwell Smart earrings. What if the music had been too loud? I quickly changed into my black skirt and top. Aurora walked in.

"What's going on? That was Dick Farquhar."

"I'll tell you later." My hands shook as I stuffed everything into my bag. I picked up my mobile. Should I try to call Alex? Make sure he knew what was going on?

The girls' room door swung in hard and hit the wall with a bang. Farquhar strode over and knocked the mobile out of my hand so it clattered to the floor.

"What do you think you're doing?" Aurora said to him.

"Keep your tits on." Farquhar winked at her. "No need to get jealous."

Jealous?

"It's OK," I told her, "I'm fine."

Farquhar followed me out of the club and down the stairs. No one tried to stop us. He hailed a cab and directed it to Queens Road where we pulled up in front of a four star hotel. He handed me a key and a bag of coke.

"Go to room twenty-seven, and wait for me to contact you."

I walked into the lobby and took the elevator to the second floor. I was alone in there and I talked softly to myself.

"Room twenty-seven, Uptown Hotel." I hoped someone could hear.

My room was typical mid-range hotel. Bed, television, desk, minibar and everything decorated in beige. A framed pastel print of a sailing boat hung on the wall. I opened the minibar and skolled a tiny bottle of vodka.

The phone rang. "Don't get too pissed," Farquhar said, "you don't want to fuck this up."

I whirled around looking for the hidden camera and Dick laughed. "Now go down to the bar next to the lobby. Lange and his mates'll be there soon. And remember, you're being watched."

The bar was decorated in a Hawaiian theme, fake palms, thatched ceiling and cane furniture. I ordered champagne off a skinny guy with a plastic lei encircling his neck and looked around. An old couple drank piña coladas by the piano player. A thirty-something man sat by himself drinking beer. I lit a cigarette from a pack I'd bought on the way to the Red. It seemed like a good time to officially start up again.

Elevators opened across the lobby and a group of men and one woman piled out, laughing and talking, wearing cheap suits and reeking of cop. Show time. They commandeered three tables near the front window, pushed them together, and a couple came up to order drinks. A young one with blond hair and full, pouty lips checked me out in the mirror behind the bar. He shook a cigarette out of a pack of Dunhill and turned to me.

"Excuse me, do you have a light?"

"Sure." I flicked my pink Bic.

"Thanks." He drew back deeply, loosened his tie and blew the smoke out with a sigh. "I'm glad that's over."

"What's over?"

"Conference. Sitting on your arse all day listening to people drone on."

"Tell me about it."

"You've been conferencing too?"

"Yeah," I said, "I'm over from Adelaide, sales rep with Lilywhite Disposables. You know, foam cups, takeaway containers, plastic forks, paper napkins . . ."

"Great," he said smoothly. "Hey, we all use those things."

"Oh yeah, it's a multimillion-dollar industry. What about you, what line of work are you in?"

"Law enforcement, actually."

"Oh my god," I said. "That must be sooo exciting."

"Not when you're sitting around all day. Listen, you want to come and have a drink with us?" He nodded to his colleagues who were looking over, nudging each other.

"Oh, I don't know," I said. "I was just about to go up to my room and get an early night. I fly out tomorrow morning."

"Come on, just one drink. I won't bite. Unless you want me to. Ha ha."

"Well, maybe just one. I'm Simone."

"Simone. That's French, isn't it? Jason." We shook hands and he ordered me another champagne, scotch for himself, and escorted me to the tables.

"Everybody," he announced, "this is Simone. She's from Adelaide, been doing the conference thing too."

"Are you all police officers?" I asked.

A man who looked exactly like the photo said, "Yeah, but it's not as exciting as young Jason makes out." He extended a hand across the table and I shook it. "Bob," he said.

"He's my boss," Jason explained.

"What line of work you in?" Bob asked.

I told them and everybody's eyes glazed over.

"And what about you guys?" I asked. "What sort of cops are you? Homicide? Vice?"

"We work for the Ethical Standards department," said Bob. "We keep the bastards honest."

Holy shit. Farquhar was trying to set up Ethical Standards. Was he insane?

A few of the cops were talking about going out but no one could decide on where to go. The casino? St Kilda? They kept drinking and it was doubtful they'd get it together to go anywhere.

Jason went to buy more drinks and I moved into his seat, right next to Bob Lange.

I flirted like I never had before, asking him about work, star sign, laughing at his jokes and playing with my hair. It was Olympic level stuff, Chloe would have been proud.

Bob was getting into it, boasting about cases he'd worked in major crimes a few years before. He wore a wedding ring but never mentioned a wife or kids. Jason could hardly get a word in and started sulking. The group became drunk and loud, got the piano player to do requests and sang along to "Piano Man" and "American Pie." Bob bought me champagnes and I drank half and poured the rest into a fake palm.

At quarter to eleven the barman called last drinks. Most had peeled off to go to bed but a couple of diehards headed off to Crown Casino. Bob, Jason and me were left. I'd made sure my leg was touching Bob's under the table and he had actually said: "You have beautiful eyes. Have you ever done any modelling?"

The bar closed.

"Let's go out," Jason whined.

"I don't think I'm up for a big one," I said. "Why don't we go to my room and get stuck into the minibar? Company's paying."

Jason brightened up, and I saw him and Bob exchange a meaningful look.

I let us into the room and poured them both a scotch and ice. Jason found some music on the clock radio beside the bed and I popped a half bottle of champagne and opened a packet of salted peanuts. I was starving.

Bob sat on the desk chair and leaned back, loosening his tie.

Jason was on the double bed. He said: "I have to tell you, Simone. Bob and I, we come as a team." He looked at Bob and they both grinned. "Remember Brisbane?"

"How could I forget?" said Bob. "Now that was teamwork."

"What happened in Brisbane?" I perched on the edge of the desk and looked from one to the other.

Bob clasped his hands behind his head.

"Let's just say we had a wonderful time with a delightful young lady fascinated by law enforcement."

"Really?"

"Have you ever been with two guys at once?" asked Jason.

"Nooo . . ." I said in a tone that suggested I'd thought about it.

"It's really good." Jason bounced lightly on the mattress and nodded his head like a dashboard dog. "The girl gets all the attention."

I tilted my head to the side. "So do you two, like, get it on as well?"

"No!" said Jason.

"God no," said Bob.

"Christ."

They coughed. Nervous laughter.

"You don't think two guys and one girl is a bit, well, homoerotic?" I asked. "I mean, it could be said that the guys just need the girl there to make it acceptable for them to be naked and sexual together."

"No . . . no nothing like that," said Jason.

"Why don't you find out for yourself?" Bob patted his lap and I sat on it thinking, come on Alex, got enough evidence yet?

Bob nuzzled his face in my hair. "God you smell good."

"So you promise I'll have a good time?"

"I can guarantee it." Jason sprang off the bed and kneeled down in front of me. He rubbed his palms up and down my thighs and nipped at the fabric of my skirt with his teeth. He looked up at me and said, soulfully, "I know how to make you feel like a woman."

"Whoa, boy." I pushed his head away from my crotch. "I just have to go to the bathroom. When I come back I want you to be all ready for me, OK?"

Christ, this cheesy dialogue was coming a little too easy. Had I been watching too much porn? I locked the bathroom door behind me and leaned against it. I'd always wondered about being with two guys at once but I refused to be the meat in a "Have you done any modelling/I want to make you feel like a woman" sandwich.

Where the hell was the cavalry? I'd done my bit. I heard shoes drop to the floor and Bob and Jason laughing and talking. I had a pee and washed my hands thoroughly and slowly, brushed my hair, powdered my nose and put on more lipstick. Damn you, Alex.

Jason knocked on the door and sang out, "Simo-one, we're ready and waiting." Fuck. I unlocked it, took a deep breath and walked back into the hotel room.

Bob and Jason sat on the bed, waiting expectantly. Jason was completely starkers but Bob had left his socks on. Nice. Their suits had hidden a multitude of sins. Jason was too skinny, with chicken legs, and Bob had a layer of waxy fat all over his body, dark wiry hair standing out in sharp relief. Sometimes a naked male can be quite beautiful. This was not one of those times. Both had erections and Jason's moved around as if it was waving to me.

Bob patted the bedspread. "Have a seat, beautiful."

I smiled. "I'll just get another drink." I took a small-screw top bottle of Queen Adelaide chardonnay from the minibar and slammed down half, thinking, I can't believe my life has come to this. I sat reluctantly between them, drinking straight from the bottle.

"So," I said.

"Relax." Bob took the bottle out of my hand and set it on the nightstand. He kissed up my arm, Gomez Addams style. Jason licked my neck and ran his hand up my thigh. My skin crawled, I was about to scream, I couldn't take another second.

Bang! A huge crash, wood splintering.

We looked at the door but it was intact, the sound coming from the room next door. A muffled announcement:

"Police!" And then a gunshot.

Jason and Bob looked at each other, dicks going limp, and I leapt up and raced for the door. I slipped through the entrance to the room next door and saw Farquhar face down on the floor with his wrists handcuffed behind him. Alex had his knee in Farquhar's back, reading him his rights, and four other plainclothes cops with IDs strung on their necks stood around him, guns drawn. Another handgun, a big one, lay on the bed. A laptop computer and a video monitor were set up on the desk. I could see Bob and Jason scrabbling around for their clothes. A female cop with a blonde ponytail saw me, reholstered her gun and started to push me out of the room.

"I'm going to have to ask you to come with me, ma'am," she said.

Farquhar twisted around in his restraints, enraged.

"You fucking dog, Christakos," he said. "You filthy maggot. You're fucked."

Alex hauled him to his feet and Farquhar saw me.

"And you, you cunt," he bellowed.

"That's enough." Alex and another cop pushed him out of the room and toward the elevators.

When Farquhar was hustled past I said, "Fucking amateur."

Alex smiled at me.

Chapter Twenty-Four

I'd handed in the earrings and was giving a statement to the female cop, Detective McCullers, when Alex knocked on the interview room door.

"Can I borrow her a sec?"

"Sure," she smiled at him. He took me into the corridor and closed the interview room door.

"Farquhar locked up?" I asked.

"Signed, sealed, delivered, baby." Alex's eyes were shining. He was pumped up like he'd just been to an Anthony Robbins seminar. Busts must do that to a fellow.

"We're about to search his house and a self-storage facility he had in a false name. I wanted to thank you before I left. You did good tonight, got a real flair for the undercover stuff."

"What about my autopsy report?"

"Haven't had time." he held out his hands. "Might be able to get it by the debriefing tomorrow."

"What debriefing?"

"Didn't anyone tell you? Be here at seven pm."

"It's really important I get the report, Alex."

"I'll see what I can do." He bent and kissed me on the cheek. A warm, tingling sensation. Not the white lightning of Mick but, hey, not bad.

"See you tomorrow," he said.

When I finished my statement I called Aurora's mobile from a phone booth in the lobby. She answered on the first ring.

"Simone, thank god, I was so worried. What happened with Dick Farquhar? Where are you?"

I told her about the sting, and how Farquhar was safely locked away.

"I'm at Betty's," she said. "Please come over. Mick's here. Don't be mad but he told me everything. About your arrest, about that prick Sal kidnapping Chloe. Don't worry. We're going to help you

146

get her back.'"

Outside the police centre the street was deserted, no sign of Sal's black car, no chance for me to explain to him what I'd been doing at the cop shop. A lone cab cruised past and I hailed it and told the driver to drop me on Chapel Street. From Chapel I ducked through the Safeway car park, down Greville Street, then followed back lanes until I slipped through the rear gate into Betty's large back yard. Paranoid? You bet.

Mick sat on the back steps in jeans and a white singlet playing "Blue Moon" on an acoustic guitar. The notes wafted eerily through the hot night air like in a David Lynch film.

I said, "The Road Goes On Forever."

He stopped playing, "Robert Earl Keen."

"Jeez," I walked across the overgrown grass, "you're good." I dropped my backpack on the ground and sat next to him.

"How'd it go?" Mick asked.

"Great. Farquhar's fucked. They caught him in the act, he shot at the cops and now they're searching his house and a storage facility."

"Teach him not to mess with Simone McCullers."

"Damn straight," I smiled.

"Simone," he said, awkwardly, "I'm sorry about the other night, at the pub. I don't know what happened, if it was stress from all the weird shit that's been going on or maybe I've been doing too much coke. I should stick with beer and weed, chemicals fucking mess with your head. Anyway, I really like you. I didn't want to push you away. I'm sorry."

"You don't have to apologise," I said. "You're gorgeous, you play guitar up on stage, and chicks are always going to throw themselves at you. Besides, we only just met. It's not like we're in a relationship or anything and my life's too ridiculous to have a boyfriend at the moment. We're just having fun, you know, casual sex, like our parents used to do in the seventies." God I was a good liar.

"Casual sex, huh? I'd hate to see what would happen if we had serious sex."

"Me too. Let's go find Aurora."

Aurora was pacing inside the retro lounge room, wearing jeans and a midriff top. She looked wired and probably was after spending the night at the Red.

"Simone." She hugged me, held my shoulders, "I can't believe that scumbag Sal. I used to work with Chloe, she's fantastic, a great girl. I'm going to help you get her back."

She twisted the cap off a bottle of Jameson and poured us all a slug. I lit a tailor-made and gave one to Mick. It was great to be smoking again. We sat on the leopard-skin couch and Aurora took the chair.

"Where's Betty?" I asked.

"Asleep, finally." Now that she wasn't pacing she tapped her foot. "Had to shove a couple of sleeping pills down her throat though. Anyway, what about telling the police? I know Detective Duval, we could go directly to him."

I shook my head. "It'll get back to Sal. He's got cops on his payroll. I don't know how many."

"Fuck," she said. "OK, Mick said Sal will let her go if he has proof someone else killed Frank. You've been investigating, who do you think killed him?"

"No idea. I told Sal it was Farquhar but I can't prove it."

Mick sat forward. "The jacks are searching Farquhar's place tonight."

"They'll find something to implicate him," Aurora said.

"You reckon?" I raised my eyebrows. It was a long shot.

"The thing is," she continued, "even if you prove someone else killed Frank, what makes you think Sal will let her go, and let you live? If I were him I'd want to tie up any loose ends, and that's you two."

I hadn't thought of that. Stupid.

"He said he was an honourable man." It sounded lame and Aurora snorted.

"We've got to find out where he's keeping her," she said.

"Simone's been talking to Chloe on Sal's mobile," Mick told her.

I nodded. "Chloe's stashed somewhere with a heavy named Blue. She seems OK and I think Blue's sweet on her. They watch videos and eat crap food. I tried to listen for clues but I couldn't hear anything.

The reception was good though, I don't think they're out bush."

"Where would Sal keep Chloe?" Aurora stared intently at the fish in the tank, swimming around the sunken galleon. "Hang on a sec, what about Frank's boat?"

"Frank's boat." I repeated. "Frank's boat." Suddenly everything fell into place, "Oh my god, she's been trying to tell me."

"What are you talking about?"

"When I talked to her on the phone she kept nattering on about the videos she'd been watching, *Titanic, Speed 2, Dead Calm.* They've all got boats in them. But how does Blue get videos and takeaway?"

"Those big cruisers have dinghies with outboards," said Mick. "They're probably anchored close to the Marina and the guy locks her in and motors out."

"Where's Frank's boat moored?" I asked. "And what's its name?"

"St Kilda marina," Aurora said, "but I don't know what it's called."

"Is there anyone who does?"

"A few of the girls, I think."

"Call them up." I was getting manic, about to leap up and go down to the marina that second.

"Darl, it's nearly five am and you need some sleep. We can't do anything until morning anyway." She poured me another whisky. "Want some Vegemite toast?"

I nodded, she went into the kitchen and I lay down with my head on Mick's lap. He stroked my hair and I closed my eyes, just to rest them for a second, and I was out for the count.

I woke up at ten in Mick's bed, with all my clothes on. There was a turn-up for the books. Rain fell on the tin roof and although I knew I had to leap up and get to the marina I just wanted to stay for a few more seconds, arm around him, breathing him in.

He was naked, back to me, and I stroked his shoulder, tracing tattoos with my fingertips. The Medusa had snakes for hair, wings sprouting from her back and a whip in her hand. The tattoo was shinier than the others, the outline precise. I kissed his back. The skin was warm, hot almost. I slid my hand from his shoulder to his hips and down along the hipbone. I lightly stroked his cock. Rock hard and velvet safe, all at the same time. A tingling started between my legs.

"You awake?" I whispered.

No reply. I pushed myself into the curve of his spine, cupped his balls in my hand, then went back to his hard-on, moving my hand up and down until it grew bigger and started to throb. He had at least eight inches down there, and thick, too. I was no size queen but it was nice every once in a while, to feel so completely filled up. Mick rolled on his back, still pretending to be asleep. I couldn't stand it anymore, enough of this hand job shit. I took off my clothes and climbed on top of him, rubbing the head of his penis on my clit. His eyes were still closed but the corners of his mouth turned up in a smile.

Afterwards Mick kissed me. "You're one hell of a fuck, girl."

"I try," I said, modestly.

"How am I going to live without you when I move back up north?"

"You're moving?"

"I've been here three months. That's a long time for me to live anywhere, specially the city. I need wide open spaces, I miss my dog."

"Enough with the cowboy shit."

"It's true," he said. "Why don't you come with me?"

"So you can lock me up in some hillbilly shack, cooking you grits and providing sex on demand?"

"Yep."

"What about the band?" I asked.

"Guitarists are pretty thick on the ground around here," he said. "Can't walk down the milk bar without tripping over about five of them."

He wasn't wrong. "Come on," I said, "let's find this boat."

Aurora was padding around the kitchen in a leopard-skin robe, making coffee. "I stayed in Betty's room," she explained.

"Still out for the count?"

"Yeah, she'll sleep for a couple of days at least, wake up not knowing where she is. Guess what? I rang Dakota. Boat's called the "Midnight Lady.""

"Poxy name," I said.

After coffee and showers we squeezed into the cab of the ute and Mick drove through the rain to St Kilda, windscreen wipers squeaking, nobody saying much. Punt Road was grey and sodden. Water pooled in gutters and the stretch between Toorak and Commercial Roads was a cluster of wet cars and red tail-lights. I checked the rearview mirror the whole way, hardly able to remember a time when I wasn't watching my back.

Mick rolled into the marina car park and I left him and Aurora and ran to Reg's shed. He sat at his desk, reading a Tom Clancy novel.

"Hi, Reg, remember me?"

He looked up. "The detective sheila. You want to go sailing today?"

"No, I need you to help me out again. Do you know a boat moored here called the "Midnight Lady"?

He nodded. "Yeah, but I haven't seen her around for awhile. Why? Has it got something to do with the murder?"

"Maybe. Is there any way you can find out where it is?"

"I could take you over to see the guy in the office. He might know."

"Look, Reg," I said, "I'll level with you. A friend of mine's been kidnapped and I think she's on that boat. I can't call the police, OK? The man who took her has people on the inside. And I don't want anyone around here tipping him off that I know where she is."

Reg nodded slowly and I continued: "The guy who's keeping watch over her has to come in now and again to get supplies, probably on a small powerboat. Or maybe he's moored at another marina. I don't know. He's red haired, chunky, looks like an ex league player. I'd be grateful if you could ask around and keep an eye out for him. Inconspicuously. Can you do that for me?"

"I know," he said, "I'll say someone inquired about buying the boat. Happens all the time."

"Good one, Reg. Here's my mobile number. Soon as you find anything, give me a call. Anytime, OK?"

"Sure thing."

I ran back to the car, large raindrops splotching my shoulders.

I told Mick and Aurora what had happened and that I'd call them as soon as Reg called me and we'd work out a new plan. We drove Aurora back to her serviced apartment in South Yarra then Mick took me home and we kissed on the front seat, steaming up the windows. I loved the way he held my face when he kissed me, twining his fingers in my hair, and how it gave him an instant hard-on.

"Can I come up?" he whispered hoarsely.

I wanted that more than anything. I had visions of a bottle of red and rainy-day sex on the lounge-room carpet.

"No, I need Sal to approach me, and that's not going to happen with you here."

"What about later?"

"I've got a debriefing with Alex at the police station at seven, but I'll call you after that, OK?"

I showered and changed into a pair of cords and an old long-sleeved man's shirt and cleaned the house to use up excess sexual energy. Didn't work. The rain fell steadily, hitting the leaves of the oak trees and gurgling down gutters. I lit some Nag Champa incense, a hangover from my hippy upbringing, and put on Chet Baker, "My Funny Valentine." It made me think of Mick. Everything did. I cooked scrambled eggs, painted my nails, and willed Reg to call and Sal to show up. Neither happened.

I grabbed an umbrella and walked to the Seven Eleven to get the paper and some Red Frogs. The pm edition of the *Herald Sun* was out and Farquhar made the front page: TOP COP IN BLACKMAIL BUST. Details were sketchy and I was relieved my name hadn't been mentioned. Sal didn't pull up next to me on my way home. Reg didn't call. I wanted to do something but I couldn't think what. I ended up watching daytime TV.

At six-thirty I caught the bus to St Kilda then the 16 tram to the debriefing. I'd dressed straight, black pants, striped blouse. It had stopped raining but was still overcast and the footpaths were covered with wet leaves. I arrived a little before seven and asked for Alex. A moment later he was by my side, looking effortlessly stylish and smelling nice.

"Come on," he said, leading me out of the station, "let's go debrief."

"Where?"

"I have a special place."

His special place turned out to be Donovan's restaurant, right on the beach where Frank's body washed up. Nice touch. We sat at a table for two overlooking the bay and Alex ordered Veuve Cliquot and a dozen oysters natural from a waiter who might have been a male model. The champagne arrived just as the setting sun broke through cloud cover and the sky was streaked pink and gold.

It was beautiful, but my thoughts were with Chloe. She was out there somewhere, and in danger despite the foot massages and action videos. I was perturbed by the fact that Sal hadn't contacted me, but comforted in the knowledge she had Blue wrapped around her little finger. I kept my mobile in my pants pocket, set to vibrate so I wouldn't miss anything if Reg rang.

We clinked glasses.

"What about the debriefing?" I asked.

He shrugged. "We had that this morning and being a civilian you don't get to go. I wanted to celebrate the bust and it's no fun going out to dinner on your own."

"You tricked me."

"It's my treat."

"What if I order lobster?"

"You can do what you want as long as you don't start dancing on tables."

The snake-hipped waiter reappeared with the oysters. I tipped one in my mouth, chewed once to release the salty juice and swallowed. Oral sex on a half shell.

"So you're telling me you had no one else to go out to dinner with?"

"I suppose there's one person I could've asked, but she's working."

I remembered how the blonde cop, Detective McCullers, had smiled at him. Interesting.

"How'd the search go?" I asked.

He leaned back in his chair and sipped champagne. "Do we have to talk shop?"

I kicked him under the table. "Give it up, you bastard, I helped you nail the prick."

"We found cash, guns, drugs, and video footage in the storage shed," he said. "And something interesting in the house."

I went to kick him again but he grabbed my ankle, put my foot on his lap and started massaging my calf. He had a nice touch.

"What?"

He pretended to study the menu. "You know the duck here is very good."

"Alex . . ."

He put it down and smiled. "We found a bloody knife in a plastic zip-lock bag. We think it's the same one used to kill Parisi."

Chapter Twenty-Five

I pulled my leg away. "What?"

"The blood's still being DNA tested but the blade's consistent with the murder weapon."

"Where did you find it?"

"Stashed under his mattress, of all places."

"Why would he keep the knife in his house? Why would he keep it at all?"

"Maybe he wanted to plant it on someone. Who knows? He's an arrogant prick, refuses to answer any questions, says none of the stuff we found belongs to him and that we planted the knife. Hey, if it does turn out to be Frank's blood, you're out of a job with the Parisi family."

My mind was racing. I had to tell Sal. The case was solved and he would have to let Chloe go. Unless what Aurora had said was right. Tying up loose ends. The more I thought about it the more it made sense.

I willed Reg to call but he was probably tucked up in bed with a cup of hot cocoa. I wanted to tell Alex but I was too paranoid. Sal had people everywhere and I suspected the waiters, the couple at the next table, and maybe even the cop across from me with his nice clothes and fancy restaurants. I gulped my champagne and he refilled my glass.

"Are you OK?" he asked. "You seem a little distracted."

"I'm fine," I said. "Let's order."

Alex had the duck, I ordered a steak and we shared a bottle of Mornington Peninsula pinot noir. Stress has no effect on my appetite and I motored through my meal. The meat was aged, cooked medium rare and my knife slid through it like it was butter. In no time I was mopping up the sauce with the last of my celeriac mash.

"Nice to see a girl with a healthy appetite," Alex said. We weren't really flirting. Well, maybe just a little bit.

After dinner we moved to the lounge area and started on cognac.

Donovan's wasn't kitted out like your usual stuffy restaurant, it was done up like a friend's beach house, if your friend lived at Palm Beach and regularly appeared in *Vogue Living*.

I sank back into the designer couch and cradled my drink. This was the life. After all this shit with Sal was over I was going to stop hanging out in grotty pubs filled with freaks and become, like, sophisticated.

Alex was telling me I should apply for the force again, that he would put in a good word. I told him I didn't know if I could handle the authority, the rigid procedure and the police culture. He said PI work was a mug's game and I was too good to be a stripper. I told him to get fucked and he said he loved it when I talked dirty.

Ah, oysters.

"I've got something for you." Alex reached into his jacket pocket and pulled out a sheaf of photocopied paper, handed it to me and studied my face for a reaction.

It was the autopsy report. "Oh my god," I said, "I love you." I leaned over the couch, kissed him on the cheek and spilled cognac on my leg.

"It goes without saying you didn't get it from me."

I held the report under the nearest designer down-light. A lot of the document used medical terminology but I'd read enough forensic thrillers to work out that a subdural haemotoma meant he'd been whacked on the head and a severed aorta was a sure bet he'd been stabbed in the heart. The knife had been long and thin and the exact make was inconclusive. Bruising and abrasions on his wrists and ankles showed he'd been restrained by rope. High levels of cocaine were found in his bloodstream—who would've guessed?—and his last meal had been a chicken souvlaki with garlic sauce, eaten approximately an hour before death. A number of hairs were found on his clothes and there were traces of two different kinds of lipstick on his penis, which had obviously not been cut off. Bloody rumours. The pathologist had also found a multitude of fibres and a couple of dog hairs. Frank's eye had been eaten by an unidentified sea creature that had slipped through a hole in his garbage bag shroud.

"Bit of a waste of time if it turns out to be Farquhar," he said. "Although I think it's cute how you're still trying to solve a murder case, kind of like a raunchy Nancy Drew . . ."

"Fuck up and die." I gave him the death stare. "And get me another one of these cognacs, I'm running low."

When my fresh glass arrived I took a sip and studied Alex over the rim. He smiled back at me. He was the total opposite of Mick, sleek, sophisticated, getting a little soft around the edges. In ten years he would be fat around the middle with receding hair but right now . . .

"You never told me what happened when you went to that illegal brothel with Farquhar." I smiled sweetly and leaned in close.

Alex actually blushed. "I was undercover."

"Was it just rub 'n' tug or did you get some extras?"

"What goes on in the field stays in the field." Alex loosened his tie. I may have had my hand on his leg. Then someone grabbed my upper arm.

"Don't look like a fucking debriefing to me."

Mick stood over us, looking huge and out of place with his tattoos and white singlet. My heart beat hard and a wave of sobriety crashed down on me.

"Calm down," I half whispered. "We're just talking about the case. He's been showing me the autopsy report."

"Don't bullshit me. I've been watching you for the last two hours. I followed you from the cop shop. A nice dinner and then a fuck, hey?"

"Mick . . ." I noticed waiters and other diners glancing over with worried looks. Alex shook his head, "Get your life together." He got up and went to the bar to pay the bill.

"Where do you think you're going?" Mick headed after him but I grabbed his arm and dragged him out of the restaurant to the footpath. He loomed over me, eyes black and features twisted with rage.

"You lied to me." He grabbed my upper arm and dug his fingers in. "You didn't tell me you were going on a fucking date."

"I didn't—" I started to explain and then I just gave up. "Fuck it, Mick, I'm not going to do this." I shook him off and started walking away and he grabbed me and spun me around.

"Don't you fucking walk away from me." His voice was a roar, his Aussie accent broader than usual. His hand hurt my shoulder and I tried to pull away.

"Fuck off," I said, and his other hand flew up to my face and hit me on the cheek and the side of my eye. It was halfway between a slap and a punch, but it hurt. My cheek throbbed and stung. Nobody had ever hit me before—my mum hadn't believed in smacking. I held my palm to my face and my eyes burned with tears.

Stylish people hurried past, careful not to make eye contact. The women had perfect waterfalls of blonde hair and the men wore European shoes. I felt ashamed. Mick let go of my arm and I ran across the road. The back door opened on a dark sedan and I got in. Sal, finally. As we pulled out into the traffic I looked out the rear window. Mick was smoking a cigarette, watching me go.

If Sal had witnessed the scene with Mick he didn't say anything.

"I've got your proof," I said, and handed him the autopsy report. "They found a knife that matches in Farquhar's place. They'll know for sure if it's Frank's blood by tomorrow and it'll be in the paper, on the news."

Sal flicked through the report and nodded. "You've done well," he said.

"How will you get your revenge if Farquhar's in protective custody?" I asked. Sal smiled. "There are ways."

"So you have to let go of Chloe, right?"

"As soon as I see Richard Farquhar is charged with the murder I'll let her go."

"Really?"

"You have my word."

I wanted to believe him but the phrase "tying up loose ends" kept running through my brain.

"Can I speak to her?"

He dialled his mobile and put it on speaker. Blue sounded sleepy and he put Chloe on.

"Hey, mate," she said, "just watching *The Poseidon Adventure*. Got any good news?"

"Great news," I said. "Looks like a corrupt cop is about to be charged with Frank's murder. They're going to let you go tomorrow."

"What time?"

I looked at Sal, he just shrugged.

"Don't know."

"'Cause I need you to book me into the hairdressers. Two weeks of dark roots, I look like some kind of scrag. And is my bong still at your place? I'm tonguing for a cone."

"We'll get you stoned and your hair fixed up soon as you get out," I said. "I can't wait to see you. You wouldn't believe the shit that's been going on."

Sal cut the connection and opened the door for me. We were outside my flat.

"Stay home tomorrow," he said, "no visitors, no phone calls. You've come this far, don't fuck it up on the final stretch."

Inside my flat I pulled on my trackie daks and singlet and went into the bathroom to examine the damage to my face. A red mark ran from my cheek to my eye, coupled with a jagged scratch from Mick's ring. I took a deep, shaky breath but I refused to cry. Why did he have to do it? He'd ruined everything.

I'd had girlfriends who'd been in abusive relationships and I'd always told them: first time he hits you—leave. And then when they didn't leave I'd thought they were fucking idiots. So there was no way I could see Mick Halliday ever again. I just couldn't. And the thought of it tore me up. What I felt for him didn't come from any rational area of my brain. It was like some primal urge dwelling in every cell, especially concentrated in my stomach and my pussy and my skin. A constant, urgent need. I rubbed my upper arm. Bruises shaped like fingertips had started to appear.

I poured a glass of cask and took it onto the verandah with my pack of cigarettes. It was ten o'clock and had finally gotten dark. The phone rang and the answering machine clicked on. Mick said: "Simone," and hung up. I looked up at the indigo sky. The stars were cancelled out by the city lights. The leaves rustled and a warm breeze brought the smell of the ocean off the bay. My mobile beeped announcing a text message: "I'm sorry, please call me. Mick."

Wasn't that what they all did? Said sorry, promised it would never happen again, and one day you were admitted to hospital with bruises round your throat and your front teeth smashed in. It was like my mother and Russell. Good god, was history repeating itself? A psychologist could have had a field day with me.

I tried not to but I wanted Mick there. Wanted to feel his hair with my fingertips, put my face into his neck and smell his skin. Push my hips against his and feel him hard.

"I am seriously fucked up," I said out loud, the wine obviously working. They say talking to yourself is the first sign of madness. I wondered about the second sign. I had another drink and thought of calling my mother but she would associate Mick hitting me with stripping. Like most people she thought the stripping world was like some B-grade movie, all drugs and violence and "hoes" getting slapped around. Hey, maybe it was. I'd been so busy trying to convince her and everyone else it was a perfectly legitimate career choice, maybe I'd been convincing myself too. Overlooking the negatives.

Now I was drunk again. I played the Cowboy Junkies' "Black Eyed Man." The song had been on when we first had sex and it reminded me of Mick. I lay on my back on the floor seeing him on stage tuning his guitar, golden lights washing over his face. And that's where I fell asleep.

Chapter Twenty-Six

I was having the weirdest dream. A doctor in a white coat who looked exactly like Sigmund Freud was holding a needle, about to test me for STDs.

"Sexual relations with a guitar player," he tutted, "you're probably riddled with disease." He roughly grabbed my arm and spiked the needle into the crook of my elbow. It hurt so much I flinched and woke up.

It was pitch black and I was on the lounge room rug. I tried to sit up but something pinned me to the floor. Someone. Mick? A huge dark shape bore down on me, I felt a crushing weight and all the air was pushed from my lungs. The room smelled sour and I heard breathing, heavy and rasping. A hand gripped my bicep, a torch clicked on and a narrow beam of light focused on my arm.

Dick Farquhar was sitting on me, a mini mag-light in his mouth and a syringe in his hand. My heart constricted in panic. This couldn't be. He was in jail. Signed, sealed, delivered.

I started to struggle and tried to scream but he pushed his elbow into my neck and no sound came out. I couldn't breathe. Farquhar grunted, sweating with effort, and a drop of filthy perspiration fell from his face to mine. The needle pricked my arm. A hot shot. Just like that prostitute. I'd never tried heroin, didn't like downers. Farquhar's knee was on my hand, keeping my arm still. I wriggled and pain shot through my vein. The needle slid out. More pressure, more of his sweat on my face and then I felt it go back in. My head swam and spots floated in front of my eyes. I didn't know if it was the drugs or the lack of oxygen. I felt like going back to sleep and then I realised my other arm was free. I hit at Farquhar's shoulder. Stupid. I tried to think of some jiujitsu moves. Nothing came to me.

Then I remembered a self-defence class I'd done years ago. Get angry, the teacher had told us. Put all your energy into it. If you think you're going to kill your attacker then you'll probably maim him. Eyes, balls, throat. I didn't have enough room to pull back and lay in a punch so I grabbed in the general direction of Farquhar's sweaty, hideous crotch, and squeezed hard until something gristly crunched between my fingers. The torch fell out of his mouth and bounced off my forehead and he bellowed and wrenched free, falling backwards.

I stood up gasping for air and clicked on the lamp. The needle hung out of my arm and I gingerly pulled it out and flung it across the room. Blood welled from the puncture wounds and ran down to my wrist. Farquhar was slumped near my front door, hunched over, retching and spitting. I was backing out onto the balcony when my phone rang. It stopped and my mobile went off but it was on the coffee table, too close to Farquhar. He got to his knees and reached into his jacket. I saw a glint of metal. A gun.

I clambered over the balcony railing, hung for a second then dropped the last two metres. My right ankle rolled under and I fell on my arse. Pain radiated through my foot but I got up, hobbled down the path through the front gate and stood there stupidly, looking up and down the street. I looked back. Farquhar stood on the balcony, pointing his gun at me, and I ducked behind the brick wall by the gate, heard him mutter, "fuck." Then a door slammed and footsteps ran down the interior stairs.

Adrenaline coursed through me but also a drowsy, sleepy feeling like I'd just taken ten Panadeine Forte. It was a toss-up between running for my life and curling up on the footpath and having a little nap.

The security door snapped shut and adrenaline won out. I turned left and did a limping run in the direction of the canal. The Seven Eleven was down that way, they would be open, they were always open. As I ran I looked for a doorway to knock on but the buildings were all unit blocks or townhouses with locked gates out front.

I'd just crossed the bridge when I heard a whip crack and bark exploded off a tree next to my head. I ducked left down the path that ran by the canal, trying to get out of the line of fire, zigzagging, limping. A row of fat palms provided shadows and cover and I slipped behind one. In the distance a siren wailed, faint at first then growing louder. I wanted to look around the trunk to see where Farquhar was but thought I'd get my head blown off. Had he seen which tree I'd jumped behind? I slumped down into a sitting position and rested my head against the rough bark. It felt really nice, relaxing. I started to nod off.

I came to suddenly. Jesus, how long had I been out? I tried to think. I needed a weapon. A stick, anything. I felt around the base of the tree and my hand came to rest on a small sign staked into the earth. They were all along the canal, giving the common and Latin names of the plants. The stake end was sharp, not much use against a gun but at least I was protected from vampires. God help me, I was going to die. The siren got really loud then cut off abruptly. I heard a shout.

"Simone! Farquhar!" It was Alex. I snuck a look. Farquhar hid two trees away, looking back at Alex. An old guy in a dressing gown was telling Alex he'd heard a gunshot and he yelled at him to get back inside his house.

Sodium orange lamps lit the path and the palms cast deep shadows. I slipped from my hiding spot and crawled slowly along the darkness to the water's edge. My plan was to wade to the other side and hide in one of the many drain holes. Like I said, I was feeling pretty out of it. I glanced back. Farquhar was still watching Alex, who moved slowly down the path, gun drawn to his chest, doing a creeping sideways walk.

I lowered myself noiselessly into the black, oily canal, bare feet touching rocks and slime. The water came up to my waist and I ducked down so only my head poked out and slowly backed over to the other side, shivering, holding the stake to my chest and keeping an eye on Farquhar and Alex.

I was almost at the tunnel-like drain when Farquhar lifted his gun and lined up a shot at Alex.

"No!" Just as I yelled Farquhar pulled the trigger. Another crack ripped through the still night air and Alex twisted and flew backwards, hitting the concrete path with a thud. The gun skittered out of his hand and he lay still. Fuck. I ducked into the drain and Farquhar turned and shot at the water where I'd just been. He took off past Alex's body and crossed the bridge, out of my line of sight.

More sirens wailed in the distance and I thought Farquhar had run off when I heard footsteps above me and saw torchlight shining in the water. When he got to my hiding spot he lowered the hand clutching the mag-light and I didn't think, just grabbed his wrist and pulled.

He somersaulted into the water with a giant splash and came up quickly but without his gun. Droplets ran down his bald pate and he grabbed me by the singlet, pulled me out of the drain and wrapped his meaty hands around my throat. I dropped the stake and clawed at his hands but he wouldn't let go. I tried to kick him but the water gave too much resistance. The world went dark, blood rushed in my ears and my head was a balloon about to pop. I lost strength and my hands dropped down into the water.

This was it, I was too tired, I was giving up.

Wet wood bumped against my hand. The stake. My fingers closed around it and with one last burst of energy I lifted it out of the water and drove it into Farquhar's armpit. The skin stretched and popped and Farquhar yelped like a dog, letting go of my throat. I drew in a raw scratchy breath and pulled out the stake, stabbed it into his chest then thrust it in his neck and left it there. He waded back, clutching at it, and I turned and hoisted myself up the concrete bank. He grabbed my foot but I kicked out and he splashed back into the water.

I ran up the path towards Broadway, pain spearing my ankle. The sirens had gotten louder and stopped and blue and red flashing lights pierced the shadows. A spotlight blinded my eyes and someone yelled at me to stop but I kept running, not daring to look back. A figure rushed me from the side, knocking me to the ground, and my face scraped gravel. Someone wrenched my arms behind my back and it should have hurt but now that I was lying down I closed my eyes, stopped fighting the drugs and felt the pain drift away. I thought I heard a helicopter, but maybe it was just the smack, and then I didn't hear or feel anything at all.

Chapter Twenty-Seven

Wednesday 26 November

Eyes closed. Throat sore. Aching all over. The flu? I couldn't afford to get sick. Try dancing and being sexy with a dripping nose and head full of cotton wool.

I reluctantly opened my eyes. Off-white ceiling. Curtain hanging from a railing. Hospital smell. I turned my head to the left, more pain, and a face came into view.

She looked familiar, a little like Lisa McCune, but I couldn't quite place her.

"Simone? I'm Detective Suzy McCullers. I took your statement after the Farquhar bust? You're at the Alfred Hospital. How are you feeling?"

I tried to speak but my mouth was so dry the words stuck in my throat. Detective McCullers poured water from a plastic jug into a frosted white tumbler and I took a sip. It was like swallowing razor blades.

Suddenly I remembered.

"Farquhar!" I sat up, looking wildly around the room as though he might appear from behind the curtain.

Suzy patted my arm. "It's OK. He's dead."

"I killed him?" I rasped.

She chuckled softly. "Not exactly. Your Buffy the Vampire Slayer act resulted in superficial wounding but it did cause a heart attack. Don't feel bad, his arteries were clogged, it was on the cards."

Feel bad? The scumbag had set me up, blackmailed me and tried to kill me. I didn't feel bad at all.

"Ambulance officers pulled him out of the canal and tried to revive him but he flatlined in the ambulance and never recovered."

"Alex? Is he . . . ?"

Detective McCullers lowered her eyes and her bottom lip trembled slightly. "He's still in surgery, it's too early to tell." She composed herself and managed a small smile. "I've got to take another statement.

165

Do you feel up to it?"

I told her what had happened up until I hit the concrete. I didn't remember much after that except for waking up suddenly in the ambulance on the way to the hospital. By the end my voice was just about gone. She handwrote my statement and I signed it.

"How did Farquhar get out?"

"He made bail, must have had something over the magistrate."

"Well," I said, pulling back the bedcovers, "I'd better get home."

"Oh no you don't. Your ankle's badly sprained, you have severe bruising, were drugged with heroin then given Narcan by ambulance officers. Not to mention the trauma you went through. The doctors want to keep you under observation for forty-eight hours and we've arranged for a counsellor."

I groaned inwardly. God no.

"Do you want us to contact anyone for you? Family? Friends?"

I wanted my mum but I couldn't tell her what had happened. I'd never hear the end of it.

"No, no one. Is it going to be in the papers?"

"Front page, I'd say. A cop gets shot by another cop he busted on corruption charges, who then dies of a heart attack after being stabbed by a stripper who is also a private investigator who he tried to murder with a needle full of heroin? I'm glad I'm not the media liaison officer."

"Do the press know who I am?"

"They'll find out."

Great. If you want to be a successful PI anonymity is your greatest asset. I could kiss that job with Tony goodbye. But right now I had more pressing concerns. I had to get home and check my phone. I had to get Chloe back.

"Thanks for all your help, Detective McCullers," I croaked sweetly, "but I'm a little tired now. Do you mind if I get some rest?"

"Not at all. If you need anything just press this buzzer. Here's my card if you want to get in contact with me. Just ask the duty nurse, OK? I'll be back to see you tonight."

"Thanks." I smiled up like a sick child and McCullers, who was probably younger than me, came over all motherly and tucked in my blanket.

I gave her five minutes to leave, reefed the covers off and swung into a sitting position. Blood rushed from my head and the room spun around. Not good. When everything stopped moving I slid carefully off the bed and limped around the room. It was a single, no bathroom, just a bedpan on a chair. Yeah right. I was naked underneath my hospital gown and went in search of my clothes. Nothing. Okey-dokey. I poked my head out the door. A sign on the opposite wall pointed the way to the toilets. Holding the gown together at the back I hobbled down the hall to the ladies', had the longest piss of my life, then examined myself in the mirror. I was a mess. One eye was black, thanks to Mick, and my cheek was grazed and raw from the constabulary crash-tackling me to the concrete. My hair was limp and stringy from the stinking canal water, my eyes bloodshot with burst capillaries and purple bruises ringed my neck and upper arms. Puncture wounds clustered along a vein in the crook of my elbow creating a fetching track-mark effect. I looked like a fucked-up junkie. Lovely.

As I left the bathroom I noticed a door ajar and peered in. An old lady was unconscious in a private room, surrounded by flowers and get-well cards. I tiptoed in and rifled through her cupboard, finding a handbag with eighty dollars, a floral polyester housedress, underwear that could double as a boat's sail, a white hat and scuffs.

I put on the dress, hat and shoes, left the underwear and stole the handbag, promising silently that I would return it as soon as possible. Pulling the hat down low I left the room and followed the exit signs to the elevators. I saw myself reflected in the elevator doors, enormous in the billowing sleeveless muu muu. Now I looked like a fat, fucked-up junkie.

The doors slid open and Sal and his driver walked right past me, carrying an elaborate floral arrangement and a cellophane wrapped basket of fruit.

What the hell? They walked off in the direction of my room and I moved to the side of the elevator, pretending to study a rack of pamphlets on prostate cancer and diabetes, my heart beating furiously. A few minutes later they hurried back, still carrying their gifts. Sal pushed the down button.

"What now?" the chauffeur whispered as they waited for the lift.

"She has most likely checked herself out and gone home, so we do her there. Then we go to Sandringham, get my speedboat and take care of the other putana on the "Midnight Lady." After that I need you to take me to the school, we've got to pick up Dominic for soccer clinic."

"You have a speedboat?" the Driver said. "Cool."

Chapter Twenty-Eight

The doors closed on their lift and the next one dinged. I got in and pressed ground. We descended slowly, stopping on every floor. I kept pressing the door close button and people looked at me like I was one of those crazy people who sit next to you on public transport. When we reached the ground floor I raced out into the lobby. Sal and his mate were walking out the double doors, heading off to the car park. In front of the hospital a TV news crew were doing their thing and I pulled the hat lower. A disabled taxi pulled up, discharging a patient in a wheelchair. Soon as the chair hit the ground I slipped into the back.

"You're keen," said the driver.

"You have no idea," I whispered hoarsely. "I need to get to St Kilda marina, and fast."

He turned to look at me. "First I'm going to need proof you can pay the fare."

"Fuck's sake." I reached into the purse and pulled out a fifty, gave it to him. "You can keep the change if you get me there in under ten."

"Hold onto your hat," he said.

We sped down Punt Road and into Barkly Street, the cabbie changing lanes like a demon, beeping wildly and driving up everybody's arse. We screeched right at Dickens and pulled up across the road from the marina.

"You're a credit to your profession," I said, and hopped across Marine Parade.

Reg had almost finished his book when I lurched into the shed. He looked up in alarm.

"Reg, it's me, Simone."

"Cripes." He peered at me. "You look like you got hit by a bus. You all right? I've been trying to call all day."

"You have?"

"I saw the redheaded guy, early this morning. He motored in, got in a Ford Falcon and drove away. Half an hour later he was back with supplies and I was ready. I followed him in the skiff, inconspicuous, just like you said. The boat's anchored three nautical miles out, she's a forty-foot Caribbean Flybridge Cruiser. I sailed past, then came back here and I've been ringing your mobile ever since. To tell you the truth I haven't had this much excitement in a long while."

"Good work, Reg, but I've got some bad news. The guy behind the kidnapping is on his way to shoot my friend. He's going to be in Sandringham soon, getting on a speedboat. First I want to call the water police, then I want to get out there." It hurt to speak so I kept it brief. I hoped Reg was up for a little more excitement.

"There's the phone," he said. "I'll get the boat ready."

I dialled triple zero and rasped down the line: "I want to report an attempted murder, it's on a boat called the 'Midnight Lady' anchored three nautical miles from the St Kilda marina. Get the water police out there."

"You'll have to slow down, ma'am. First, can I have your name and location?"

"Simone McCullers, St Kilda marina. I have to get to the boat, Salvatore Parisi is going to kill Chloe Wozniak. Send the police. Please. I gotta go." My voice cracked. I hung up, shuffled out to the sailing school yacht and climbed aboard. The engine was going but Reg wasn't on deck. Then I saw him, swinging open the wire gate and striding down the decking, big gun in hand. I swear, it seemed to happen in slow motion like a Jerry Bruckheimer movie. I may even have heard a guitar riff.

"Is that a shotgun, Reg?"

He nodded. "Smith and Wesson twelve gauge pump action. Mate of mine keeps it on his boat in case of sharks. May need it if we're going up against a fella with a gun." He untied the boat, jumped in and manoeuvred out of the marina onto the open waters of the bay. The boat was slow and the engine laboured. I wanted to get there before Sal and convince Blue to let Chloe go.

"Can't you go any faster?" I squinted as the sun reflected off the water. Reg cranked up the engine until it whined. My head pounded, my body ached and when the boat slammed over small waves I felt sick in the guts.

At the same time I was wired, indignant, jumped up on anger.

How dare Sal betray me. I'd done everything he asked, been a good girl, found his brother's killer, not sicked the police onto him. And for what? So he could whack Chloe and me anyway?

And then there was Farquhar. Even though he was dead I was still livid when I thought about him breaking into my house, trying to kill me. And Mick, I didn't want to get started on him. What was with these violent, power-tripping men? Where did they get off? And it was such bullshit, hiding behind their heavies and their guns. Penis substitutes, no doubt. Well I had a big dick of my own now and I wasn't afraid to use it. I picked up the shotgun. "How's this thing work?" I asked.

Reg steered the rudder as he explained it to me. "Pretty easy. Bullets are along here and to load you just move the slider back. She's got five rounds, couldn't find any more ammo."

I loaded and the gun made a chick-chick sound like it does in the movies.

"Aim, press the trigger and fire, then reload. I warn you though, a shottie doesn't have much of a range so you'll have to get up close and it's got a big kick. Watch your shoulder."

"How come you're such an expert on guns?" I asked.

Reg smiled. "There's a lot you don't know about me."

I held up the gun and was practising my aim when a boat came into view. A speck at first, gradually growing larger.

"That's her," said Reg. The "Midnight Lady" gleamed white with blue trim, the wheelhouse high up top and a small square deck at the back. My pulse rocketed. Please let Blue be so in love with Chloe he lets her go. Then I heard Reg: "Did you say the bad guy had a speedboat?"

It was coming up from the opposite direction, moving rapidly.

"What do you want me to do?" Reg shouted.

"Keep going! I'm not going to lay down and take it up the arse from these cocksuckers any longer."

Reg's forehead creased into a frown. "Language," he said disapprovingly, but he didn't turn back. I could see the two figures on the speedboat pointing at me and Reg. We were closer to the Caribbean but they were coming up twice as fast.

They pulled up to the "Midnight Lady" when we were still a hundred metres away and Sal's chauffeur trained his pistol on us while Sal crouched behind him. I crawled to the bow of the boat and lay down on deck, aimed the shotgun and fired. A deafening boom, a whack in my shoulder and the pellets dropped uselessly into the water. The chauffeur returned fire and I heard a bullet thwack into the mast. Reg, god bless him, kept heading for the speedboat and I held my head down as the guy continued shooting. He was useless at hitting a moving target, probably only killed people execution style, or used the gun for show.

As we got closer I fired again, more shoulder pain, and the chauffeur was hit in the arm with a spray of pellets. He yelped and dropped his gun into the water, staggered back and fainted. Sal climbed up a small ladder and onto deck then ducked down out of sight. Reg expertly manoeuvred the sailing boat alongside the speedboat and tied off. I grabbed onto the ladder, floral tent billowing, still holding the shotgun. I looked back briefly and saw Reg tending to the unconscious man, ripping off part of his shirt to tourniquet his arm. I hoped he wouldn't look up and see I wasn't wearing undies. I peeped over the railing to the rear deck but Sal wasn't there. That's when I heard the gunshot.

Oh god, I thought, Chloe, no. I hauled myself onboard, raced to the hatch and plunged in, gun first like they do in the cop shows. It was a really dumb thing to do. The cabin was dark and I heard a click and felt hot metal against my temple.

"Drop the fucking gun," said Blue.

Chapter Twenty-Nine

I dropped the shottie. "Don't shoot," I said, pathetically.
"Put the gun down, babe." The voice was Chloe's. "It's Simone."
She turned on the light and pushed Blue's hand away. He was
sweating, his face as red as his hair.

Sal lay dead on the carpet, a hole in his head and a dark pool of
blood soaking into the shag pile. My stomach turned. I looked at
Chloe. Her roots were dark and she'd put on a couple of kilos but
otherwise looked good. The tracksuit wasn't ugly at all. It was pink
velour. Very J-Lo.

"At least I think it's her," she said. "What's with the smock? You
pregnant?"

And then, "Fuck, mate, look at your face, your neck . . . what
happened?"

"It's a long story," I said. She held out her arms and I hugged her,
a proper hug, with no awkwardness or back patting. Then, like an
enormous sook, I started crying and couldn't stop. Sobs wracked
my body and my nose ran with snot.

That's how the water police found us when they burst in with
guns drawn. We surrendered and they took us all in, even Reg.

Sal's chauffeur was taken to hospital under police guard and
they interviewed the rest of us in separate rooms back at their
Williamstown headquarters. I was getting no love from the water
rats, what with the stolen purse and track-marks, so I used my
phone call to contact Detective McCullers. Once she arrived things
moved a little quicker, but she was real pissed off with me for not
telling the police about the kidnapping. She started to lecture me
but stopped when I told her Sal had someone from St Kilda Road
on his payroll. She told me she'd look into it.

"How's Alex doing?" I asked and her face opened up and
seemed to flood with light.

"He's going to be OK. The bullet hit high in his chest, deflected
off the second rib and lodged in his scapula. They've managed

to remove it and he's being shifted from ICU to a private room sometime tonight."

Blue was charged with kidnapping and manslaughter, and Chloe, Reg and I saw him on our way out. Two police officers were escorting him down the corridor, hands cuffed behind his back, when he broke free, ran over and kissed Chloe on the mouth. "I did it all for love," he announced as they dragged him away. Chloe rolled her eyes.

I apologised to Reg for getting him involved.

"You're right, love," he smiled. "Haven't seen so much action since the battle of Long Tan."

Chloe and I caught a ride back to my flat in a squad car. She flirted with the young constable all the way and got him to pull into a drive-through and shout us cigarettes and champagne.

"You're incorrigible," I whispered.

"That's a good thing, right?"

Soon as we got into my place, using the spare key I'd cunningly hidden in the communal laundry, I ripped off the itching polyester dress and jumped into the shower. I used every fruit flavoured, foaming, moisturising unguent I possessed. Finally I smelled good, even though I still looked like shit. I swallowed four painkillers, threw on my second favourite pair of trackie daks and collapsed on the couch. Chloe was cross-legged on the floor, simultaneously sucking down a bong and booking herself in for a bleach job and a Brazilian.

"You'd better have a lot of wax," she told the beautician, "I've gone feral. It's a fucking forest down there."

We cracked open the Yellowglen and unwrapped the pack of Winnie Blues. I told her everything, my voice a hoarse whisper. Even about Mick.

"So while I was kidnapped you still managed to find time for a root?"

"Hey," I said, "a girl has urges."

Chloe nodded. "True."

"What about you and Blue?"

"What about us?"

"I did it all for love?"

She shook her head and packed another cone. "I didn't screw

him till the second week. He's not exactly my type but there was fuck-all else to do and I was getting horny, you know? I think he's in love with me but I just like him as a friend. What's going on with you and this Mick dude?"

"It's over between us," I said. "It has to be."

"You still want him though." She could read me like a book.

"Yeah, but I'm not going to have him. Fucking men, I'm over them. I'm going to turn lesbian."

Chloe laughed, coughing out bong smoke. "Yeah right. You like cock too much."

When Chloe left for her beauty appointments I went to bed to have a small nap. I don't know if it was the stress, my injuries, or some canal-borne virus, but I was out for two days.

Chapter Thirty

I wandered out to the lounge, yawning and scratching the back of my head where the hair had clumped into dreadlocks. Chloe was on the couch watching Oprah, painting her toenails fluorescent pink and eating Barbecue Shapes. I sat down and hugged her.

"What's come over you?" she asked.

"Dunno, what day is it?" I had my voice back.

"Friday."

"What'd I miss?"

"About three thousand phone calls and us being the lead news story for the last two nights. Don't worry, I saved it all for you." She showed me a scrapbook of newspaper clippings and a videocassette. I hugged her again and she looked at me suspiciously. "I reckon Farquhar injected you with E, not smack. Want a coffee?"

I nodded sleepily and flicked through the scrapbook while she went to the kitchen. The journos had mixed up my real and stage names and referred to me as Vivien Kirsch, which was good, but had included a publicity still of me in a sequinned bikini, which was not. There were heaps of photos of Chloe, some from her picture spread and paparazzi shots of her in dark glasses, coming out my front door. She put the pot and two mugs on the coffee table.

"You're famous," I said.

"I'm about to get more famous."

"What are you talking about?"

She smiled proudly and pushed down the plunger, "I'm going on telly. 'A Current Affair,' mate. The kidnapped stripper who fell in love with her captor. It's a crime story, it's a love story, and there's tits and arse. At least that's what the producer said. They want to do a story on you too, but I told them you wouldn't be into it."

"You told them right. They paying you?" I poured myself a cup. The first sip was heaven.

"Three grand for an exclusive. I'm going to split it with you."

"You don't have to—"

"You saved my life."

"Blue saved your life," I said. "He shot Sal."

"Sal told Blue he was coming to let me go. If it wasn't for all the commotion you and that old bloke started we wouldn't have known anything was up. I'll split the money with you, fifty-fifty. No argument."

I remembered I had a month's rent overdue and stopped arguing. "When do you film the segment?"

"Tomorrow, so they can screen it on Monday."

"You'll be the most famous stripper in Melbourne," I said.

Chloe clapped her hands with excitement. "Isn't it great?"

The phone rang and I groaned, but reached for it. Time to get my life back in order. It was my agent Kelvin, and he was freaking out.

"I'm sorry to bother you, Simone. I've seen the news and I know you're injured but you've got to help me. Sabrina's fucked me around again. I booked her and Jamie to do a bi-twin show at five thirty for an office party and they've gone AWOL. Mobiles switched off. Do you know anyone who can fill in?"

I held the phone to my chest. "Want to do a double show in two hours?" I asked Chloe.

"What? With you limping around?"

"You could ask Aurora."

She thought about it for a second. "OK. She's hot."

"Kelvin," I said, "I'll call you back."

Aurora turned up half an hour later with champagne and a bunch of orchids for Chloe and me. She hugged us both. My life was turning into a regular love-in.

"You two crazy chicks have been all over the news," she said. "I was supposed to be in the rescue party but someone forgot to call me."

"I was a little pressed for time," I said.

"So I've read."

"Aurora figured out about the boat though," I told Chloe, "Since I was too dense to work out your clues."

"They were good clues." Chloe wrestled with the wire around the cork. "I spent ages working out those clues."

Aurora sat on the couch and crossed her long legs. "Guess what?" she said. "I'm moving to the Gold Coast."

Chloe popped the champagne and poured three glasses. "Really, when?"

"Next week. I just decided on the spur of the moment. Apparently the table-dancing scene in Surfers is really good, kind of like Melbourne in the early nineties."

"Wow," I said. "What's Betty think about that?"

"She's not too happy. She wants to come up with me."

"Do you want that?" I asked.

Aurora shrugged. "Betty can be hard to handle. Exhausting. I mean, I love the girl but she's doing so much coke at the moment. One minute she's arrogant and bitchy and the next teary, clingy and paranoid."

"What about Johnny?"

"He told her last week he wanted to break things off for a while."

"Shit," I said.

"Anyway, I'm having a going away barbie at Betty's on Sunday. I'd love it if you could both come. It's starting about three. Pretty casual. Bring a plate if you want."

"We'll be there," said Chloe, "but right now I need to know what I'm wearing for this show."

They decided on a bondage theme, and Chloe borrowed my latex outfit, a pair of handcuffs and a riding crop. I have some really cool things on the top shelf of my closet, up the back near the X rated videos.

Not long after, Wesley pressed the buzzer. Chloe went downstairs first and Aurora turned to me at the front door: "Mick asked me to give you this." She handed me a present shaped like a CD, crudely wrapped in old Christmas paper. "I don't blame you if you don't want anything to do with him but for what it's worth, he's sorry."

I opened the package when she left. It was the Lucinda Williams CD.

I tipped out the dregs of my champagne, brewed some more coffee and fried up bacon and eggs, no toast. I sat at the dining table and scarfed down my first meal in forty-eight hours while playing back the answering machine tape. There were messages from reporters, a couple from Mick and Aurora, one from Alex in the hospital, and the last from Tony Torcasio, asking me to call. I pushed my plate away and dialled his number.

"A1 Investigations."

"Tony, it's Simone. Do I still get the job?"

"Simone Kirsch," he said slowly, "the one who was obviously absent from class the day I taught everyone that it's not worth risking your life for twenty bucks an hour."

"I risked it for free."

He sighed. "You've got balls, I'll give you that. Even though you're not right in the head."

"True."

"And you can't take direction."

"I can work on that."

"And you lied about being a stripper."

"By omission."

He was silent.

"You're right," I said, "I lied."

Another pause. I screwed up my face. Please, please, please let him give me another chance. Then I heard the smile in his voice.

"Famous PI like you, all over the news, might be a bit boring at my little agency."

"Boring's good, I love boring."

"I suppose you could still be useful for the odd bit of surveillance, long as you don't wear those sparkly swimmers."

"I live for surveillance," I said. "And I can piss in a funnel, I did it following Farquhar."

Tony laughed. "That's all I ask of my investigators, the ability to piss in a funnel."

"So I've still got the job?"

"It's just a bit of subcontractor work but, yes, it's yours if you want it."

"Thanks, Tony. You won't regret this."

"Just keep out of trouble till then."

At that point I thought it was entirely possible.

Chloe got home at seven, pissed and hyped up from doing the show, a bag of McDonald's in her hand. She went straight to the bowl and started mulling up.

"How'd it go?" I asked.

"Great. I was freaking because we didn't have anything choreographed but it went fine. Aurora's very good at eating pussy."

"Really?"

"Yep, and she's got this wicked tatt, I want to get one just like it."

Chloe had one, a Playboy bunny on her arse.

"Aurora doesn't have any tattoos," I said.

"Ever been up close to her snatch?"

"No."

"That's where it is. Just to the side of her pubes." Chloe showed me the exact location by pulling down her capri pants and pointing to the edge of her neat racing stripe. "If you stopped waxing it would be totally hidden. If you ever wanted to stop waxing." She shuddered at the thought.

"What's it of?"

"It's hard to explain. It's like this ancient chick, with wings and snakes and a whip."

My face felt hot and my stomach twisted. It was the exact same tattoo Mick had. "Did she say what it meant?" I asked.

Chloe sucked back on the bong, the water bubbled and smoke escaped her mouth as she spoke. "It means passion."

Chapter Thirty-One

The next day Chloe went home to get ready for filming and I visited the hospital. First I slipped into the old lady's room and dropped off her stuff, then I saw Alex. He was propped up on pillows, bandaged around the chest and left shoulder, and had tubes coming out of his arm. His eyes were glassy and he smiled when he saw me.

"Hey."

I kissed him on the cheek. He still smelled good, even swabbed in disinfectant.

"How you doing?" I asked.

"Fine," his voice slurred. "Feelin' no pain."

"No wonder," I said. "Your pupils are totally pinned. What have they got you on?"

He laughed. "I dunno, but whenever I want more I just push this little button." He demonstrated and his eyelids fluttered closed.

I'd wanted to talk about the Parisi murder but I wasn't going to get any sense out of Detective Morphine. Oh well, I could at least have fun watching a big macho control freak all helpless in bed, off his mind on painkillers.

He opened his eyes. "You shoulda told me about your friend," he said, "but thass OK. I forgive you."

"Thanks," I said, looking him over. On the part of his torso not covered by bandage he had a chest rug Sean Connery would've been proud of. "You're a hairy son of a bitch, aren't you?"

"Whaddaya expect? I'm a wog."

I reached over and stroked the hair.

"Lower," he growled.

I gasped and held my hand to my chest. "Detective Christakos, what's gotten into you?"

"Too much time with nothing else to think about."

"Don't you have a nurse to give you sponge baths?" I inquired sweetly.

"Male nurse!"

"Oh dear."

There was a knock at the door and Detective McCullers came in, clutching an oversized white teddy bear with a red bow. She pulled up a bit short when she saw me and we nodded hello. Alex seemed happy to see her and started singing, badly.

"Suzy! Suzy Q. Woo! I love you."

Me and McCullers looked at each other and raised our eyebrows.

"Less have a party," Alex said. "You know I had a dream about the two of you the other night. One of those dreams." He winked and McCullers' eyebrows shot up so far I thought they'd fly off her head.

"Detective McCullers," I said, "can I speak to you outside?"

She nodded, relieved, and set the bear down on a chair.

"Seeya, Alex." I waved.

"Aw, come back, don' be like that," he said.

She closed the door on him. Out in the corridor nurses padded past in cushioned shoes.

"Sorry about Detective Christakos." McCullers blushed. "He's on some strong medication."

"I wanted to ask about the Parisi murder," I said. "Are Homicide sure Farquhar did it?"

"Pretty much."

"Do they know why he killed Frank?"

"I doubt anyone will ever know exactly what was going on in his head. But the general consensus is Farquhar demanded more money from Parisi, who then threatened to report him to Ethical Standards. Threat of exposure seems to have been the thing that motivated him to murder."

"Like that prostitute in the eighties?"

She nodded. I continued.

"I just think it's weird that Farquhar used a knife, when you guys found a whole stash of unregistered guns in his storage unit. I mean, a knife, that's messy, personal, heat of the moment stuff."

"So you're an FBI profiler as well as a stripper and an inquiry agent." McCullers crossed her arms. I ignored her comment.

"And why would he keep the knife in his house. Under his bed?"

"He was going to plant it."

"But why keep it there? That's just stupid."

McCullers sighed, exasperated. "The public doesn't seem to realise that most criminals are not evil geniuses. They get caught precisely because they are stupid. And arrogant. The case is closed. Give it up, Simone."

But I couldn't give it up. I went home and stewed about it and looked through my notebook. What I knew didn't square up with the facts. Why would Frank Parisi go anywhere with Dick Farquhar? Where did Farquhar tie him up and kill him? How did Farquhar get Frank into the water?

I went over my notes until the words were swimming in front of my eyes. I was obsessing over it. But the alternative was obsessing over Mick and Aurora and their shared tattoo. Had they had a fling and celebrated it with a mutual tatt? Why had neither of them mentioned it? I told myself I shouldn't care. I wasn't seeing Mick anymore, and it was none of my business who he was screwing before we took up. But I did care, a lot.

Chapter Thirty-Two

Chloe turned up at two-thirty wearing cut-off denim shorts and carrying plastic shopping bags full of munchies and cheap champagne. I asked how the filming had gone the day before.

"It was so much fun." She sat on the lounge and put the bags down with a clink. "We did a re-enactment on a boat down at the marina, an interview at the studio and then got some footage of me dancing at the Red. The sound guy sat in as a lap dance customer."

"Jim didn't mind?" I asked.

"Are you kidding? Free advertising. After the shoot me and the crew went to the pub. Man those guys can put away some piss."

I didn't ask what happened after the pub had closed. "So you'll be infamous by Monday night."

"Yep." She pulled out a tiny plastic bag. "Bit of Louie before we go?" Speed.

"Nah. I'm starting with Torcasio next week. Better stay on the right side of the law."

"Suit yourself. Get hideously pissed. Throw up. I'll be too busy talking some poor bastard into a corner to hold your hair off your face." Chloe went into the kitchen and poured Coca-Cola into a glass. She grabbed a teaspoon, scooped some speed out of the bag and stirred it into the drink, then licked the spoon and drank the coke in one go.

"More lamb for me then." I took a lunchbox and a wooden salad bowl out of the fridge. The lamb cutlets were marinating in a mixture of Dijon mustard and chopped rosemary and the salad was Greek with Dodoni feta, kalamata olives and a sprinkle of fresh oregano. Chloe had a party pack of Twisties, a jumbo box of chicken-in-a-biscuit and a quarter ounce of weed.

We caught a taxi to Prahran. The speed was kicking in and Chloe wiggled around in her seat, asking the driver if she could smoke and he could turn up the music.

I watched Punt Road slide by, feeling nervous inside. I had to see

Mick again, not to mention a whole bunch of people I'd lied to and deceived. And I wanted to find out about the tattoo, but couldn't think of a way to bring it up without sounding like a jealous bitch.

The front door was open and we trekked through to the large back yard. Girls from the club and members of the band sat in the sun, drinking and listening to James Brown from speakers facing out the back door. Some had come with children and partners and the kids ran around in circles, screaming, just like at any normal suburban barbecue. Well what had I expected? It was just weird seeing everyone in the daylight, unnatural almost.

I did a quick scan and couldn't spot Mick. His ute hadn't been out the front—maybe he'd already gone back to New South Wales.

Aurora and Betty stood by the barbie. It was a big Beefmeister, old and weathered with a rusted plate and rotted wood. The laminex kitchen table was full of salads and supermarket packets of sausages and chops. Aurora waved us over.

"We brought food." I held up my bowl.

"Simone brought food, I brought chicken-in-a-biscuit," said Chloe. We put our stuff down on the table and Aurora kissed us and thanked us for coming. She handed us plastic cups filled with champagne.

I studied Betty from behind my sunnies. She wore fifties film star sunglasses, red with diamantes at the sides, and a rose printed halterneck dress with a full skirt. She looked thin and pale but otherwise all right. No blood streaming from her nasal passages, no convulsing on the ground.

Betty smiled. "If it isn't the Agatha Christie of the stripping scene."

She may have been insulting me but I decided to take it as a compliment.

"I love your dress," I said. It was true.

"A friend of mine got it for me from a vintage clothing store in LA."

Well well. We were actually having a normal conversation. The day was looking up. If I could get on with Betty then everyone else was a cinch.

Chloe held up her clinking plastic bag. "Where can I stick these bottles?"

"The fridge is pretty full," said Aurora, "but Johnny and Mick will be back soon with some ice." She looked at me when she mentioned Mick's name and I kept my face neutral and pretended to be interested in the overgrown pumpkin patch by the back fence.

"Well," said Betty, "I've had enough of being straight. Who's for a line?"

Aurora shook her head. "Later,"

"No thanks," I said.

Chloe smiled. "Why the fuck not. I've got some Lou and some smoke." They linked arms.

"Speed is such a gutter drug," said Betty as they headed toward the house.

"Well la-di-fucking-da. You don't have to have any."

My cup was empty so I grabbed one of Chloe's bottles and began unwrapping the foil.

"When do you leave?" I asked Aurora.

"I fly out tomorrow afternoon."

"Soon."

"Yeah. Actually I was packing and there's a whole bunch of books I was just going to throw out. You're welcome to them if you want. I'd give them to Betty but she doesn't read anything written after nineteen fifty-nine. There's some true crime, a novel by Hanif Kureishi, and a great book on evolutionary biology."

"Sure, that'd be great." I popped the cork and Aurora waved to Jim and Flame, standing at the back door. He wore baggy shorts and had skinny white legs and she was practically unrecognisable in jeans and trainers, a baseball cap hiding her red curls. Even in flat shoes she had a good couple of inches over her boyfriend.

Aurora went over and hugged them. They both had the bewildered look of nocturnal animals, removed from their burrow in the middle of the day.

I stood alone by the table, feeling awkward. I wished I had a cigarette but they were in Chloe's bag.

Dakota approached me, a little blonde girl hanging on to her hand.

"Hi, Vivien," she said. "I heard what happened. How you going?"

"I'm all right."

"This is my daughter Tahnee."

The girl grabbed on to her mother's miniskirt.

"Tahnee, say hello to Vivien."

I crouched down. "Hi, how old are you?"

"Thwee." She hid her face against Dakota's leg.

"She's shy," Dakota explained. "Not like her ma." She refilled her plastic glass with champagne. "You know I wanted to apologise for being nasty the last time I saw you."

"You were nasty?" I vaguely remembered one time at the club when she had acted a little weird.

"I feel really bad. It was after Sexpo. Ebony told me you were a private detective and I just thought you were, like, lying to us all, spying on us, so that's why, you know. But now I know about Sal kidnapping Chloe, well, I can see you were doing it for the right reasons. So, like, yeah, I'm sorry."

"That's OK." God, how could I have been so naive as to think it wouldn't have got all over Sexpo? I wondered who else had known I was investigating the murder. And when. I turned my gaze to the house where Aurora was talking animatedly to Jim and Flame. Johnny squeezed past them carrying two bags of ice, wearing frayed shorts, a Hawaiian shirt and lipstick.

"We come bearing ale," he announced theatrically. Mick was right behind, a case of Coopers on each shoulder, the sunlight hitting him. How was it that Mick always seemed to get himself lit just so? On stage, in broad daylight, he seemed to catch the light and reflect it. I became aware of a voice in my ear.

". . . to the club?" Dakota was talking to me.

"Sorry, what?"

"Are you coming back to the club?"

"No. I've actually got some real life detective work coming up." I tried to focus on her but it was difficult.

"How exciting. I should get you to check out my ex. He says he's not working, to get out of paying maintenance, but I reckon he's getting cash in hand."

"Can I have a cigarette?" I could see Mick out of the corner of my eye, breaking down the bags and pouring the ice into a concrete laundry tub. He ripped open a carton and arranged stubbies in the ice. Dakota handed me a Horizon and lit it while Mick grabbed a beer and held the bottle to his forehead. He leaned back against the peeling weatherboard wall, twisted the cap off the bottle and looked directly at me as he drank. I felt an electric jolt in my chest and groin.

"Hi, Vivien." It was Jim, grinning behind opaque black Raybans. His short-sleeved navy shirt showed off his jail tattoos and he stuck out his hand and I shook it.

"Congratulations," he said.

"What for?"

"You've become a bit of a celebrity around town."

I wondered what part of town exactly. "Shucks," I said.

"You know I'm in negotiation to buy the Red from Sal's wife," he said, "so if you ever need a job . . ." He ripped a bourbon can from a four-pack and wandered off to talk to some dancers. I looked around, trying to avoid Mick's gaze. The place was really filling up. At least thirty people stood around drinking, some more kids had arrived and a couple of dogs chased each other around. Johnny had started blackening steaks on the Beefmeister and the music was louder, faster, some kind of neo-rockabilly. Half the Red had turned up, as well as the rest of the band and their assorted hangers-on.

"Vivien!" Anais crossed the yard in pinstriped pants and a tight black singlet, the outline of her nipple rings visible. She threw a container of falafels and tabouli on the table and hugged me. "Way to go, knocking off that pig Farquhar."

"I didn't exactly—"

"Anais!" Chloe bounded into the yard like an overexcited puppy and jumped on her so that they both tumbled to the grass, squealing. Chloe was going off today, and who could blame her? Stuck on a boat for two weeks. I wished I could have shared her enthusiasm but I felt kind of flat. Mick had disappeared from the laundry tub and I took the rest of the champagne over. I shoved the bottles in the ice, my fingers smarting from the cold, wiped my hands on the back of my jeans and went inside to the toilet. All that cheap champagne. When I left the loo I heard music coming from down the hall, Mick's room. I took a deep breath and walked to his door. It was open and Mick sat on the bed playing his guitar along to a Johnny Cash record, a cigarette hanging out of his mouth. He put the guitar down when he saw me.

"Hey," he said.

I closed the door behind me and crossed my arms. "Hi."

"I missed you." He stubbed out his cigarette and stood up and moved toward me. I stepped back. "How come you and Aurora have the same tattoo?"

"What?"

"You know what I'm talking about. The one that looks like Medusa. Yours is on your shoulder and hers is next to her pussy."

Mick hesitated. "I dunno. I saw hers and liked it. Got it done. You can never have too many tattoos."

"You saw hers? Must have been getting up close and personal."

He didn't reply.

"What did you say the picture meant?" I asked.

"Strength, I think."

"Not passion?" I turned to reach for the door but Mick held me from behind.

"Is that what this is about? You don't have to worry about me and her. It was just a short fling. Over before it began."

I felt the heat of his body pressed against mine and smelled his scent: sweat, tobacco and clean washing. Mr Cash was singing about falling into a burning ring of fire, and Mick pushed my hair away and kissed my neck. One of his hands was on my breast and the other trailed down into my pants and I wanted him so much I was instantly wet.

One more time, I thought, one last hit then I quit for good.

But I surprised myself. I turned around, pulled my arm back and punched him in the face.

Pain radiated out from my knuckles and Mick touched his cheek, more shocked than hurt. Now we were even.

"Goodbye's all we got left to say," I said.

"Steve Earle," he replied.

I walked to Chapel Street to find a cab and saw the tattoo parlour's neon lights. It was worth a try. I pushed the door in and a buzzer went off. Thousands of pictures of tattoos plastered the walls and a couple with multiple piercings sat on a couch flipping through plastic folders full of photographs. The high whine of a tattoo needle filled the air. I went up to the counter and a guy with a goatee came out from the back, through a red beaded curtain. The multicoloured tattoos down his forearms reminded me of Mick and I was sure I'd seen him before at one of their gigs.

"How can I help you?" he smiled.

I smiled back. "I think a friend of mine got a tattoo done here and I'd like to get the same one."

"What was it?"

"I could draw you a rough picture."

He handed me a pencil and a piece of scrap paper and I drew Mick and Aurora's tattoo and slid it over to him.

"So you're friends with Betty?" he said. I nodded slowly. Betty? "Yeah, she got this one about a month ago. Came in with a guy and a hot blonde chick and they all got the same tatt."

Chapter Thirty-Three

My mind reeled. It was suddenly hot and airless inside the small shop.

"What does the picture mean?"

"Fucked if I know. Looks a bit like Medusa though, from those ancient Greek legends." He looked at me. "Are you all right? Do you want a drink of water?"

"I'm fine."

The sound of the needle stopped abruptly and the curtain clicked as the blonde with the wrist tattoos came out. The one Mick had shagged.

The counter guy turned to her. "You finished up, Delores?"

Delores. Yeah right. Her real name was probably Tracey.

"Yeah, I'm off to the barbecue—" She stopped short when she saw me.

"Hey, Delores," I said, "better get your arse into gear, everyone's wondering where you are. Mick in particular. He's all yours. Go get him, tiger." I gave her a wink and she stared at me, dumbfounded, while I walked out of the shop and into a Silvertop taxi.

By the time I got home I was distressingly sober. I contemplated getting stuck into the cask but made a plunger of coffee instead and took all my case notes and spread them on the lounge room floor. I checked dates. I thought back to what had happened after Sexpo. I wasn't sure of a motive and a lot of things didn't add up but I was getting a very bad feeling about the whole thing.

I needed to make a couple of phone calls. First I called my mum. The phone rang for ages and when she finally answered she sounded drunk. Drunk was good. I could handle drunk.

"Simone! How are you?" She drew out the "are."

"Good," I said carefully.

"Steve and I just got back from a week in the Hunter Valley. We found some fabulous aged semillon so now we've got a few people over for a barbecue to help us drink it. It's a great day for a barbie.

How's the weather south of the border?" She said the last bit with a Mexican accent.

Jeez, she was pissed.

"Yeah, it's good, mum, uh—"

"It's funny you should call," she said. "Brian was just telling us he read about a shooting in Melbourne a couple of days ago that involved a stripper with the name Kirsch. He wondered if it was you and I told him to stop being ridiculous."

"That's ridiculous."

"That's exactly what I said!"

"Kirsch probably isn't even her real name," I said. "Listen, I need to ask you a favour. You've got a classics department at the uni, right?"

"Of course."

I heard *The Big Chill* soundtrack start up in the background. Good god.

"I've got a rough sketch of a figure that looks like it's from ancient Greek mythology and I need to know what it represents. Can I fax it to your office tomorrow and you take it round and—"

"I don't know, everyone's pretty busy. Why don't you just email them or something?"

"I need to know as soon as possible. It's urgent."

"Is this part of your detective work?"

I told her it was and she gave me her fax number, then went off to dance to that song that starts with Jeremiah was a bullfrog.

Next I pulled Curtis Malone's card out of my wallet and dialled his mobile.

"My name's Simone," I said. "I met you at the Miss Striptease comp in Melbourne. You said I should call if I wanted to do some modelling."

"Oh yeah."

Cheering, loud music and a strange squelching sound came from his end of the phone.

"Where are you?" I asked.

"The Oxford Hotel, Sydney, reporting on the baked bean wrestling. Hang on, I'll step outside." The noise became muffled. "That's better. So you want to do some glamour modelling, eh?"

"Yeah, but I need you to do something for me first."

"What's that?" He sounded amused.

"I read a story from the *Sydney Tribune* with your byline, published a few years ago. Restaurateur beats rape charge. Frank Parisi, who owned Deluxe, was acquitted of raping a young waitress. I need to know the name of the girl."

"Whoa," he said. "I remember the case, I covered it, but this is wrong on so many levels. First of all I don't have to do anything for you, you come in, take your clothes off, and we pay you. Second, it's unethical. We don't print the victim's name—"

"But you know it. From being in court."

"I may have it somewhere—god, all my stuff from the *Tribune* is in my mother's garage, but, thirdly, why should I? We've got no shortage of would-be models and I don't need the hassle."

"Have you been keeping up with the news, Curtis?" I asked. "Been following the story about two strippers and the shooting on a luxury yacht?"

"Yeah."

"Well I'm Vivien Kirsch."

"The kidnapped one?"

"No, the private detective one. The kidnapped one's my friend. She's going on 'A Current Affair' tomorrow night and the story's about to get even bigger. She's had offers from *Penthouse, FHM,* you name it," I lied, "but if you get me this information we'll both pose for you. For *Picture Premium* even, all the hot stuff."

"Open leg work?"

"You betcha."

Curtis didn't speak for a while. I could practically hear the cogs turning in his brain.

"What I'm seeing," he said, "is like a Chandler-esque kind of thing. You're sitting in an office, venetian blinds, desk fan, wearing a trenchcoat with black lingerie underneath. Then your friend—she's blonde right?"

"Uh-huh."

"Beautiful. A blonde walks into the office. We could do her up forties style, gloves, dress, then the dress comes off and the two of you go for it on the desk. I could call it The Big Sleep-over. Or maybe Lesbo Confidential."

"That's great, Curtis. Just get me the name by midday tomorrow or the deal's off."

I gave him my mobile number and he assured me he'd call.

The next morning I dropped by the post office to fax a rough sketch of the tattoo through to my mum before going to Aurora's place to pick up the books. A sign in front of the building read "Pinewood serviced apartments, daily, weekly or long-term."

I bypassed the reception desk and headed straight for the elevator, got to her floor and rapped on the door. I stood there a long time, until finally she opened it wearing a red kimono and messed-up hair.

"Hi," she said sleepily.

"Sorry, did I wake you?"

"I had to get up and get my shit together anyway," she said. "Come in."

The apartment was one bedroom, with a kitchen and laundry and decorated like a hotel. A balcony looked out over the leafy streets of South Yarra.

"Nice place," I said.

Aurora was in the kitchen boiling water for coffee. "A bit soulless but it beats buying furniture and dealing with share house politics. You can up and leave whenever you want. I like to travel light. That's why I'm unloading stuff onto you."

We took our cups onto her small balcony. There was a hot wind blowing, whipping up leaves and dust.

"Enjoy your going away party?" I asked.

"Most of it. What happened to you?"

"I didn't feel too good, I had to go home." Which was true in a way.

"Betty lost it right at the end."

"Really?" I blew on my coffee.

"It was about me leaving. She said some nasty things. I'd had enough so I left and came back here. Chloe and Johnny were trying to talk her down when I walked out."

"Glad I missed that bit," I said. "What's her problem, do you think?"

"Drugs. Abandonment issues. Johnny used too much smack for them to have any kind of sex life. Her parents, her upbringing, shit, I don't know." Aurora put down her coffee and looked at her watch. "I'm going to have to jump in the shower. I'll show you the books and stuff, just go through and take what you like."

We went into the living area. A neat pile of books and clothes sat on the coffee table and a suitcase was closed but unzipped on the couch. She handed me a couple of plastic bags.

"Go for your life," she said. "Whatever you don't want I'm just going to throw in a charity bin."

She closed the door behind her and I heard the shower start up. I piled a couple of books and some tops into one of the bags, glanced nervously in the direction of the bathroom and flipped the lid of the suitcase. I went through it and found nothing but clothes. Aurora's handbag sat on the kitchen counter so I tiptoed over and opened it, heart beating fast. I found a plastic wallet for travel documents and picked it up with shaking hands. A passport and air ticket were inside and I slid the passport out and opened it up.

At first I thought it was stolen. A pale, slightly overweight woman with dark hair and thin lips stared out of the photo, a serious expression on her face. It looked nothing like Aurora.

Then I noticed the eyes. They were the same. And the chin, and the general shape of the face. Talk about a makeover. It was more like a total transformation. I checked out the vital statistics. Name: Hermione Gallagher. DOB: 1/2/70. Eyes: Brown. Hair: Brown. The passport had been issued four years earlier.

I slipped the passport back and took out the ticket. It was British Airways, the destination London.

I suddenly realised I couldn't hear the shower anymore, shoved the ticket back in and zipped up her handbag. I'd just got back to the books on the coffee table when the bathroom door opened and Aurora emerged in a towel and a cloud of strawberry scented steam.

I felt sweaty and out of breath and pretended to read a dust jacket. I couldn't look her in the eye.

"Whereabouts you going to work on the Gold Coast?" I forced myself to sound natural.

Aurora padded to the kitchen and stuffed the few items from her cupboard and fridge into another plastic bag. "I don't know, there are so many places. Bad Girls, Players. I might take a couple of weeks off first, lie on the beach and then find somewhere." She held out the bag to me. "You may as well take this too, otherwise it'll just go in the bin."

"Sure." I took the bag.

"Do you want to go down to Toorak Road and get something to eat?" she asked.

"I'd better get going," I said. "I've got to be in the peeps in half an hour." There was an awkward silence.

"Don't you hate goodbyes?" she said.

"Yeah, I'm no good at them. You feel like you should say something profound, but it just comes out corny."

Aurora hugged me. Her breasts felt hard against my chest. I couldn't hug back because of the shopping bags.

"Well, see you later," she said, "and good luck with the detective thing. You'll be great, I know it."

"Thanks. Have a good time in Queensland. Send me a tacky postcard."

"I will," she said.

Yeah right.

I ascended the stairs at the Shaft, disinfectant and cheap air freshener getting up my nose. Dean sat in the bookshop, surrounded by every porn magazine known to man, reading the latest Harry Potter novel. He looked up when I said hello.

"Read about you in the paper," he said. "Didn't think you'd be coming back here."

"Being in the paper doesn't pay the bills," I told him.

"Guess not."

Three booths were going as I lay in the peeps, feigning masturbation, my mind not on the job at hand. I was thinking of Aurora, Hermione Gallagher. Telling everyone she was off to the Gold Coast when she was going to London. Getting the tattoo a month ago. Lying about her relationship with Mick. Befriending me. Transforming herself from plain Jane into Super-stripper. I kept trying to find reasonable explanations for her behaviour, but couldn't. It was just too suss.

The guys in the booths were putting in a couple of coins then leaving. I couldn't really blame them, my act was about as erotic as watching Parliament question time.

My mobile rang and I snatched it up.

"Hello?"

It was my mother.

"I know what the picture means," she said.

Chapter Thirty-Four

I jumped in a cab on Swanston Street and got the driver to take me to the Pinewood Apartments. I'd just walked out halfway through my peeps hour and would probably never masturbate publicly in this town again. Oh well.

I paid the cabbie, took the elevator and knocked on her door. No answer. I went down to reception and spoke to the woman behind the desk.

"My friend in number twenty-six, did you see her leave?"

"The blonde girl? She's vacated the apartment. She left in a taxi a few minutes ago. You just missed her."

Out on Punt Road I hailed a cab to Tullamarine. Now I was officially broke. It took fifteen minutes to get to the freeway but once on Citylink we reached the airport in ten. As we pulled up outside international departures, excited travellers pulling suitcases and backpacks out of car boots, my phone rang. It was Curtis.

"I've got the name for you." He told me what it was. "Now when do you want to do the photo shoot?"

"I'll call you back." I switched the phone off.

Inside the terminal I looked up at the departure display board. British Airways flight 227 to Heathrow was boarding in an hour. Aurora wasn't far ahead of me so she had to be around somewhere. I circled the BA check-in counters and the overpriced cafeterias but couldn't see a statuesque blonde. Just as I was starting to think she'd already gone through customs I spotted her in a duty-free store buying Issey Miyake perfume.

I stood behind her. "Hermione" I said quietly.

"God I hate that name," she said. She paid for her purchase and turned to look at me. Her eyes weren't violet anymore, they were brown, and she studied me intently like a hawk zoning in on its prey. The lady at the counter placed the perfume in a sealed bag and Aurora grabbed it and walked out of the shop, me following.

"I've got to board my plane soon," she said, and then, "you went through my stuff while I was in the shower. Nice."

"I know you killed Frank," I said, "and I know why."

We were passing the women's toilet and Aurora abruptly pushed the door in, grabbed my hand and pulled me in after her. It was empty and she dumped her bags on the floor, pushed me up against a wall and started frisking me.

"What are you doing?"

"Checking for wires."

"In this outfit?" I was wearing a small singlet with no bra and tight hipster jeans.

"You do have a reputation, honey." She patted me down and I felt a small thrill when her palms brushed my nipples. For god's sake, not very professional. She checked my backpack too and, satisfied I wasn't wired up, left the bathroom. I trotted after her to the airport bar. I needed a drink 'cause I certainly didn't have a plan.

Aurora bought us both champagne, just like old times, and we took our drinks to an out-of-the-way table.

"What are you actually doing here, Simone?" she asked. "You're not stupid enough to call the cops. You know you only have circumstantial evidence. Planning to leap on me and make a citizen's arrest?"

I shook my head, "I just want the truth."

"How very X-Files. Okay, well the truth is I didn't kill Frank Parisi."

"You didn't? Then who—"

She held up her hand to stop me. "Tell me what you've worked out first. I'm interested to know."

"Chloe saw your tattoo and told me about it. Mick has the same one and yesterday when I left the party I dropped into the tattoo parlour on Chapel Street and found out Betty has it too, and you all got it around the time Frank was killed. My mum works at Sydney uni and I got her to contact the classics department. The tattoo is a picture of one of the Erinyes, or Furies as the Romans called them. In Greek mythology there were three, and they were the underworld goddesses of vengeance and retribution."

I looked at her to make sure I'd got it right and Aurora nodded. I went on: "In nineteen ninety-eight Frank opened restaurant Deluxe in Bondi. He was charged with raping a waitress but never convicted. Her name was Myfanwy Gallagher."

"My parents had god-awful taste in names," Aurora said. "Miff was my younger sister."

"Was?"

"She died of a heroin overdose a year ago. Never touched drugs until after the assault. It really fucked her up. She blamed herself, if you can believe that." Aurora sipped her champagne and looked into the middle distance. "She was just out of high school and it was her first job. Her only job as it turns out. Bastard."

My silence prompted her to go on.

"Soon as I found out what he'd done to her I wanted to kill him. Especially when he got off scot-free. And when she died, well, that was it.

"It wasn't hard to find him. I just typed his name into an Internet search engine and pulled up a newspaper article about an ex-restaurateur running a strip club in Melbourne. A strip club! A guy with his background shouldn't be allowed anywhere near women.

"I quit my research job at the uni and dipped into my trust fund. I knew I had to look like a stripper and I didn't want Frank to recognise me from the trial. I'd already lost weight from stress after my sister died and the rest was easy, except for the boob job. I bleached my hair, got a good eyebrow wax, coloured contacts, Restylane in the lips. I probably went a bit overboard. All I really needed was the tits. With a rack like this nobody looks very closely at your face.

"Frank interviewed me and didn't have a fucking clue who I was. It helped that I'd stolen the driver's licence of another blonde who looked a bit like me. He fell over himself to hire me, even tried it on, but I kept refusing him. He went for the younger, weaker ones. Girls he could intimidate and push around. Everything I saw him do at the club strengthened my resolve to kill him. But I had to wait for the right time."

"Where do Betty and Mick fit in?"

"He raped Betty."

"Oh."

"Yeah, you didn't know that, huh?"

"Hang on," I said. "What I don't understand is why the girls kept working at the Red after Frank raped them. Why didn't they just go to the police?"

Aurora sighed like she thought I was a bit dense. "You know how they photocopy your ID? Frank had files on all the girls, knew where they lived, knew if they had kids. He threatened them, even said they'd be sorry if they left and worked at another club."

"What about Mick?"

"Needed someone physically strong and we were friends, we'd been sleeping together. He hates pricks like Parisi. Did Mick tell you what he was in jail for?"

"Assault."

"He almost killed a Catholic priest. The guy had abused him at school when he was twelve. Mick was eighteen when he hunted him down and beat him almost to death. A passer-by called the police and Mick served three years."

"He didn't tell me."

"I told him not to."

"Did you tell him to sleep with me?"

Aurora looked away again. "I needed someone to keep an eye on you."

I felt white-hot rage surge up like bile but forced it back down. I had to know everything.

"When did you find out about me?"

"I suspected you from the start," she said, "but I'm pretty paranoid. Paranoid is good, keeps you out of trouble. That night at Expansion when you asked the questions? You put on this kind of stupid, naive voice which I knew wasn't you. But I still didn't know for sure."

"So that first night we went out?"

"I wanted to see the band with you, I liked you, but I still wanted to suss you out."

"And Mick?"

"He didn't know, he was just being Mick. It was Dakota who told me. She found out about you talking to Ebony at Sexpo. I asked her not to tell anyone else, I didn't want you knowing I was onto you. At that stage I didn't know about Sal kidnapping Chloe and I thought you'd been retained by the family or something. It was then I told Mick it would be a good idea if he got closer to you."

"And people just do whatever you tell them, do they?"

"If what I tell them makes sense. Don't freak out, Simone.

He really did fall in love with you, if that's what you're worried about."

"Did you break into my flat?"

"Yep."

"Fuck," I said, angry. "How'd you plant the knife on Farquhar?"

Aurora didn't answer and I suddenly remembered what Farquhar had said at the club. Don't get jealous . . .

"Oh no," I said, "you didn't . . . sleep with him?"

Her mouth twisted up at the memory. "It wasn't my finest hour."

"I can't believe you fucked Farquhar."

"Oh calm down, Simone, it's just sex. Jesus."

"Tell me about the murder," I said. "The one you didn't commit."

"First I got Mick to call up Shane and two hours later Shane was in the club, wanting to kill Frank. The same night Dick Farquhar came in and argued with him, which was quite fortuitous, nothing to do with me, but it made me think the time was right. At least two other people had a motive, and with my fake ID I didn't have any at all. At the end of the night, when just about everyone had left, I asked Frank if he wanted to have a threesome with me and Betty. That was Frank's thing, you know. Come to think of it, it's every guy's thing. I told him to keep it quiet and not tell anyone, the way gossip flew around the club. Frank was really into it. He'd pretty much given up on the idea that he was going to get to have sex with me."

"Where'd he meet you?"

"A motel on Ormond Esplanade, Elwood. Mick rented it that night, dressed up like a salesman in a shirt, tie and glasses. He was unrecognisable, looked like Clark Kent, and he paid cash.

Soon as Frank walked in the door Mick hit him a couple of times and he passed out. When he came to he was gagged, tied to the motel chair, and there were plastic drop sheets everywhere. Scared the shit out of him, as well as the fact we were all wearing gloves and hats and those awful junkie tracksuits that don't shed many fibres. We took his coke and lined up. It all felt kind of surreal."

"Did you have a weapon?"

"Yeah, the knife."

"Shane's."

"No. But it was similar." Aurora sipped her champagne, her hand shaking slightly. "I told him why he was there, for what he'd done to Miff, and Betty, and god knows how many other girls, and I smacked him around the face a few times. I unzipped his pants. I wasn't really going to cut his dick off but I told him I was. It was disgusting. A shrivelled little thing. And he'd pissed himself. I'd had enough and I felt sick. He was so pathetic that I just lost interest. I'm telling you revenge is better in fantasy than reality, like a lot of things. And anyway, the Erinyes didn't necessarily kill their victims, they pursued them relentlessly, driving them to madness and despair for their crimes until, through ritual purification, they were cleansed of their sins. Maybe what we'd just done was like ritual purification. I don't know. I was off my tits.

"I had to get out of there to clear my head so I told the others I was going for a walk on the beach and sat on the sand for about ten minutes, watching the moon shine on the ocean. Finally I decided we'd leave him there and piss off out of town.

"I went back to the motel to tell the others. When I got there Frank was dead, stabbed, and Mick was wrapping him up in the plastic sheets, then covering them with garbage bags and taping them up. Betty was wiping small specks of blood off the furniture with cleaning products we'd bought just in case. It was three in the morning and the streets were deserted. Mick put the body in the back of the ute and dumped it in the bay. I drove Frank's Beemer to Prahran with Betty in the passenger seat. We parked the car down a side street, chucked the trackies, gloves and everything in a garbage bag, stuck it in someone's wheelie bin and went to the Dome nightclub.

"A few girls from the club were around, so off their heads they didn't know we hadn't been there for hours. We stayed until six. Betty scored some Es and then we met up with Mick back at Betty's and dropped and drank champagne all morning. We were so fucked up we even had a threesome. Betty was really into it because she'd fancied Mick for ages. It's probably why she didn't like you. Anyway, we finished the rest of Frank's coke and went up the road and got tattoos. I went home and slept like a baby and the next day it all seemed like a weird dream."

A voice over the loudspeaker requested Hermione Gallagher

make her way immediately to the departure lounge.

"Oh shit, that's me." Aurora drained her glass. "It's been nice, all this confession stuff. I feel light, kind of unencumbered." She slid out of her seat and hurried toward customs. I jogged after her.

"So who did it?" I asked. "Who killed him?"

"I don't know."

"Bullshit."

"I don't. I never asked. They never said. Believe it or not, we never spoke of it after it happened. We talked about what we were going to do about the police, about you, but not the actual act. It made it less real. The hardest part was the police interview. I was fine, but I had to dose Betty up on a whole heap of Valium."

We were at the doors to customs. Did I believe her? I didn't know. Should I try to call airport security and turn her in? I had a feeling there wasn't enough evidence for a conviction and I didn't want Aurora to go to jail. I had a sneaking suspicion that if I'd been in her shoes I might have done the same thing.

"What are you going to do in London?"

"What do you think? Strip. I love it, I'm addicted. It's art, power, self expression and you can't beat the money."

They called her name again.

"I guess this is it, Vivien Leigh," she said. The hawk-like look was gone and sugar-coated Aurora was back. Which was the real her? Perhaps they both were. She tilted my head up and gave me a full, lingering kiss on the mouth and a fat businessman did a double take. She put a finger to her lips. "Sweet," she said, and disappeared through the automatic doors.

Chapter Thirty-Five

Too broke to catch a cab I got the Skybus back to town, my heart thumping and my brain going into overdrive. Who killed Frank? Mick? Betty? Both of them?

Or was Aurora lying?

Mick had lived on a farm. He'd slaughtered animals, gone pig and roo shooting. If you could kill an animal was it really such a stretch to kill a human? But then Frank had raped Betty. She had a real reason for revenge. And she was kind of unhinged, to put it mildly.

I had to find out what had happened or I'd drive myself crazy wondering for the rest of my life.

The bus pulled up at Spencer Street Station and I took a train to Flinders Street then hopped on the Sandringham line to get to Prahran. It took me five minutes to walk to Betty's place and when I got there I saw no cars parked outside. Nobody answered when I knocked so I took the key out of the potplant, shook the dirt off and unlocked the door.

"Hello?" I called.

The house was gloomy and smelled of cigarette smoke, beer dregs and a long burned out incense stick. I walked into the lounge, then through to the kitchen, the beaded curtain clicking as it fell back into place. The kitchen was a mess of paper plates dotted with limp salad and smears of tomato sauce, and cigarette butts floating in beer bottles.

"Anyone home?" My voice sounded weird and loud. Where was everybody? Had Aurora called them from the airport and warned them that I knew?

I poked my head into Betty's room—no one there—then went to Mick's. His things were packed ready to go, clothes stuffed into a duffel bag and records and books in a milk crate.

Sitting down on the bare mattress I looked through the crate. A lot of junk was stuffed down the bottom, old batteries, a couple of screwdrivers, a square of sandpaper. I found a photograph of Mick and his dog. The dog had brown fur, like forensics had found on the garbage bag. I slipped the photo into my back pocket. Faint traffic sounds drifted through the air and the roof ticked as it expanded in the summer heat, but the house was cool.

Back in the kitchen I opened the fridge. Force of habit. A container of mouldy takeaway sat next to three individually wrapped cheese singles. I grabbed one, peeled off the plastic and was nibbling at the edges when I sensed someone behind me. Just as I started to turn something slammed into my head, bang, and I saw the pain in rainbow colours as I fell to my knees on the black and white checked lino. I spat out the cheese, unchewed, and put my hand up to shield my head while I looked at my attacker, vision brown around the edges.

Betty came into focus. I saw her drop a thick wooden breadboard on the floor and turn and pull open the cutlery drawer so hard it crashed to the floor. She rummaged around and picked up a knife. One of those stay-sharp ones they advertise on TV.

I got to my feet, holding one hand out in what I hoped was a placatory gesture.

"You fucking bitch." Betty held the knife in one hand and ran the other through her hair so her fringe stood up at an odd angle. She was grinding her teeth, chewing on nothing, and her eyes were glassy and unfocused. "Aurora called me," she started raving. "I knew we should have got rid of you, or fucked off as soon as you came on the scene, but Rory said if we kept you close it would be just as good. Said you were just a stupid bimbo, all talk no action.

"That's the only reason Mick was with you, you know, to see what you found out. The only reason—oh, and to get an easy fuck," she spat. "He was screwing other people. Everyone knew except you." She laughed and her face twisted so she looked like a witch.

My head was pounding but I forced myself to sound light-hearted: "What makes you think I was so in love with Mick?" I said. "He's a good root, sure, we all know that, but he's not the only one."

"That cop."

"Among others."

"You could be a cop yourself." Betty alternated between pointing the knife at me and smacking it on her bare arm. She fluttered it lightly over her skin until thin red scratches appeared.

"Yeah, but I'm not." I didn't know where this ridiculous conversation was going but as long as we were talking she wasn't stabbing me.

Betty said, "You've been out to get me from the start."

I held both hands in front of me, the universal gesture for: I'm harmless, no need to whack me.

"Listen, Betty, Aurora told me about the night Frank got killed. I don't know who killed him. And I don't want to know. The bastard deserved it. I'm not going to go to the police. I'm not going to dob in my own ex-lover, my friends. The police think Farquhar did it anyway."

The front door opened then slammed shut and Mick walked into the kitchen wearing his work clothes and holding a Coopers.

"What the fuck," he said.

"She's going to turn us in." Betty was wild eyed. "We've got to get rid of her."

"I'm not turning anyone in," I appealed to him.

"He killed him." Betty pointed at Mick. "He stuck him like a pig."

Mick shook his head in that laconic, country way. He actually looked bored. "I'm out of here," he said. "I don't need this shit." He stalked out of the kitchen toward his room, leaving me there with the knife-wielding bitch. Don't need this shit?

"Mick!" Betty and me called his name at the same time. We heard him slam his bedroom door.

"Yeah, just leave then, cunt," Betty yelled so he could hear. "Everyone fucking leaves me. Johnny. Aurora promised she'd take me with her. She's gone, everything's gone, except this fucking tattoo." She lifted her skirt to show me the winged woman on her thigh. I'd never seen it at the club, she'd always covered it with makeup. "I've been cursed by Frank, by this tattoo, and now the fucking Erinyes are coming after me."

Holy shit, Betty was off her jang. A big fat tear rolled down her cheek, taking with it a long line of black from her eye makeup. She put the knife down on the kitchen bench and I went to grab it but she snatched it up again.

"Stay back." She pointed the knife at me, then at herself, and started stabbing at the tattoo, little test stabs at first, gradually going deeper. Blood welled up. She was making a mess of her leg.

"Betty don't," I said, and lunged for the knife.

She slashed out and the blade burned into my palm. I retreated, curling my hand in a fist and holding it up to my chest, blood seeping through my clenched fingers.

"Mick!" I yelled.

I heard his bedroom door open and footsteps down the hall. Finally, thanks a lot.

Betty heard him too and in one sweeping motion she stabbed the knife into her chest right up to the hilt. Mick reached the kitchen and just stared.

Betty looked surprised. She let out a little sigh, fell back against the wall, and slid down until she was sitting on the floor, legs out in front of her. Her hands still clutched the knife-handle and her blouse was becoming soaked with blood. I tried to remember some first aid training I'd done years ago but my mind was blank.

"Should we pull the knife out?" said Mick.

"No." I looked frantically around the kitchen, picked up a couple of filthy tea towels, removed her hands and bunched them around the knife.

"Call an ambulance," I yelled. Betty was starting to slump over and I held her up against the wall with my shoulder.

Mick came back into the kitchen. "I've called them," he said. "Should we lie her down?"

"I think you're supposed to keep the bleeding part elevated," I muttered, "or maybe that's limbs, shit, I don't know." I felt for a pulse in Betty's wrist. It was still there. What if I had to do CPR? How could you do CPR if there was a knife stuck right where you were supposed to push down?

Mick looked at me. "I'm sorry," he said.

"This really isn't the time, Mick."

He got up and went to his room, then carried his stuff out to his ute. Blood seeped through the tea towels, soaking my hands.

"What the fuck do you think you're doing?" I yelled at him as he came back in. "Help me out here." He went into Betty's room and returned holding a small book. It was a diary, the front and back covers plastered with pictures of Betty Page.

He crouched down in front of me. "This is Betty's. Read it then destroy it. I'll contact you in a couple of days." My bag lay on the kitchen floor and he slid it in. Sirens wailed in the distance. "After the ambos the cops'll come. I have to get out of here."

I just stared at him. He picked up his beer and left and I heard his ute start up with a low rumble. The sirens got louder until the ambulance stopped in front of the house.

Epilogue

The paramedics took me and Betty to the Alfred. I got stitched up and Betty got operated on. I had to talk to some more cops. It was getting to be a habit.

When they'd finished with me I went to see Alex. He wasn't on so many painkillers and if he remembered what he'd said under the influence he didn't mention it.

"What happened to you this time?" he asked when he saw my bandaged hand.

I shrugged. "Friend of mine took too many drugs, went crazy with a knife and tried to kill herself."

"You have got to get out of the stripping industry," he said. "Put in an application, join the Victoria Police."

"I wouldn't want to join a club that doesn't want me," I said, then paused and looked out the window. "Alex, what if, hypothetically, I knew that Farquhar didn't kill Frank Parisi, and I knew who did?"

"Got any evidence, hypothetically?"

I thought of the diary in my bag. "No, but if someone confessed to me?"

"Recorded confession?"

I shook my head, no.

"Hearsay," Alex said. "Circumstantial evidence. Not enough for a court case. No one would touch it. So which nut-job colleague of yours confessed?"

"No one. I was just speaking—"

"Hypothetically."

"Yeah."

Betty had just missed her heart and she lived. After hospital she was admitted to a psych ward for a while which got her off certain drugs and onto other ones, and I heard she moved back to the country after she was released.

I read her diary. She admitted stabbing Frank and confirmed

everything Aurora had told me. I burnt the diary in my kitchen sink and set off the smoke alarm.

I got home from the hospital that day in time to see Chloe's segment on "A Current Affair." There were a lot of gratuitous T&A shots, and despite mugging shamelessly for the camera, Chloe looked great. She called me right after the show had aired and told me her good news. The TV station had offered her a hosting gig on a TV special, a six part series called "Sin City," exposing the seamy side of Melbourne, peepshows, strip clubs, brothels. She was over the moon. She'd finally gotten her fifteen minutes of fame.

After the special she did a couple of magazine articles about her life, and ended up posing sans me for Curtis at *Picture* magazine. She got two lines in a "Stingers" episode, playing a stripper, showed up at the opening of an envelope for a season, and auditioned for a hosting gig on an afternoon cartoon show, losing out to a former soap star. Her stripping career was going great guns though, everyone wanted the celebrity stripper as seen on TV.

I received a letter from Mick a week later, one page of childish looking scrawl. He apologised and wrote that although he first pursued me because Aurora told him to, he really did fall for me. I rolled my eyes when I read it but I kept the letter and the photo I'd stolen all the same. And memories of the sex we'd had kept me going on long lonely nights when I let my fingers do the walking.

I thought about Aurora too, wondered if getting away with Frank's murder had helped her get over her sister's death. I doubted it.

I did the surveillance job with Torcasio. Most of it was deathly boring until we caught the guy with his mistress pashing on the promenade at Southbank.

Tony gradually gave me more and more work and taught me all the stuff they never did at the security academy. It was a real mentorship, kind of like Yoda and Luke Skywalker, or the karate kid and that old Chinese guy. He couldn't always promise me regular hours so I still did the occasional show for Kelvin, but didn't tell my mum.

When Alex was released from hospital his unit threw him a party and I was invited. It took place at an Irish pub in the city but I ended up leaving early. I felt excluded from their tight-knit cop club, suspected everyone there had heard the surveillance tape of Mick and me having sex, and Suzy McCullers kept hanging on Alex's arm like a limpet on a rock. I liked Alex, there was something sexy about him, but I wasn't the type to go and cut another chick's lunch.

Three weeks after Betty stabbed herself I was sitting in the Turtle Café drinking a long black that was giving me heart palpitations and flipping through *Inpress*, checking out the band listings. Doug Mansfield and the Dust Devils were playing at the Greyhound. I called Chloe, but she was shooting the "pub strippers" segment of her show so I decided to go it alone.

As usual there weren't many punters on a Wednesday night. I sat at a table by myself getting gloriously drunk on mini bottles of champagne and smoking Winnie Blues from the cigarette machine. I'd decided I would only smoke when I drank. I sang along under my breath to all the songs, and swayed and swished my hair around. When the band took a break the spunky bass player came up and sat at my table.

"I'm Jack," he said.

I already knew his name from the liner notes of their CD.

"Simone." I shook his hand. It was damp from the Melbourne Bitter can he'd been holding.

"You always come and see us play, and you never come up and say anything," he said.

"I'm shy."

"You weren't shy when you danced on the table that time. You must have been pretty pissed."

"Not pissed, happy."

"Who was that guy who dragged you out? Boyfriend? Husband?"

"Nah, he was an undercover cop."

Jack's eyes widened. I could see him decide to let that one go.

"It's surprising, a girl who's into country music," he said.

"I'm full of surprises." I smiled and played with my glass. Flirting 101. Like shooting fish in a barrel.

"Can I buy you a drink?" Jack asked, emboldened.

"If you promise to play 'She Dances on Tables.' "

"What's so special about that song?"

"I used to be a stripper."

"I can imagine you would have been very good. What do you do now?"

I leaned over. "It's a secret," I whispered drunkenly into his ear. "If I told you I'd have to kill you."

Jack laughed. "You wanna go out sometime?"

I sat back in my chair. "No offence, but you're a guitar player and I'm trying to cut down."

"What does that mean?"

"You guys are trouble." I sipped the last of my champagne, leaned forward and looked him intently in the eye. "With a capital T."

I would like to thank the following people for inspiration, advice and technical support: Anthony Larsen, Donna Shoebridge, Julie Lamont, Damien Powell, Alan Rice, Stuart from Melbourne Sailing School, Barry Watts, Marele Day, the Northern Rivers Writers Centre, Gary Ovington, Jesse Blackadder, Peter Mitchell, Annette Barlow, Colette Vella, Jemma Birrell, Jo Jarrah, Kevin Jansz, Mario, The Colonel, Sable, Larry, JB, the CIB detective I flirted with at the Chelsea pub, Scott Wales, Greg Thorsby, Adrian Brown, Mick Watson, Matt Rassmussen, Gareth Lindsay, Matt Dwyer, Simon James, Josh Burgoyne, Steve from America, Tony Redhead, Thea Woznita, Jesse and Kate and Jasmine Redhead, Stella and Jean O'Connell, and Keith Larsen.

Some of the venues described are based on reality but the characters are fictional. Except for Doug Mansfield and the Dust Devils. They're real and they are: Doug Mansfield, Gerard Rowan, Nick Del Rey, Jack Coleman, Bruce Kane and Peter Mullins.

Lyrics from "She Dances on Tables" are reproduced with permission from Doug Mansfield.

All the mistakes are my own.

Leigh Redhead
March 2004

www.ingramcontent.com/pod-product-compliance
Lightning Source LLC
Chambersburg PA
CBHW050527260626
47157CB00004B/1497